KILLING BY COLOURS

KILLING BY COLOURS

Wonny Lea

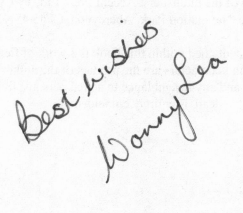

Best wishes
Wonny Lea

Killing by Colours

Chapter One

Martin sat at his kitchen table surrounded by the smells of freshly brewed coffee and baking croissants, but his mood of complete contentment had just been wiped out and he had an awful feeling in the pit of his stomach.

Shelley, the reason he had woken up feeling on top of the world this morning, was half-asleep in his bed, waiting for him to return with the coffee and croissants and the promise of not getting out of bed until lunchtime. Just ten minutes ago everything had seemed idyllic, and he hadn't even minded when he'd lost the coin toss and been the one who had to leave the warm bed and rustle up the breakfast.

He'd prepared the food in the kitchen of the cottage he'd shared for years with his Aunt Pat – she'd left everything to him when she died. Almost daily Martin thanked his aunt for her choice of house and for the way in which she had transformed the end-of-terrace cottage into a comfortable home. Typically, she'd retained most of the period features – but being a very practical woman she had installed all the latest mod cons, and had brought the old and the new together perfectly.

Shelley was the first woman Martin had brought to the cottage since his aunt had died and he knew beyond doubt that Aunt Pat would have been over the moon with his choice. He was sorry the two women had never had the chance to meet as he was certain that they would have become really good friends.

Aunt Pat had been a really good judge of character, and on one of the few occasions that Martin had not listened to her opinion he had made a big mistake. He had married Bethan, a woman whose sole mission in life was to be a perfect homemaker and produce beautiful babies. Nothing wrong in principle with that, but there had to be something else for Martin – and unfortunately, with Bethan, there wasn't. Within a few short months he had been bored by the lack of decent conversation and looked to his job and work colleagues for the stimulation his mind needed, which left his attractive young wife feeling neglected. The marriage had lasted two years, but that was only because of the time needed to secure a divorce.

He now realised that he had never loved Bethan. He had been flattered by the attention of a woman almost ten years younger than him, but getting married to her had been one of the biggest mistakes of his life. It was because of this mistake that Martin, since his divorce, had been reluctant to form any serious relationships with women, and although he was attracted to Shelley from the time he first met her, it had taken almost a year before things really took off.

Shelley worked in the same building as Martin but she was not a police officer – she was an expert in all matters relating to Health and Safety. She did a really good job at actually making this potentially mind-numbing subject come to life for all the officers who attended her training sessions. Martin regretted the wasted months when the two of them could have been together, and now he was determined to make up for lost time. She was waiting for him, but instead of rushing back up the stairs as he so desperately wanted to do he was sitting at the kitchen table.

The reason Martin now sat with his head in his hands had nothing to do with Shelley and everything to do with the A5 sized orange envelope that he had picked up from his front doormat and put on the kitchen table. He hadn't opened it and was trying desperately to ignore it.

He got to his feet and finished preparing the mini-feast of coffee, croissants, butter, and honey for the pair of them, and then piled some small sweet strawberries into a bowl as a finishing touch. Even with all that done he still didn't touch the envelope, and with considerable resolve he left it unopened on the table and carried the breakfast tray up the stairs.

Shelley squealed with delight when she saw him with the

tray of goodies and said, laughing. 'Hey, you know how to treat a girl – had a lot of practice, have we?'

Almost before she had finished the sentence Shelley regretted teasing Martin and hopped out of bed, grabbed a robe, and poured them each a cup of coffee. 'That was just a joke, you know.' She started to say she hadn't meant anything when Martin interrupted.

He kissed the top of her head as she handed him a cup of coffee and forcing a smile he quickly reassured her. 'I know you were teasing,' he said. 'It's nothing you've said or done, Shelley.'

'Then what?' she asked. 'You were full of the joys of spring earlier, and so was I – even more so when I saw the feast you've prepared. That was until I saw your face ... oh my God!'

Shelley stared directly into Martin's eyes. 'I thought I heard the postman. You've had another one, haven't you?'

Martin took a large mouthful of coffee before slowly answering. 'Yes, I think so, but for now it's sitting unopened on the kitchen table. And I'm leaving it there, and it's not going to spoil our weekend.'

For a few minutes nothing more was said as they both picked at the croissants and Shelley managed a few strawberries. Pouring them each a second cup of coffee Shelley broke the silence. 'You know I love you, Martin, and there's not one bit of you that I would change – not even your job. I've always known that any plans we make are likely to take second place when your job gets in the way and I can accept that. There is no way that you're going to spend the weekend forcing yourself to forget what you know could be in that envelope and at least we had a brilliant Friday night. So, Detective Chief Inspector Phelps, do what you have to do and I'll do the domestic bit.'

Martin knew how much trouble Shelley had gone to so that they could have their first real weekend together in the cottage. It was just three weeks since they had returned from Edinburgh having spent five memorable days at the Fringe festival, but for that trip and for this weekend Shelley had had to make arrangements for the care of her diabetic father and that wasn't always easy.

They both knew the weekend at the cottage would mark a milestone in their relationship and they had been looking forward to it. Martin reflected that many women would have been furious to realise that such a carefully planned weekend was likely to end so early on the Saturday morning.

'No wonder I love you, Shelley Edwards,' said Martin and then after a kiss that would normally have taken them straight back to bed he pulled himself away.

The man that was Martin Phelps wanted desperately to stay in the bedroom – but the officer that was DCI Phelps knew he had to open the orange envelope that beckoned to him from the kitchen.

It had been on a Saturday morning, exactly two weeks ago when Martin had found an almost identical envelope on his doormat. The only difference between the two envelopes was that the first one had been red and this one was orange. Both were formally addressed to Detective Chief Inspector Martin Phelps and that had been the first surprise for Martin. When he had picked up the red envelope he had expected it to be for Mr Martin Phelps – he had never before had mail arriving at the cottage for DCI Phelps. He valued the fact that the cottage was his refuge from all that his title and rank could mean.

But obviously whoever had sent the letters knew where he lived as well as his full name and rank and initially he hadn't thought that there were too many people who knew that combination. Since he had received that red envelope he and his colleagues had spent hours trying to think of anyone who did fit into that category, and there were many more than Martin had first thought.

He remembered clearly opening that first envelope, and before opening the second one he allowed his mind to take him step by step over the frustrating events of the past two weeks, starting with the opening of the red envelope.

Inside that red envelope, written on a single sheet of

4

matching red paper, was a poem, and as poems go it wasn't particularly good, but Martin could remember it clearly.

Think of red as it rhymes with dead
and dead she now will be.
She could have had a better fate
if she'd been kind to me.

She bullied me and made me play
the games I hated most.
But now she hasn't much to say
for she is but a ghost.

This dragon now has met her match
no longer will she preach.
No more the teacher for this time
the lesson I will teach.

Find her now if you think you can
but you will be too late.
If you're so clever Martin Phelps
let's see you take this bait.

During the time that he had been in the police force Martin had known of a couple of people who had been singled out for special attention by criminals, but there had always been some personal element involved and he struggled to find anything to connect himself to the woman whose body had been found.

Yes, as he was to discover a couple of hours later, a body had been found. At first there was no way of linking that body, discovered in the car park of the Red Dragon Centre, with the letter Martin had received as Martin's team had not been the ones to attend that particular crime. He had not rushed into the office with the red letter as his first thoughts were that it was some sort of hoax but he had phoned a few colleagues for their opinions.

It had been just after eleven on that Saturday morning when

5

he received a call from one of the people he had spoken to earlier, Detective Inspector Steven Hall.

'Hi, Martin,' said Steven. 'We have just come back from a call-out to the Red Dragon Centre where a woman was reported slumped over the wheel of her Ford Mondeo in the car park. Apparently the man who noticed her looked into the car and saw that she was sitting in a pool of blood. He told the security staff at the centre and they called the police and the ambulance service.

'Alex Griffiths and the SOC team arrived the same time as I did with DS Cotter, and within minutes Prof. Moore had turned up, so I left them to do the business at the crime scene. It was on my way back to the office that I remembered our earlier conversation, and the poem you read out – it had something in it about a dragon and the finding of a body. Do you think there's any connection?'

Martin had the advantage of having the letter in front of him and scanned the lines. 'Well, apart from the observations you've already made, the poem mentions is the colour red – that could be a reference to the Red Dragon Centre or the pool of blood the victim was sitting in.'

'Or it could be the red cord that had been tied around her hands in what according to Alex is a reef knot,' Steven added.

Martin said nothing for a moment but the cogs in his brain went into overdrive. 'Steven, I'm sure you remember that this should have been my weekend on call, but you asked me to swap – and I can't help thinking that the letter I received this morning is relevant and it's me who should have discovered this body.'

'Bloody hell!' exclaimed Steven. 'So what do you want to do?'

'If it's OK with you I'd like to take on the case. The super won't be happy with that but if I come in now I should be well into it by Monday and you can always say I pulled rank.'

'No problem from my point of view,' came back the reply. 'As it happens I've got two weeks leave from next Thursday so it's likely I would've needed to hand over anyway. The only

6

thing that worries me is that if there is a personal element to this case, then perhaps you should, , take a back seat for your own safety.'

'I appreciate your concerns, but I don't really see how I can take a back seat. The letter was sent to me so we can assume that any further correspondence will come via the same route. I'll see you in about half an hour and you can give me the handover.'

So two weeks ago to the day, on a glorious September morning, Martin had set aside his plans to give his garden a much needed clear-up, leaving the tranquillity of his cottage in the small coastal village of Llantwit Major and heading for Cardiff.

His destination was Goleudy, the headquarters of the South Wales Crime Investigation Services. The imposing Victorian building, with its history dating back to the days when Cardiff was the coal-exporting capital of the world, was now home to all the agencies needed for crime prevention and detection in the twenty-first century. Martin knew from past experience that the head of SOC, Alex Griffiths, would by now have a complete picture of the crime scene and Professor Dafydd Moore would be making arrangements for the body to be brought back to Goleudy for post mortem examination. Martin would have preferred to visit the scene himself but DI Hall had already been there and it would have been unprofessional for Martin not to rely on the report of a fellow officer.

The two men met in the incident room that had only recently been cleared following the protracted investigation of a spate of premature deaths at a nursing home in the area. At some point in the future Martin would be required to give evidence at the trials of a number of people either responsible for or complicit in these crimes but for now it was the business of the CPS and lawyers on both sides to untangle the detail.

The room was quiet and peaceful for the moment and Martin sat down with Steven Hall to be briefed on what was now the latest DCI Phelps murder investigation.

'We got a call at 09.35.' began Steven. 'Actually, it was

almost as soon as I had put the phone down after speaking to you about your letter and by the way have you got it with you? I'd like to take a look.'

Martin nodded and as he reached into his jacket pocket he encouraged Steven to continue. 'The local police responded to the 999 call and arrived alongside the ambulance. That vehicle and crew was certainly not needed as the woman was dead but according to the Prof had not been dead that long. Her hands had been tied behind her and she had been stabbed in the abdomen, probably more than once, and that's why when she slumped forward onto the steering wheel she looked as if she was sitting in a pool of blood. There was no weapon as far as I could see but Alex and his team will let you know more when they get back.'

Steven paused and then concluded. 'The only other thing I can give you is the detail of the car and a simple phone call will give you the registered owner.' Before he left to resume writing the reports he had been doing when the call came in, Steven looked at the letter and made no comment other than, 'Weird – really weird.'

Martin shook his head as Steven Hall left the room and not for the first time wondered how his colleague had made it to the rank of detective inspector. He speculated on how long it would be before Steven took early retirement. At the moment he was lucky to have DS Cotter working with him but Cotter had applied for a transfer and his departure would leave the inadequacies of DI Hall somewhat exposed.

Martin set about organising the room in his usual manner, knowing that for him the devil was always in the detail and he had learned from experience that recording and sharing every piece of knowledge was vital when solving crime.

Incident Room One was set up with a number of whiteboards and the two largest were always used by Martin in the same way. The one that was most central was the one on which he drew his renowned three columns with the headings 'Absolute Facts', 'Facts to be Checked', and 'What Ifs'. He liked to give the case a name but as yet he wasn't sure if the things he knew from his letter and what he had heard from DI Hall about the murder had any connection. He provisionally put a bold side heading – **RED DRAGON**.

On one of the smaller whiteboards he wrote out the poem in full and seeing it displayed in this way made it look even more sinister. It would have been more effective if the board had been red too, but to ensure everyone got the picture he wrote '(written on red paper)' underneath the verses.

By the time Alex and his team returned from the scene Martin had obtained a number of facts for his first column. He had written the date and time of the 999 call, a list of the attending officers, and had recorded the location as the Red Dragon Centre, underlining the word 'Red'. Where he had noted that the woman's hands were tied behind her back with red cord the word 'red' was again underlined. For the moment he wrote nothing about the cause of death, as although DI Hall had said it was a stabbing he was light on facts. Martin decided to wait for Alex before filling in the details.

He had discovered that the car was a black automatic 2000cc Ford Mondeo hatchback which looked practically brand new, registered to a Miss Mary Rossiter,. Miss Rossiter's address was recorded as 12 Merlin Crescent, Caerphilly, and Martin had found out that there was only one occupant listed for that house. Of course, it didn't necessarily follow that it was the owner of the car who had been killed – someone else could have been using the vehicle.

The door opened and Martin's thoughts were interrupted by the appearance of a tall, solidly built man with a smoothly shaven head. It was Alex Griffiths, and he stood in the doorway for a few moments, taking in the information on the whiteboards, before smiling broadly.

'Never in a million years would DI Hall be responsible for this level of order, and there's only one "columns man" that I know and that's DCI Martin Phelps. What are you doing here, mate, and what's with the macabre poetry?'

Martin returned the smile. He and Alex had known one another for many years, since before either of them had joined

9

the force, and they had worked together on a number of complex cases. When it came to SOC investigators Alex was one of the best and not just because he was meticulous about detail; he had a natural instinct for knowing when things just did not add up.

'The poem is something I rang you about earlier but your phone went straight through to voicemail.' Martin showed Alex the red envelope and the paper on which the poem was written, explaining that it had been delivered to his cottage earlier that day. Just as Martin had done, Alex immediately picked up on the fact that it was addressed to 'DCI' and not 'Mr' Martin Phelps. The separation of their professional lives and their private lives was something most of the senior officers tried desperately to achieve, and this piece of correspondence had clearly crossed the line.

It didn't take more than a few minutes for Alex to take on board all the facts that Martin had gathered, and to reach the same conclusion. 'The person who murdered the woman I've just seen sent you that letter, and you weren't meant to get it until after the crime was committed. But why send it to you? You weren't even on the rota to be the senior CID officer on duty this weekend; I know because I always check who I'm going to be working with when I get a call out.'

'No, but I would have been if I hadn't swapped weekends,' replied Martin. 'Maybe our killer is someone with inside knowledge but not up-to-date information.'

'Oh, I bloody hate it when things get personal,' said Alex. 'Murder is bad enough anyway without the killer playing some sort of game with us. Have you got any idea who could have sent the letter and *de facto* could be the killer?'

'None whatsoever,' Martin said. 'I've been racking my brains thinking of the people who know my full name and rank together with my home address, and it's basically just the people I work with here plus a few close friends and relatives. I can't get my head around any of those people being responsible for this.'

'Good God, no!' interrupted Alex. 'Even I would be on that

10

list, as would Shelley and Charlie. That's what I mean when I say I hate it when things get personal – we're forced into considering possibilities that would never normally enter our heads.'

Charlie was Alex's wife. As a result of a hit-and-run incident when she was a teenager, she had received irreversible spinal injuries and was unable to walk. Amazingly she had not given up on life. In the years immediately following the accident she had been confined to bed and used the time to learn all there was to know about IT. Now in her early thirties, she had forgotten more about computers and electronic information systems than most people would ever know, and she was frequently headhunted by the big names in the industry.

Under different circumstances one would say that Charlie kept her feet on the ground; in her case it was the platform of her wheelchair – and that wheelchair seemed to propel her forward in life rather than hold her back. She was the Head of IT at Goleudy, and it was there that she had met Alex. Her black hair, hazel eyes, and Irish charm had been a mixture he'd found himself unable to resist. There were some who had been surprised at the match, as prior to their meeting Alex was known as a fun-loving man with an eye for the ladies, and his six-foot plus frame, good looks, and shaven scalp had attracted them like a beacon. But Alex only had eyes for Charlie once they got together.

Martin thought about the two of them and couldn't even contemplate having to consider them on any list of possible suspects, but he knew that his meticulous attention to detail would have to take him there at some point, though only so that they could be completely discounted.

Martin asked Alex what had happened at the crime scene and if DS Cotter was on his way back. 'I was just going to ask you,' countered Alex, 'if Cotter would be staying on the case or if Matt and Helen would be working with you. I presume you've taken the case, but I don't think Steven Hall has told his team and so, like me, they'll be surprised to see you in charge.'

'Well, I know that Matt's away this weekend,' said Martin.

11

'I've got no intention of calling him back, as apparently all four of his sisters plus his twelve nieces have taken a shine to his new girlfriend Sarah, and 16-1 odds against interruption of their mini-break are more than I can handle.'

Matthew Pryor, more commonly referred to as Matt, was the detective sergeant who normally worked with DCI Phelps and the whole force regarded Martin, Matt, Alex, and Professor Dafydd Moore as the 'A Team' – a reputation gained from the level of success the four of them had in crime solving.

Alex grinned and Martin continued. 'I'll speak to David Cotter, and if he's in agreement he can continue working with us until Monday morning and then hand over to Matt. However I did call Helen a while ago and she's on her way in. This will be her first experience of a murder from the CID angle and it's a pity she didn't actually see the body at the scene, but I'm sure your photography will fill us both in. I was going to say treat her gently, but I think she's quite a tough cookie and when it comes to dealing with the Prof women seem to come off better than men.'

Alex nodded in agreement. 'The miserable old git was at his most objectionable this morning,' he said. 'You know what the Red Dragon Centre is like – there's the bowling and the cinemas and as you can imagine the area was busy with families having Saturday morning treats and such like. There was a pile-up of traffic as soon as the security staff from the centre, at the request of DI Hall, closed the barriers. Prof honked his horn and did his "don't you know who I am thing" and for a while it was chaos.'

Martin smiled as he imagined Professor Dafydd Moore arriving at the crime scene in his cream-coloured Lexus, and in the manner of many leading academics expecting the world to be awaiting his arrival. When it came to forensic science he was a world leader, and moved and lectured in circles where his reputation went before him, so he was used to being instantly recognised.

Perhaps unusually for someone of his academic standing, he was dextrous and possessed practical skills that made him

12

invaluable when reading the clues left on a body, but one thing he lacked was common sense. It would never have occurred to him that everyone at the Red Dragon Centre did not know who he was or how important he was likely to be to the officers involved in this crime.

Alex continued. 'To be fair to our uniformed colleagues, they had matters in hand quite quickly and they'll be there for hours scrutinising everyone that goes in and out of that parking area, although I suspect the killer was gone before any of us arrived.'

'I'll have to tell Helen to be careful what she wishes for, as it was only Thursday when she said she could do with a good murder to get her career with CID started. This is certainly going to be an interesting one, what with the poem relating to a number of key elements already discovered and maybe a clue to more – it's a new one on me anyway.'

Helen had transferred from uniform to CID just a couple of months ago. To date she had only seen the more mundane side of the job, and had wondered if she had made a mistake. Even as a police officer she had experienced mounds of paperwork, but it had been peppered with opportunities to meet the public and get out and about. The last couple of months had seen nothing but paperwork, and although she had helped with two cases of fraud and criminal deception she was feeling vaguely dissatisfied.

When DCI Phelps had telephoned she had been taking her dog for a walk, and Oscar had not been happy when she made him turn tail and head back home before they had even reached the local park. Helen shared a flat with her brother and she knew it would be hours before he surfaced from his duvet, as sometime in the early hours she had vaguely heard him return from his Friday night partying.

She left a note to say the dog would need to be taken out later and headed for Cardiff Bay in her silver Mini Cooper, on the one hand feeling excited and on the other hand telling herself to remember that some poor woman had been murdered and that was hardly a cause for celebration.

The officer at the front desk told her that DCI Phelps was in Incident Room One, and she went straight there to be greeted by Martin and Alex. Just one of these men could make her feel small, but with the two of them standing together she felt as if she was in the land of giants.

Helen had never considered herself to be short, as at five feet five inches she was on a par with most women she knew and taller than a few of them, but she had always struggled with her weight and her rounded shape had made her seem shorter. Since transferring to CID she had joined a gym, and in a couple of months she had lost over a stone and was looking good. No longer wearing a uniform she was able to wear heels that boosted her height a bit but she still needed to lift her head to greet her colleagues.

'Good morning,' she said, and her eyes moved swiftly around the room before resting on the whiteboard where Martin had written out the poem. 'Not exactly written by one of the Romantic poets, is it? Byron and Keats certainly haven't been outdone by this modern-day rhymer – what is it exactly?'

''Morning, Helen,' responded Martin. 'Sorry to mess up your weekend but as I appear to have been selected by the murderer to solve this crime I feel justified in getting my own team to support me.'

Martin was about to explain the poem and the circumstances that had led to her being called in when the door opened again and this time it was DS Cotter who entered. As expected he looked surprised to see Martin and initially apologised for interrupting, believing he had walked into the wrong room.

Martin assured him that he was in the right place and suggested that they all get a coffee while he explained what was happening.

'Is DI Hall OK?' asked David Cotter. 'He seemed fine earlier although he didn't hang around and if anything was gone even faster than usual. I'm beginning to think he's allergic to the sight of blood, but seriously he's not ill or anything is he?'

'No, he's perfectly well,' Martin replied. 'It's just that under the circumstances, which I am about to explain, I feel I should

14

be the one leading this case.'

As Alex was already in the picture he offered to get them all some drinks while Martin briefed the other two as to why he was now heading the investigation instead of DI Hall.

Less than five minutes later Alex returned with four coffees and a plate of toast. 'We don't have breakfast until about ten on a Saturday,' he explained. 'So I missed mine this morning and suddenly felt hungry, help yourselves.'

Martin swallowed a mouthful of coffee and then spoke to Alex. 'David and Helen are now in the picture regarding the letter and why I have decided to take over this case, so now I need you and David to bring me up to date on the crime itself.'

Alex was still standing and picked up a second piece of toast before sitting at the table and pulling out his notebook. He asked David to start the ball rolling.

David looked at the details that Martin had already written on the large whiteboard. 'Well, that's it exactly,' he said, looking at Martin. 'You've got the names of the officers who were the first on the scene and it was PC Davies who contacted CID. I went to the scene with DI Hall. We had barely been there five minutes when Alex and his team arrived and then Professor Moore.' Alex looked up from his notebook and gave Martin the precise time he and the Prof had arrived.

David consulted his notes and gave Martin some information about the man who had made the emergency call. 'He is a Mr Carl Pearce and he's one of the security staff at the Red Dragon Centre. We're getting a full statement from him but from what he has said so far it was a member of the public who alerted his attention to the fact that a woman was slumped across the wheel of her car in the car park. Unfortunately he is unable to give us the name of the gentleman who told him as he didn't see him again.'

'Where was the security officer when the gentleman told him?' asked Martin.

'Walking about inside the Red Dragon building,' came back the reply. 'Apparently the man gave an exact position for the car and also the colour and make but instead of following security to the vehicle the man seemed to disappear and probably didn't want to get any more involved.'

'Or possibly,' said Martin, 'they didn't want to be arrested for murder!'

Chapter Two

'Surely not, sir?' DS Cotter stared at Martin. 'You can't think the person who murdered the woman had the brass to walk away from the murder and alert the security staff to what he had done. He would have wanted to get away as quickly as possible, wouldn't he?'

Martin considered the question before he responded. 'This is not someone who has committed a random murder, this is someone who has thought for a long time about what he wanted to do and has planned it carefully. It may well be that part of the thrill will be associated with taking risks and watching us all run around trying to put together the clues to his identity.'

'My guess is that he was still in the area when you all arrived and may even still be there now. This person is intelligent, he knows me, and I get a gut feeling that he knows the systems we operate, which is going to make it more difficult for us to find him.'

Alex had loaded his pictures of the crime scene onto the computer and now played them on the second large whiteboard. As neither Martin nor Helen had actually been to the crime scene they took a particular interest in the images.

The car, as Martin had already discovered, was a black Mondeo and looked in tip-top condition, but the front passenger side window had been smashed to allow the police entry to the vehicle. Alex told them a bit more. 'The car doors were all locked and there were no keys in the ignition so we can assume that after the stabbing the killer locked the doors remotely and took the keys with him. The same applies to the knife he used as there was no weapon found in the car.'

Martin interrupted and asked DS Cotter what instructions had been given regarding searches of the area and the other cars in the car park. 'It's all in hand, sir,' he assured Martin. 'Sergeant Evans had arrived on the scene before I left and there are now more than twenty officers combing the vicinity and vetting all the cars that leave the area. Of course, every car will be stopped – but any car occupied by just one male driver will be particularly scrutinised.'

'Will you please ask them to look out for people walking as well as driving – drivers would be the obvious suspects and that's why I think this killer may not have used a car.' Martin sat thoughtfully for a moment and then asked Alex to continue.

The next image on the screen showed the woman with her head face down on the steering wheel, and it was followed by shots from all angles of the car's interior.

One picture showed a handbag and a blue lightweight jacket. 'That handbag will belong to the victim, won't it?' suggested Helen. 'A woman might lend her car to someone else – but her handbag, never!'

The men laughed, but they all agreed that Helen was the best judge of that, and then David told them what had been found in the handbag.

'The bag is with Alex's team but it doesn't look as if it was disturbed in anyway. We found it on the passenger seat and all it contains is a purse, a hairbrush, a nail file, a lipstick, and a very old-fashioned mobile phone.' Alex confirmed that his team were taking a look at that and he had asked Charlie to see if she could get into the mobile phone. 'It's locked with a password,' he explained, 'but I've managed to get my wife away from the shops, and if she can't unlock that phone no one can.'

'Was there anything in the purse?' asked Martin.

'Not much, really,' replied David. 'Some loose change, one twenty-pound notes and three tens, - and an HSBC debit card. Oh, and one library card; I didn't even know they issued them anymore.'

'Very neat and tidy,' remarked Helen. 'If anyone did a random check through my handbag when I was out and about on a Saturday morning they would find it stuffed full of till receipts, packets of wine gums, a couple of folded plastic bags, and all sorts of random stuff.'

'Judging by the images I guess this woman was as near to seventy as damn it, and it looks as if she was previously in pretty good shape, but she's not one of your modern elderly women, the way she dresses and her belongings are quite dated.'

'Do you know when the Prof is planning to do the PM?' Martin asked Alex.

'Immediately,' came the reply. 'He has some sort of reunion dinner with his university colleagues tonight, and he told me that he'd be available until about five o'clock if there was going to be a briefing. What time is it now?'

Helen responded. 'It's a quarter past twelve. Mrs Williams from the Prof's department arrived at the same time I did so I suspect the PM will be well underway. What's the plan now, sir?' she asked Martin.

'I'm torn between going up to the fourth floor to see what's happening with the PM and going to the home of the car owner to ascertain whether or not she is our victim. I think it must be the latter.' Turning to DS Cotter he asked. 'Will you chase up anything you can find out about Mary Rossiter and then get an update from the crime scene? I want all the tapes covering today from the surveillance cameras in the car park and see if you can get the security officer to give us a description of the man who reported the incident. Helen will come to Caerphilly with me and you can let all the relevant people know that the first official briefing on this case will be here, at 4 p.m. Is that OK with you?' he asked Alex.

'Fine,' Alex responded, turning to DS Cotter. 'I need to speak to the professor so I'll tell him about the briefing arrangements.'

With everyone certain of the tasks that needed to be completed Martin led the way to his car, and about fifteen minutes later they had left the M4 motorway and were heading northwest on the A470 towards Caerphilly. Martin had tapped the postcode into his sat nav and switched it on for the last part of the journey. 'I hate that woman's voice,' he explained to Helen. 'That's why I only turn her on when I get to the part of the journey where her knowledge of the area is better than mine.'

'I know what you mean,' laughed Helen. 'She sounds like a really posh robot, but you can turn her off if you want to because I know exactly where Merlin Crescent is – I have a cousin living in Merlin Place and it's the next block of houses.'

'Brilliant,' said Martin, and he immediately switched off the robotic voice in mid-sentence. He looked around as they drove through Merlin Place, and he could see that there were some large detached properties and some buildings that were divided into flats.

He turned into Merlin Crescent. As the name suggested, all the homes sat back along the extended half-moon shape of the road, and he slowed down as they came close to the number he was looking for. The house was one half of a semi-detached pair and the adjoining one was a hive of activity. Three young children were running up and down the short path knocking into one another and screaming with laughter. They all came to the edge of the path to get a better look at Martin's car and the oldest one called out to his mother who was, presumably, in the house.

'Mammy, some people have come to see Miss Rossiter but she's not there.'

Martin heard a woman's voice. 'Come in here and mind your own business,' she said. 'If you don't get yourselves sorted in the next few minutes there'll be no party this afternoon.'

Helen pointed to the banner across the front door indicating that someone was eight today and gave a friendly wave to the children as Martin rang the doorbell of Miss Rossiter's house.

'Mister, she's not in – I told you she's not in,' the boy shouted to Martin. 'She said she'd buy me a birthday present but she hasn't, and if she's not back soon she'll be too late for the party, 'cos it starts at two.'

The boy's mother appeared at the door and took over the conversation. 'I'm sorry about my son,' she began. 'He seems to have formed his own neighbourhood watch scheme. Miss Rossiter is very kind but she'll soon get fed up with his pestering, and he's even invited her to his birthday party. Archie is right, however, about her not being at home, and according to him she left just before nine o'clock this morning. Can I help? Do you want to leave her a message or something?'

Martin had walked towards the woman as she spoke and as he approached her he took out his warrant card and formally introduced himself and Detective Constable Cook-Watts. 'Is there somewhere we could speak without the children hearing?' he asked and the woman called up the stairs. 'Danny, can you come down here, there are some detectives that want a word.'

'Yes, right, pull the other leg,' shouted a voice from one of the bedrooms. 'I'm trying to blow up these helium balloons and pack a pass-the-parcel at the same time, so tell Archie I'll play detective games later.'

'Danny, I'm serious, will you please come down here now?'

Something in the tone of the woman's voice must have got the message through as a man holding three purple helium balloons came to the top of the stairs and looked down. 'Sorry!' he said descending the stairs two at a time. 'What's up? Has there been an accident or something – s it someone in the family?'

Martin re-introduced him and Helen and explained that their visit was regarding Miss Rossiter. The man introduced himself as Danny Lloyd and his partner as Mandy Pugh. 'We don't share the same name,' he told the detectives, 'but we do share all the same children and as you can see they're in birthday mode. Sorry if they've been a pain.'

'Not at all,' replied Martin. 'I need to talk to you about Miss Rossiter, and preferably without the children hearing.'

A moment later Martin and Helen were sitting in a lounge strewn with wrapping paper and birthday presents and speaking to Danny Lloyd while the children were upstairs continuing with the balloon-blowing and parcel-packing which their father had abandoned.

'What's this all about?' asked Danny. 'Has something happened to Miss Rossiter? Sorry, I don't even know her first name, but maybe that's the way it is with retired teachers – she's Miss Rossiter to everyone.'

Martin's mind snapped back to a couple of lines from the poem he had received that morning.

'*No more the teacher for this time the lesson I will teach.*'

So another thing was falling into place, as it looked as if the victim had been a teacher. If there had been any doubt that there was a connection between the murder and the letter, there was no more, and Martin knew that when he got back he would be concentrating on every word that had been written.

'Is it at all likely that Miss Rossiter would lend her car to anyone?' asked Martin.

Danny shook his head. 'She doesn't seem to know many people and although she goes out quite a lot I've never known her have visitors to the house. It's about nine months since she moved in and there was a middle-aged couple who helped her with the move but that's about it. Look, it's obvious that something serious has happened, are you able to tell me what it is?'

'Yes, of course,' replied Martin. 'I just wanted to make sure we were jumping to the right conclusions. The fact is that Miss Rossiter's car was parked in the Red Dragon Centre this morning and a member of the public noticed that she was lying across the steering wheel and he alerted Security to a potential problem. When the police arrived they discovered that Miss Rossiter was dead, and I'm afraid she didn't die from natural causes – she was murdered.'

'Oh, my good God! That can't be right, surely? Murdered in her own car, and in broad daylight.' Danny struggled with his words. 'What did they do to her? Perhaps it was some sort of accident. I can't think why anyone would want to murder her.'

'Well, as you can imagine,' replied Martin, 'I am unable to give you the details but I'm afraid that the idea of an accident is out of the question – all I can say at the moment is that she was stabbed.'

'Stabbed!' echoed Danny. 'Then it must have been a case of mistaken identity. Why would anyone single out Miss Rossiter and stab her and on Archie's birthday? I can't get my head around this.'

'What can you tell us about Miss Rossiter?' Helen asked gently. 'You said earlier that she moved in about nine months ago; have you got to know her well in that time?'

Danny raised a smile. 'Archie is the only one who has had anything to do with her, really,' he replied. 'We're all sociable, in that we speak to her in passing, but we've taken our lead from her and she gave us the impression that she wanted to be left alone. Archie has not yet reached the age of discretion and he's knocked on her door several times – and to be fair, she's helped him with a couple of school projects.'

'When she moved in one of my mates from the pub told me that she used to teach in the school that his kids went to and she had the reputation of being quite a strict disciplinarian – "a bit of a dragon" is what he actually said! But he did say that his two boys achieved more in her class than at any other time in the school.'

Martin heard the words 'a bit of a dragon' and matched yet another connection between the poem and the murder.

'I take it from what you've said that you wouldn't know how to contact Miss Rossiter's next of kin or anyone who could help with a formal identification? I hate to ask you this especially, as you are in the middle of sorting out your son's party, but would you consider helping us? Your neighbour has not been disfigured in any way, and it would just be a question of you stating that the body is indeed Miss Rossiter.'

Martin didn't know what the reaction would be to his request but Danny didn't hesitate. 'No, I'm sorry, I can't help you with contacts, but I will help with the formal identification you need, it's the least we can do. Do you want me to come with you now?'

While the two men had been speaking Helen had received a

call on her mobile and told Martin that a set of keys belonging to the victim's car had been found. Sgt Evans had made the call and was able to tell Helen that there were two other keys on the keyring and one was almost certainly a house key.

Martin accepted the information and then turned back to Danny and thanked him for his cooperation. 'You carry on with your party plans,' he said. 'I wouldn't say anything to the children and let Archie enjoy his day. It looks as if we may have recovered the keys to Miss Rossiter's house and so an officer, DS Cotter, will be here in a little while to look around the house. When he has finished and if it fits in with your plans, he can bring you to the station, where you will be able to make the formal identification, and then we'll arrange for you to get a lift back.'

'That's fine with me,' replied Danny. 'Poor sod. She wasn't that old by today's standards and she was certainly active and seemed to be in good health. Why would anyone want to murder her?'

'Hopefully it won't be too long before we find the person responsible and maybe then we will have an answer to your question,' was Martin's reply. 'In the meanwhile thank you for being so helpful and if you think of anything that may help us please give me a ring.'

Martin left his card, and it was a few minutes into the journey back to Cardiff before any conversation occurred in the car. When Helen did eventually speak it was clear that she and Martin had been sharing the same thoughts. 'There's no doubt that the poem you received was written by the killer, is there? I can't remember it exactly but there is a reference to the colour red and something about a dragon.'

'No doubt whatsoever,' said Martin. 'Having read it several times and then written it on the board I think I know it word for word. The actual word "red" is only mentioned once but the killer wrote it on red paper and used a red envelope. The crime was committed at the Red Dragon Centre and we know that the victim's hands were tied behind her back with red cord.'

'The poem tells us the woman is dead – we were never

meant to find her alive – and the writer indicates that he or she knew the victim. We now know that Miss Rossiter was a teacher, so that bit fits, and if she was strict she would certainly have been seen by some kids as a bit of a dragon.'

'Well I thought that a number of my teachers were fire-breathing dragons,' said Helen, 'but I never seriously contemplated bumping them off.'

Martin laughed. 'We would be working around the clock if every pupil had that idea but in this case I believe we are being directed towards an ex-student and one who is harbouring an unnatural grudge. I wonder how many children Miss Rossiter taught during the years when she was working as a teacher? I guess it narrows it down from everyone in the country being a suspect, but it will still run into hundreds if not thousands of people.'

Helen nodded. 'The murderer obviously knew Miss Rossiter, but the thing that worries me, sir, is that he or she knows your home address. That's more than most people would do and I don't like the thought of that.'

'You and me both,' replied Martin, as he parked the car and led the way back to Incident Room One.

Finding no one there he suggested to Helen that he could have an idea regarding their colleagues' whereabouts and changing direction headed down the backstairs to the staff dining room. It was no surprise to find DS Cotter and Alex finishing off a late lunch.

'Sorry we didn't wait for you,' said Alex. 'It was coming up to two o'clock and I needed something more than those couple of slices of toast we had earlier to keep me going.'

'No problem,' replied Martin. 'I was awake early this morning with the intention of sorting out my garden, so I had scrambled eggs on toast before the noxious letter arrived. I'll get a sandwich or something now and then we can have a session going over what we know before the briefing.'

Martin turned to David Cotter. 'I understand we have recovered the victim's missing keys.'

'Yes, sir,' was the reply. 'They were handed into Security by a couple of teenage girls and I get the feeling that we were meant to find them.'

'What makes you say that?' questioned Martin.

'Well, there was no attempt to hide them, and the girls just saw them sitting in the middle of the bonnet of their mother's car as she was about to drive off. It's probably just a coincidence but that car is a red Mondeo – exactly like the victim's car, but red, not black.'

'No,' replied Martin. 'That is no coincidence. We're dealing with one sick bastard who likes playing games, and I suspect we'll see more things linking the murder to the poem as we get further into the case.'

The three men discussed the keys and Alex confirmed that there was nothing he would be able to get from them in the way of links to the killer. He shrugged his shoulders. 'Getting prints from keys is difficult at the best of times. Here we have a situation where the murder was planned and the killer is likely to have worn gloves followed by at least three people handling the keys since they were found.'

Helen brought an orange juice and a sandwich to the table, and as she sat down Martin suggested she update the other two regarding the visit to Merlin Crescent. He returned a few minutes later with a ham salad baguette and a coffee in time to hear Helen summing up. 'So we know that Miss Rossiter left her home, driving her black Mondeo, just before nine o'clock this morning – and we were told that she is a retired teacher, apparently with a reputation for being something of a dragon.'

'Everything we know so far fits in with the letter you got this morning,' said Alex to Martin. 'Any thoughts on what it could all be about?'

Martin replied. 'At this moment in time none whatsoever, and before we have our first briefing I would like some thinking time.' He turned to DS Cotter. 'Helen knows where the victim lives and you have her house keys so I'd like you both to go there and take a look around. Don't go in a squad car as I don't want you upstaging an eight year-old's birthday party that should by now be well underway. You can bring the neighbour back with you as he has agreed to do the formal identification. I think we should move the planned briefing forward in time to 4.30, to allow you to get to Caerphilly and back and for me to think things through.'

Helen finished her sandwich and headed towards the car park with DS Cotter, leaving Alex with an opportunity to air his concerns. 'We have worked together for many years, Martin, but we've been friends for much longer, and I'm seriously worried that someone, someone we know now to be a killer, has picked on you as the focus for whatever sick game he is playing. I say "he" although it is possible that the person responsible is a woman – but my gut instinct is that it's a man.'

'I had just finished a call from the professor before I came to lunch and basically all he had to say was he had finished the PM and that the woman had been stabbed twice. He's happy with the revised time of four thirty for the first briefing as it will give him more time to pick up some colleagues from Cardiff Central station. I think he said one was coming by train from London and the other from Manchester.

'Anyway, they and several others have a reunion do tonight at the St David's Hotel. He plans to meet them within the next hour or so and take them to the hotel. I guess he should be back here by four thirty, but then he wants to be away by five.'

Martin laughed. 'Well at least that will ensure a shorter than usual pathology lesson for us all. I don't personally see a reunion of aging, probably brilliant pathologists being a fun-packed evening but what do I know about it?'

'Who knows?' replied Alex. 'I wonder what the collective noun is for a group of eminent pathologists.'

'What about an autopsy of academics?' suggested Martin as the two men parted, each with a couple of hours of work to do before the start of the first briefing session.

Barely had Martin sat down at his desk when, without ceremony, his door opened and Superintendent Bryant walked in. There were three things unexpected about this and the first was that Martin had never before known the super to be around at the weekend. Secondly, Martin couldn't remember ever having been paid a visit, as the norm was for Martin to be summoned upstairs. The third thing was that Martin had never seen Superintendent Bryant wearing anything but his uniform.

This afternoon he was dressed in what could be described as this season's 'must have' attire for a weekend on the golf course. For a few seconds Martin took in the whole ensemble, from dark green and tan coloured shoes that looked decidedly expensive to the wide-brimmed black hat with the Galvin Green logo. Not being a golfing man, the relevance of the matching V-neck sweater and cotton trousers was lost on him, but he suspected that whatever the superintendent's handicap was it was not his dress code.

One could be forgiven for thinking that anyone dressed so well and obviously set for an enjoyable afternoon on the golf course would be in a good humour, but Martin was soon to discover that this was not the case.

'I was on my way to my club when my partner for this afternoon rang to say he had been held up in the car park of the Red Dragon Centre because the police were crawling all over the place. Apparently even before he and his family left the area there was an announcement on a local radio station that the body of a woman had been found stabbed in one of the cars in that very car park. Is that right, and if so why haven't I been informed?'

Martin's first thought was to wonder who had leaked the information to the media. He had already given a brief statement but it had only said that the body of a woman had been found and that the police were treating her death as suspicious. Quite deliberately he had not mentioned the cause of death.

'Good afternoon, sir,' he began. 'Yes, it is true that we are investigating the murder of a woman probably between nine and nine thirty this morning – and in exactly the place you mentioned.'

Martin didn't bother to explain why he hadn't notified the super because he knew from past experience that he was damned if he did and damned if he didn't, and on this occasion he had not wanted it known that he had taken over the case from DI Hall.

'I can't tell you much at the moment other than that the victim was a retired teacher and that she was stabbed. The PM has already been done and the first full briefing on the case is set for 4.30. Do you want me to update you after that, as it's likely to be when you're still on the golf course?'

Superintendent Bryant looked horrified. 'Mobile phones are frowned upon during the round and we're already forced to tee off at a later time because of the delay, so I'd rather not be disturbed again. Just let me know what's being released to the press and anything else can wait until Monday.'

With that he left Martin's office, and Martin sat wondering what the visit had been all about. A simple phone call would have been sufficient but he had better things to do than second-guess his senior officer. He opened his desk drawer and took out a pencil and a couple of blank sheets of paper that would help focus his mind on the facts of the case ahead of addressing the team.

The victim had been a teacher, and even in today's society teachers had a degree of respect – and the murder of any public servant always grabbed the interest of the media. Martin knew that the horror of a woman being murdered in a busy public car park in broad daylight would strike a note of terror with the general public.

He also had to consider the personal element that the poem had thrown up, and although it worried him slightly he was fully committed to solving this case. He wished he could come up with some ideas regarding why the poem had been sent to him, and what the last couple of lines were all about. In preparation for the briefing he wrote down everything that came into his head and managed to cobble together four pages of organised scribble.

About ten minutes before the briefing was due to start he got a phone call from Charlie. She had received the CCTV tapes from the Red Dragon Centre and had transferred the images to her computer. What she had seen had caused her to contact

Martin immediately, and within minutes he had joined her to watch some of the most chilling CCTV evidence he had ever seen.

Chapter Three

It was a few minutes before 4.30 and the room was buzzing. Placing his papers on the table at the front Martin listened to the opinions that were being voiced about the killing and the way in which a normal Saturday had, for hundreds of ordinary people, turned into an occasion they would never forget. He heard some of the uniformed police officers relating stories of the abuse they had taken from drivers, who were unaware of the crime that had been committed and just angry at the disruption to their day.

Martin missed Matt, and knew that if his usual sidekick had been around they would by now have had a session of bouncing ideas to and fro and possibly come up with a few more ideas than Martin had done alone. His temporary DS and the recently appointed DC Cook-Watts had returned from their visit to the victim's house and were deep in conversation.

Alex was leaning over one of the computers and advising Charlie on the order in which he wanted scenes of the crime presented and she was explaining that Prof. Moore's images would need to be first because he had to get away early.

At the mention of the professor's name Martin looked around and realised that their esteemed friend was not there, but as it was now exactly 4.30 Martin got to his feet to bring the meeting to order.

Talk about being upstaged! The room fell into immediate silence but it had nothing to do with Martin's leadership skills and everything to do with the person who had just made a grand entrance.

The professor's hair was only slightly less dishevelled than

31

usual and the familiar half-rimmed glasses were still perched on the end of his nose but apart from that there was a complete transformation. Shiny, black leather shoes replaced his usual open-toed sandals. The much loved baggy khaki trousers had been substituted by immaculately pressed, black fine woollen ones with a black silk stripe that matched the material on the lapels of his jacket. Under the jacket the professor wore a brilliant white dress shirt and a perfectly knotted deep burgundy bow tie that matched the colour of his cummerbund. The final touches came in the form of a pair of thick, square gold cufflinks and the overall effect was certainly a showstopper.

Martin had no control over the situation as the room erupted with spontaneous applause and comments, such as 'he scrubs up well' and 'would hardly recognise him,' followed the professor as he made his way to the front of the room. 'OK, the show is over.' The Prof spoke in his usual miserable way, so no change there. 'I need to be away in thirty minutes, so may we get started?'

The question was directed at Martin, and although the voice had been the one of the miserable old git they all loved to hate, Martin had spotted a twinkle in the professor's eyes and knew that he had enjoyed his entrance and the resulting response.

Martin held up his hand and this time the audience responded to the DCI's cue and there was silence. 'I suggest that DS Cotter gives us the background to today's events and then, as Professor Moore has to leave by five o'clock, we go straight into the results of the post mortem.'

DS Cotter got to his feet and outlined the details of the 999 call and the subsequent response. Nothing he said caused Martin to add anything to what he had already written on the whiteboard, but it did ensure that everyone was up to speed on the precise facts that were known up to that point.

Martin picked up from where DS Cotter had left off but spoke only briefly to inform every one of the identity of the victim. 'Before I arrived for this meeting I spoke briefly to a Mr Danny Lloyd, who had just identified the body as his neighbour, Miss Rossiter, a retired schoolteacher. DS Cotter will tell us more about her later, but for now it's over to Professor Moore to tell us what he has found.'

Instead of immediately enthralling the audience, as he usually did, with the precise details of his forensic examination, the Prof turned to Martin and asked about the poem that was written on one of the smaller whiteboards. Martin briefly explained the origin of the poetry, and to the wider audience he added that they would go into it in more detail later.

'It's a pity I have to rush off,' said Prof Moore. 'I would have enjoyed watching you tease out that puzzle – but maybe on Monday you could give me an update.'

Martin nodded and the first post-mortem image appeared on the large whiteboard. For the next twenty minutes the room was quiet as the professor gave a detailed account of his findings.

'First thing to say is that the woman, who we now know to be Miss Rossiter, had very likely reached her three score years and ten, and if her life hadn't been cruelly ended in this way she could well have gone on to the day of receiving her telegram from the Queen. She was five feet seven inches tall and weighed one hundred and thirty-six pounds, and for those of you into the metric system that's 1.7 metres and 61.7 kilograms respectively.

'She looked after herself and I doubt if she has ever smoked or had more than the occasional alcoholic drink in her life. Prior to the stabbings all her major organs were in very good shape and I found no sign of any abnormal pathology anywhere. It is obvious that she had had a hysterectomy, but not recently and I would put the time of surgery at more than twenty years ago, so possibly around the time of her menopause.

'Miss Rossiter had the hands and nails of someone who has done very little in the way of manual work. She had a "port wine stain" birthmark at the top of her right arm but I doubt if many people even knew of its existence, and the only other thing to mention is that although she had several well-cared for fillings most of her teeth were perfect and they were certainly all her own.

'So, as you can deduce, when this lady left her home this

morning she was fit and well and so now I will go on to show you the damage done by her murderer.'

The professor nodded in Charlie's direction and she hit one of the buttons at her fingertips and an image of Miss Rossiter filled the whiteboard. This image was not of the healthy mature woman just described by the Prof, but of a pale, lifeless body covered in a white mortuary sheet with just the head, neck, and shoulders visible.

The professor continued. 'As you can see, there is a gaping hole at the side of her neck, towards the back, and I believe that we are looking at the second stab wound.'

The next image showed the rest of the body with the sheet folded back to the top of the pubic bone and slowly zoomed in on an abdominal wound that looked lethal. 'This, I believe, is the first stab wound inflicted by the killer and it is what killed her. I have had the opportunity to see some of the CCTV footage that you will be viewing later and it confirms what I believe happened.'

'Detective Chief Inspector Phelps will take you through the possible reasons why this woman would have opened her car door to a man with a knife but I can tell you that within seconds of her doing so she was dead. A long sharp knife was plunged into the abdomen just beneath her ribs and followed exactly the correct upward direction to make contact with some important blood vessels to the right side and immediately below her heart.

'The inferior vena cava is the large vein in this area and its purpose is to carry de-oxygenated blood from the lower half of the body into the right atrium. As I'm sure you all know the heart is made up of four chambers and the right atrium is the one that is situated above the right ventricle. In this case our killer either knew exactly what he was doing or was extremely lucky, as his knife went through the large vein and into the right ventricle.'

He asked Charlie to zoom in still further so that the damage to the internal organs could be witnessed clearly.

'Would that have killed her instantly?' asked DS Cotter.

'Well, she wouldn't have had time to get her parking ticket, that's for sure, and my guess is that she would have immediately lost consciousness and been dead within a minute.'

With another nod towards Charlie the images returned to the neck wound. 'That's why I don't really understand this second stab wound. I didn't need to scientifically work out which order the wounds were inflicted because as you will see, when you are presented with an actual video of the murder, my forensic science genius was surplus to requirements.'

'The only thing I can add is that both incisions were made with a sharp knife and it would have had to be long to cut through the upper abdominal contents and make contact with the heart.'

'Thanks for that,' said Martin, as he realised that Prof Moore was finished and heading for the door. 'Hope your evening goes well.'

Even before Martin had finished speaking the Prof had left the room, and the level of conversation had drowned the last words of the DCI's sentence. The excitement had obviously been caused by the professor's reference to the possibility of there being a CCTV recording of the actual murder. It was the one that Charlie had called Martin to see before the briefing started, and it certainly showed how the murder had been committed, but it asked as many questions as it answered.

Martin didn't want to go straight into viewing the CCTV records as he wanted to go back to the order in which things had been discovered, and he shouted above the noise to Alex, who responded by displaying the first of the images from the crime scene.

The room fell silent as the body of a woman whose head was positioned in an awkward angle, face down on the steering wheel of her car, came into focus. The injury to her neck was obvious, but in the position she was sitting the only clue to the fatal abdominal wound was the colour change of her clothing. The cream cotton skirt was emblazoned with an extra scarlet waistband of sticky red blood that had seeped up the material of her floral blouse, creating bizarre patterns.

Alex painstakingly took the meeting through every detail of

the SOC operation and then handed back to Martin, who in turn asked DS Cotter if there was anything he wanted to add at this point. He replied. 'Just to say that we are looking for the weapon, known to be a sharp, long-bladed knife but so far nothing has been recovered.' He explained how the car keys had been recovered and with them keys to Miss Rossiter's home.

'DC Cook-Watts and I have just returned from the house and basically there was nothing found that at first glance is of any help. The only thing that caught our attention was a desk drawer that we opened with the third key on her keyring. The drawer contained old school reports and exercise books, some over as forty years old, and appear to be just a random selection of her pupil's efforts. We have brought them all back and will study them in more detail, but on the face of it they don't appear to be connected to her murder.'

'Thank you.' said Martin. 'The only other thing to mention, before turning our attention to the CCTV footage, is the mobile phone found in the victim's handbag, and Charlie will tell us more about that.'

Charlie smiled. 'It's a long time since I have seen one of these second generation prepaid phones and it reminded me of how far the technology has developed over the past twenty years. It's a very old Vodafone, I guess it's about eighteen years old, but it was easy to get into and I was able to retrieve eleven names and telephone numbers. Can you imagine that? – having a mobile for all those years and only having eleven names and numbers registered in the memory.

'The last time the phone was used was four months ago, and that was an incoming call from her dentist. However the numbers that were registered have been useful and one enabled us to contact a Mr Simon Rossiter, who is her brother's son and apparently her next of kin. He lives in Cambridge and the last time he saw his aunt was at his mother's funeral eight years ago.'

'I will need to speak to him,' said Martin, 'but I understand he was in Germany when you spoke to him; has been for the past week, and lots of people can verify that. So at least we can cross him off our non-existent list of suspects.'

Martin continued. 'I have already seen the footage you are about to watch and it is one of the most chilling things I have ever experienced. It looks a bit like something we would see at the cinema or watch on the television, but this is real – this is a real murder. Please watch carefully and if you spot anything that could help us identify this killer, no matter if you think it's trivial, jot it down and we will discuss it at the end.'

Charlie pressed the button and the first images from the CCTV camera showed the area of the car park where Miss Rossiter would be parking her car. The time was displayed in the top right hand corner and the seconds were seen ticking along and when they reached 09:13:03 the black Mondeo car was seen entering the car park and by 09:13:59 Miss Rossiter had parked the car.

She didn't get out of the car and just sat there. It wasn't possible to see what she was doing as the camera was not picking up that level of detail. The officers watched and waited as the CCTV showed other cars around her arriving and departing. Having watched the action once already Martin was concentrating on the people on foot rather than the movements of the vehicles. He was therefore one of the first to spot a man approaching the black Mondeo.

The man was tall, probably around six feet, and wore black jeans and a navy polo-neck sweater. His head was well covered by a baseball-style cap with a large rounded peak that made it impossible for the camera, from its high vantage point, to show his face. He carried a dark blue canvas sports bag with no visible logo.

The man was obviously aware of the security cameras and looked down at the floor as he purposefully made his way directly to Miss Rossiter's car. The time displayed was now 09:19:02. It seemed as if she had been waiting for him as she started to open the car door when he approached it. Keeping his head well down the man, who it could now be seen was wearing gloves, took charge of the door and swung it wide open. As he did so he stepped between the door and the car and took something out of his sports bag. Still keeping his head down he ducked into the car and was seen lunging in a forward and upward movement.

There were gasps of horror from some of the people watching as they realised they had just witnessed a cold-blooded murder. The killer didn't stop there and he seemed to yank something forward at the same time as he pulled something out of the body. That first something must have been Miss Rossiter's head but before her head reached the steering wheel the killer made a second stabbing movement and the head rolled forward into the position it had been discovered just a short while later.

It looked as if he was pulling her arms backwards and he must have returned the knife to his bag because he was using both hands to do something.

Because the killer's body was, for the most part, preventing a full image of what was happening in the car there was no sign of the knife and the only reason the audience knew a knife had been used was because they had seen the post-mortem results. They knew that what they had witnessed was a knife being thrust into the woman's upper abdomen, just below her ribs and aimed in an upward direction to sever her inferior vena cava and pierce her right ventricle. They also knew that the second stabbing of her neck was an unnecessary affront on a body already damaged to the point of death.

He appeared to take the glove off his right hand and put it in his bag before carefully removing the keys from the ignition and closing the door by pushing it with the toe of his trainers. The killer didn't rush and when he moved away from the car he exercised the same care. There was not a moment, throughout the whole episode, when anything other than his back was facing the camera. He gave the impression of having all the time in the world as, still with his head kept down, he mingled with men, women, and children enjoying their Saturday morning freedom from work and school. No one gave him a second look and he did nothing to attract their attention. If they

38

had only known!

As the murderer disappeared from view the time showed 09:22:16 and so from arriving to exiting it had taken him just over three minutes to commit an act of unspeakable horror.

Instead of the usual buzz that tended to follow a CCTV presentation there was an uncanny silence and Martin could tell that there was no one who had not been affected by what they had seen. He allowed everyone a few minutes reflection before suggesting a five-minute break and maybe a coffee before they went into analysing the detail of the CCTV footage.

Helen spoke to Martin. 'Hell, that's one cool character. At any point someone could have noticed what he was doing and did you see that even when he was standing outside but with his body inside the car there were people walking past. We are all so busy with our own lives, aren't we? Still, to be fair to those people you are hardly likely to think, when you're parking your car, that someone in the next parking space is being murdered.'

'I'm going to take up your suggestion of a coffee, do you want one?'

Martin replied that he would love a coffee and Helen left him to update his whiteboard with a few facts and figures, such as the exact time the murder was committed. He couldn't remember another occasion when he or any of his colleagues had been able to do that and for a moment his mind went back to something DCI Austin had once said. He had told Martin that an officer could only be certain of the exact time of a murder if he had been the one committing the act.

Martin had worked with DCI Austin when he first joined CID, and although he had applauded the detective brain of his senior officer Martin had intensely disliked the man – and some of his methods of obtaining evidence had been, to put it mildly, unethical. Anyway, the DCI had been wrong about only knowing the time of death if you committed the murder, because in this current case they had positive evidence regarding the time and the exact method used by the killer.

The room started to fill up again and a couple of minutes later Martin re-started the briefing session by drawing everyone's attention to the poem he had written out earlier. 'We've jumped about during this session,' he explained. 'Now I want to take you back to first thing this morning when I received a red envelope through the post and written inside, on an A4 sheet of red paper, was this poem.'

All eyes were on the whiteboard and Martin explained that when he had first read it he thought it could be some sort of sick hoax. 'The envelope was sent to my home but was addressed to *Detective Chief Inspector* Martin Phelps, and that in itself is very odd,' he continued. 'I try, like most of you, to keep home and work at arm's length from each other and I will be working with my CID colleagues to get a comprehensive list of anyone who knows me well enough to have my full name and rank as well as my home address.

'Anyway, aside from that I couldn't make any sense of the poem and I called a few people who were not able to help. It was DI Hall who remembered the poem on his way back from the crime scene and called me to ask if I thought there was a connection.

'Since then we have come to know a number of things about the victim and I am now going to go through these verses line by line and tell you what I think are the linking factors and please let me know if any others spring to your minds.

'I believe that the first verse simply refers to the fact that the writer intends to commit a murder and that he knows exactly who he is going to kill and why. It appears to be someone who has not treated him well, perhaps even bullied him and he is making it known that by the time I read his words the deed will be done. Does anyone have anything to add to that?'

DS Cotter initially shook his head but then added, 'I agree with that and would just like to add that we were never intended to prevent this killing; it's more like he is teasing us and he obviously thinks he's very clever.'

Martin nodded and as no one else wanted to contribute to the discussion he continued. 'The second verse confirms the bullying and seems to me to specifically relate to a schoolteacher/pupil relationship. Where else would you get one person forcing another to "play games"? I certainly remember a few of the kids in my school year saying they hated one of our teachers who made them play rugby. Anyone got any other ideas?'

PC Davies made a suggestion that people in the army were sometimes pushed into games. 'But then I realised that the victim was a teacher, so your suggestion is probably right. The only other games that seem to get people in trouble are boardroom power games and perhaps sexual games. Neither would seem likely when you consider our victim, but you did ask for ideas.'

'Yes I did, and thank you for that,' replied Martin. 'It's all too easy to get tunnel vision when you think you have hit on the right interpretation, so thanks for reminding us that we need to consider all possibilities.

'Let's take a look at the third verse, and here I can shed a bit of light. When I went to the victim's house with DC Cook-Watts we were told by her neighbour that she was a retired teacher, and although he was only repeating pub gossip he seemed to think she had the reputation of being a hard taskmaster – "a bit of a dragon" was coincidentally his exact phrase.

'Given all of this I have reached the conclusion that at some time the killer was one of Miss Rossiter's pupils, and that as far as he was concerned she bullied him and so now he has turned the tables and has killed her.'

'A bit extreme, sir,' suggested Helen.

'If we were dealing with a normal person then I would agree. It is said that under the right circumstances we could all resort to killing someone, but it would usually be to save our own life or the lives of people we love. Extreme anger or jealousy, as in your crime of passion, can cause someone to commit murder, and then of course we have our psychopaths and paid assassins.

'I'm not an expert profiler, but of the scenarios that I have just mentioned the one that seems to fit the killer in this case is the one that labels him as a psychopath. I know that there are hundreds, possibly thousands, of definitions of a psychopath and if we were to consider just a dozen so-called psychopaths we would probably get a dozen different disorders.

'All we can be sure of at this stage is that this was no random killing, no crime of passion, and that the murderer was not acting in self-defence. We saw the act for ourselves – actually saw him commit the crime – and I believe he knew that we would and that is part of the game he is playing with us. The poem sent to my home with all the clues that fit the murder was written before it happened. The car was parked where the CCTV camera had a clear view of the actual killing. These things were carefully planned by one sick bastard, and if the term "psychopath" is not the recognised medical term for him it will do for me.'

There was general consensus and some nodded their heads in agreement while others shook their heads, unable to believe that someone had not just killed this woman, but had orchestrated the murder so that it would be witnessed by the very officers investigating the crime.

'Look at the last verse of the poem,' Martin added. 'It is clearly aimed directly at me and it seems likely that I will know this killer. Please God don't let him be on the list of people I consider to be friends or colleagues. During my time in the force I have been instrumental in bringing countless villains to justice, and like most of you here I have been warned by some that they will get back at me in some way.

'It's likely to be one of those but as yet no one comes to mind and I am really struggling to formulate any connection between me, the killer, and the murdered woman.

'It looks as if we have tons of evidence, not the least of which is an actual recording of the killing and we know a bit about the victim, but what do we actually know about the killer?' Martin asked. 'We will look at this CCTV footage over and over – it is bound to tell us something. We need to have his image enhanced – anything that will give us a clue to his identity.'

'There are things I would really like to know, such as, why

42

the elaborate set up? Why the colours and the poems, and is this a one-off murder or are there more people he wants to get even with?'

Chapter Four

By the time Martin had sorted a few loose ends it was approaching seven o'clock and as he left the city and took a familiar route towards the coast there were already signs of the daylight fading. The journey always comforted him and he looked forward to closing his cottage door and leaving the cares of the world behind him.

That was how he had always thought of his life in the small seaside resort of Llantwit Major, at least until today. Now he felt that his home and his private life had been violated by that vile letter. He knew he had to reverse that feeling and instead of walking up his path when he had parked the car, he turned around and walked back towards the village – but then changed his mind and headed for the beach.

He walked quickly, as if trying to throw off the shackles of the day and made a conscious effort to think about his surroundings rather than the case and he silently thanked his Aunt Pat for giving him the skills to do this. He had been just a young boy when his parents had died and initially he had been resentful about having to live with his maiden aunt. Although she had never married, his aunt had not lacked company. She was great to be with, being both amusing and interesting, and most of Martin's friends thought he was very lucky not to have to live with boring old parents.

Her job as a costume standby had given her many opportunities to mix with the great and the good of the entertainment world and she had encouraged Martin to go along to film shoots and other projects during his school holidays. She had constantly told him to open his eyes and really notice things

45

instead of just seeing them and he had lost count of the number of times he had been given cause to thank her for just that one thing – although there were countless others.

The evening was still, and as he reached the rocky beach he saw a few groups of surfers making their way across the pebbles and heading for the small café. Maybe they were hoping for larger waves later. Aunt Pat had known all about the history of Llantwit Major, where she had lived for most of her life, and had shared her love of the area with Martin. So he knew that the pebble beach and the old, crumbling cliffs formed part of the fourteen miles of Glamorgan Heritage Coast stretching from just beyond Southerndown in the west to Gileston in the east and he had walked it many times.

He and Shelley had talked about doing the walk, but so far talking about it was as far as it had got, as they were at the stage of their relationship when any time they had together excluded the rest of the world. Martin smiled as he thought of her and felt certain that they would always be together, and so would have plenty of future opportunities for walking when their physical love was a bit more controllable.

He looked out to sea and over the Bristol Channel towards Somerset, and although it was now getting darker the coastline was still visible. Maybe that was the reason he had been drawn here this evening because it was in the village of Milverton in the Taunton Deane area of Somerset that Shelley was staying this weekend.

She had taken her father to visit his sister and Martin remembered her saying that they would all be enjoying a pint or two at The Globe, the pub that had been her father's local when he had lived there.

The idea of a pint made Martin turn back towards the town and head for the Old Swan Inn. Although he sat on his own drinking his two pints of beer he did not feel alone, and had recaptured the feeling that living in this village had always given him. The killer had not won on that count and Martin would do everything in his power to ensure that he would not get away with the murder of Miss Mary Rossiter either.

He made his way back to the cottage past some of the oldest buildings in the town that dated back to the Normans. The people of Llantwit Major, and he included himself as one of them, were fortunate to live in a place where others had worked and played for over three thousand years. Bronze Age and Iron Age had left evidence of their life there, as had the Romans. The history mingled well with the more modern aspects of the town and overall it gave him a really good feeling.

When he returned home he telephoned Shelley, and she confirmed that at the time he was looking out towards Somerset she was indeed having a pint with her father and his friend Stan. 'Didn't you see me waving,' she teased. 'I was the one wearing a skirt!'

She had gone on to say that she had heard about the murder in Cardiff as it had been mentioned on the BBC news. 'It's lucky you aren't on call this weekend.'

Martin said nothing and changed the subject. He would of course tell Shelley how he had become involved, but it was not the subject for a telephone conversation and if she thought there was a personal element to the case it would give her cause to worry. After he had told her how much he loved and missed her Martin ended the call and had a quick shower before crashing out. Getting to sleep before 10 p.m. was really unusual for Martin and he paid the price for his early night by finding himself awake before 5 a.m. He had slept solidly for seven hours and that for Martin was something of a miracle.

It was Sunday morning and immediately his eyes opened his brain visualised the calculated killing of Miss Mary Rossiter. Nothing unusual about that but what was unusual was the fact that he had slept so well. Usually during the first night following the start of a murder investigation his mind went racing around in ever-decreasing circles. If a bracing walk down to the beach and a couple of pints had prevented that, then it was a recipe he would use from now on.

Thinking back, Martin remembered how on that Sunday morning he had not rushed to work but because he had woken so early he had got there ahead of the rest of the team and was

47

already watching the CCTV recording, for the third time, when DS Cotter arrived. He froze the image at the point where the killer had committed the murder and was taking off the glove from his right hand.

'Why did he do that?' questioned David Cotter. 'He was in danger of leaving prints as soon as that glove was off.'

'I've been asking myself the same question,' replied Martin. 'The only thing I can think of is that he used his right hand for the stabbing and the glove would surely have been blood-stained. He took the keys from the ignition carefully, we can see because he has turned his body slightly to do that. There is no sign that he wants to get away quickly. All his movements are measured. He is either a seasoned killer or this particular murder had been acted out in his mind so many times before that he is crime-perfect.

'I am inclined to go for the latter,' Martin continued. 'It's obvious from the way the victim started to open the car door as the man approached that she'd been waiting for him, and couldn't possibly have suspected that she was in any sort of danger.'

For a while both men said nothing, and then Martin restarted the tapes and they watched as the killer disappeared from the bottom right-hand corner of the screen.

'Do we pick him up on any of the tapes from other CCTV cameras?' asked Martin.

'No, sir, and we have now looked at the footage from five cameras covering the period between 9 a.m. and an hour after the murder. Some of the cameras are static and others pan over two or three parking bays, but we have not picked our man up on any of them.'

'Well he can't have disappeared into thin air,' said Martin. 'We know that at some point he left the victim's car keys on the bonnet of that red Mondeo.'

'We can see on one of the tapes that the keys are on the bonnet, and that is the camera that would have shown them being placed there. Unfortunately the camera was not on that particular car at the time, and we have an earlier shot when there are no keys and a later shot when there are keys – but nothing between, if you see what I mean.' David Cotter shook his head. 'This man is either a lucky son of a bitch or he knows enough about surveillance to be able to second-guess the cameras – you and I could do it, sir, especially if we had taken time to check them out in advance.'

Martin agreed and not for the first time the thought that the killer could be someone he knew through work crossed his mind. Both police officers and villains would know a thing or two about security cameras, but he didn't even want to think that one of the former could be responsible for this.

'I take it no knife has been found?' he questioned.

'No, the whole area has been searched and absolutely nothing found,' replied David Cotter. 'Given the cool of the killer I don't think we expected him to just dump it. How do you want to play things, guv?'

Martin replied. 'You were at the Red Dragon Centre yesterday but I haven't been there in connection with this case so I'll take DC Cook-Watts with me to look around and hopefully interview some of the security staff.'

'One of them was interviewed on the news last night,' said David. 'It wasn't the one I spoke to when I was there, so perhaps they do twelve-hour shifts and the man who actually called in the crime will be there again this morning. DC Cook-Watts is here, I saw her talking to one of the constables who has been involved with the weapon search.'

'I deliberately avoided watching the news,' Martin said. 'Did they get it right?'

David replied and was obviously annoyed. 'I would say they got it more than right. They knew a lot more than we have officially told them.'

'Such as?' questioned Martin.

'Well, the news crime reporter said that there had been a fatal stabbing at the Red Dragon Centre at sometime between nine and nine thirty that morning. He said the victim was a retired schoolteacher and that she had been stabbed twice, with one stab wound to her heart.'

Martin wished he had been surprised but he knew that the press were fed information from within the police force, and one of these days he was going to find out the source of the leaks.

David continued. 'The reporter went on to say the police are looking for a tall man who may have been known to the victim. They then identified her as Miss Rossiter and showed some pictures of the school where she taught until she retired in 2002; apparently she stayed on a few years after the usual retirement age. It's a primary school in Newport, and they had managed to get hold of the headmaster who told the interviewer that Miss Rossiter had been well respected as a teacher who was able to keep order and get good results from her pupils.'

'There were also interviews with some of the people visiting the Red Dragon Centre, including one with a woman who hugged two of her children and proclaimed that no one was safe anymore and that in this crime-infested city we all need protection just to go the cinema. Both the children were screaming but it looked as if it was the mother who had scared the living daylights out of them. Where do the press get these people? It's always the extremists and never anyone who gives a rational view of what's happened.'

Before Martin could reply DC Cook-Watts walked in and she was holding a copy of the *Wales on Sunday* tabloid newspaper. 'It's all over the front page,' she began. 'They've managed to get hold of photographs of Miss Rossiter with children from her school, some going back to the 1970s. There's a picture of her car in the car park, obviously after the killing because Alex, in his crime scene clothes, is standing alongside it and you can actually see the victim's head on the steering wheel. The headline is "KILLER STABS AT THE HEART OF OUR COMMUNITY". How corny is that?'

Martin took the newspaper from Helen as she continued. 'The paper is full of every sort of serious crime that has been committed in Cardiff over the past twenty years and I guess if I was just an ordinary member of the public reading this I would be wondering if I was safe in my bed at night. A bit of a balance on the clear-up rates and the reasons for those crimes would be helpful. Every one of the murders mentioned was committed by someone the victims knew, not by random killers stalking the Welsh Valleys.'

Martin had always tried to keep the press on side, and had to admit that there had been times when the media had been instrumental in getting important messages into the public domain. If only they would temper some of the emotive language that they used, but then their business was to sell newspapers and there was a part of the public psyche that loved to be scared and that had to be pandered to – in their best interests, of course.

There was a photograph of Danny Lloyd and his family holding purple helium balloons and looking forlornly at their late neighbour's house. The storyline here told how the eight-year-old boy next door had waited in vain for Miss Rossiter to come to his birthday party. She had, through the process of poetic licence, suddenly become his best friend and his mentor, so creating another human interest angle to the story.

Martin handed the newspaper to DS Cotter and then suggested that the three of them have a quick brainstorming session, and for the next hour or so that was exactly what they did. Anything and everything that was mentioned was written down by Martin, and after the first half an hour one of the smaller whiteboards was turned black with scribbles, not just of the known facts but with even the most fanciful of possible motives for the crime.

'I need a comfort break,' said Martin. 'Just continue to rack your brains and feel free to squeeze any additional points on the board, if you can find a space.'

Martin left DS Cotter and DC Cook-Watts to continue their deliberations, and as soon as the DCI was out of ear shot David Cotter spoke. 'I hope you know how bloody lucky you are to be working with Martin Phelps,' he said. 'I can't tell you what a difference it is to be investigating a crime alongside someone who knows what he is doing.'

Helen nodded. She had enjoyed the last thirty minutes or so

and was learning that it was not just OK, but was actually essential, to just say anything that popped into her head. The crowded whiteboard was a mass of random data and she was looking forward to seeing how it could be translated into manageable chunks of information.

'I don't mean to knock DI Hall,' continued David. 'He's a decent bloke but he's one of those people who was promoted too early and out of his comfort zone. As a result he's been far too many years at DI grade watching men like DCI Phelps catch up and overtake his ranking. In an ideal world I think he would like to go back to being a DS, and he would be very good in that role, he can do the nitty-gritty stuff but not the "blue sky thinking".'

'Well, Matt will be back tomorrow,' responded Helen. 'So make the most of today and, who knows, we may even crack the case before you leave us.'

David laughed. 'I don't think so,' he said turning back to the board. 'Although this stuff is going to give us some direction there is nothing to actually give us positive clues regarding the identity of the killer.'

'Not positive clues,' affirmed Martin, who had returned with three cups of coffee. 'Not at this stage, but we can start to build a profile of the man with what we know.

'We have actually seen him so let's start with that. Before he stoops to lean into the victim's car he is seen walking towards it with his back to the security camera and I would say he is a few inches shorter than I am and considerably more than a few pounds heavier.' They watched that part of the tape again and all agreed on a height of approximately five feet ten inches, and a weight of around fifteen stone.

'Anything else about the man?' asked Martin.

'Yes,' replied Helen. 'He doesn't really walk. It's more like a sort of march. Possibly like someone who has been used to wearing a uniform.'

The two men nodded and David commented. 'Possibly army, or any one of the forces if it comes to that – even the police force.'

Martin nodded. 'I don't get the impression of a young man, although I am struggling to bring any rationale to that thought. Helen is right, he does sort of march but it's also as if all his movements are measured and deliberate and that's the case throughout the period when we see him walking to the car, actually committing the murder, and then walking away. At every stage I get the feeling that this is a man who is at least middle-aged and used to being in control.'

Martin finished his coffee and turned to DS Cotter. 'Helen and I will pay a visit to the Red Dragon Centre now, and while we're there I would like you to go through that drawer full of papers you brought back from the victim's house. I had a quick look yesterday and although there were a few recent official letters, things like electricity bills and bank statements, the majority of the papers are reports and exercise books which belonged to Miss Rossiter's teaching days.'

David nodded and asked, 'Am I looking for anything in particular?'

'No,' replied Martin. 'It would be too much to hope that she had kept a list of all her ex-pupils with whom she had disciplinary issues. At best you may just pick up a few clues regarding the character of our victim that may help us build up a picture of her. That will then enable us to consider the sort of person who may have had a reason to hate her to the point of murder. It's all a bit speculative at this stage but quite often the picking through of the minutiae is what brings results.'

Martin reached for his jacket and minutes later he and Helen had reached the Red Dragon Centre and Martin was attempting to park. They had been met by a security officer some way back from the usual barrier entrance and he was directing all the vehicles away from car park.

'There are no more spaces,' he explained as Martin approached. 'I'm trying to prevent a queue at the barrier because we'll be keeping them closed until things calm down a bit.'

Seconds after Martin had shown his warrant card the barrier was lifted and they were not only through but en route to a space that had been reserved since Helen's call to the centre earlier. When Martin's Alfa Romeo had driven through the raised barrier it had attracted blasts from the horns of some of the cars that had been refused entrance and a few shouts of abuse aimed at the security guard. Suggestions of bribery and corruption were amongst the ones being voiced.

'I'm glad I thought about ringing ahead to tell them we were coming,' said Helen. 'I would have given them your car registration number but I'm so used to travelling in marked police cars I assumed they would see us a mile off.'

Martin smiled but then his smile disappeared as even before they were out of the car he spotted a few familiar faces approaching. The two men and a young woman, who could have been mistaken for a schoolgirl, had obviously been waiting for their arrival.

'Told you this space had been reserved for the CID lot, didn't I?' The girl tossed her beetroot coloured hair and looked triumphantly at her fellow reporters. 'Was it worth the wait or what?'

'Depends on what he can or will tell us,' answered the taller of her two companions. 'First off, I wasn't expecting the CID presence to be Detective Chief Inspector Martin Phelps, and he won't tell us as much as DI Hall would have done.'

Thinking that a bit of light banter would ease their way in, the young woman smiled broadly and aimed her first remark at Helen. 'So it's Detective Constable Cook-Watts now is it? – what's that, promotion or just a means of getting out of those shapeless uniforms?'

Helen did not justify the remarks with any sort of response and continued walking alongside Martin in the direction of the security office. The woman's tall colleague addressed Martin. 'I was expecting to see DI Hall,' he said. 'He was the one here yesterday and you lot don't usually change riders once the race has started. Someone up there must think this case warrants the top team – and talking about the top team, where's your usual sidekick, DS Pryor?'

It was now Martin's turn to ignore the statements and the

54

question from the press but inwardly he was getting really annoyed with this trio. The young woman who had commented on Helen's appearance looked as if she had been dragged through a hedge backwards and what business was it of theirs who was conducting the investigation? However he knew that unless he set the record straight they would concoct their own version of events and so he spoke calmly, but with a definite note of sarcasm.

'Good morning, your powers of observation do you credit, I am not DI Hall and DC Cook-Watts is not DS Pryor. The reason you have the pleasure of meeting us this morning has nothing to do with some covert masterplan but is simply a matter of us all achieving some sort of work/life balance.'

Martin's sarcastic comments were wasted on the threesome and the third member of the group made his opening gambit. 'We're getting a lot of information from the public and our sources about this murder but precious little from the police. Rumour has it that the killer is known to you personally, DCI Phelps – is that true? Is it a fact that prior to the murder he wrote to you telling you exactly what he was going to do?'

With some effort Martin kept his composure. 'I can assure you that if the killer was known to me he would be under lock and key by now, but he is not. Obviously some of the facts surrounding the murder will not be made public until we know whether or not they are significant. We will be speaking officially to the press later today and appealing to the public for help. There were lots of people around yesterday and there is a chance that someone will have seen something that was not picked up by the CCTV cameras.'

'Oh,' responded the third reporter. 'Do you mean the tapes that actually show the woman being murdered? Even as we speak our legal teams are looking at the pros and cons of publishing some stills from those tapes. The public will be amazed that the police are unable to capture a killer when they actually have a pictorial view of the whole event.'

Inwardly Martin was shocked. How had they managed to get hold of photographs from the CCTV tapes that he believed had only been handled by the police since their removal from the machine? He would do all he could to prevent those pictures being published and the tragic circumstances of someone's murder being turned into a grisly front-page exposé. What about the victim's human rights, didn't they continue posthumously – and what about the effect such publicity would have on the killer? Martin was getting the feeling that the man they were looking for would be elated if his actions were given such a high profile.

The reporters continued to ask random questions but Martin now blanked them completely and a few minutes later was in the security office talking to the officer who had been on duty the previous morning.

It was only ten minutes after that when Martin restarted his engine and he and Helen made their way back to Goleudy. 'That was not a lot of help,' he admitted. 'It confirmed what we already know but I was hoping that the security officer would remember something more about the man who reported the crime to him. What he does remember certainly fits the details of the killer, in that he was wearing a black baseball cap, but he appears to have been faceless.

'The officer says, quite rightly, that his first priority was to see if the woman was all right and it didn't strike him as odd until later that he had been given an exact location for her car. Most members of the public have difficulty remembering where they leave their own car but this man gave the bay number and the location within the bay.'

Helen looked thoughtful. 'So you think it was the murderer, who had the nerve not to leave the scene of the crime straight away, but to calmly walk up to the security officer and in essence tell him what he had done? It's almost as if he is boasting, isn't it?'

'It's exactly like boasting,' replied Martin. 'It's a part of the sick game this monster is playing with us all.'

Martin recalled how for the next couple of weeks the usual investigations following a serious crime had been completed.

Public appeals had been launched but had only resulted in countless interviews with people who had been at the Red Dragon Centre and seen nothing, or from cranks who had witnessed the whole thing in spite of being miles away at the time.

The car had been meticulously examined by Alex and his team, but no evidence of the killer had been found, and the knife used in the stabbing had not been recovered either.

DS Pryor had returned to work on the Monday following the crime and Martin had welcomed him back, hoping that a fresh mind would see something he was missing. Martin had managed to keep the actual images of the murder off the front pages, but as time was passing and there was no sign of the case being solved the press was getting restless. Headlines suggesting that the police knew more than they were telling the public were making the top brass angry and Martin was feeling more under pressure than on any other case he had headed.

The past two weeks had certainly been a nightmare and as he sat at his kitchen table, having left Shelley upstairs, Martin stared at the mail he had been dreading receiving. It certainly looked as if the killer either had or was about to strike again and Martin picked up the orange envelope and opened it carefully.

As soon as he saw the layout of the poem his heart sank and by the time he got to the final verse his heart had reached his boots.

What was the killer doing? If the last verse was correct, the letter wasn't intended to give prior warning – just to taunt Martin about a crime that had already been committed. If that turned out to be the case, all he could hope for was that this time the killer would make some mistakes.

What was it all about?

His next action was a call to Matt. 'See you in thirty minutes,' said Martin. 'I've had another set of verses but it looks as if, like before, the killer will have already struck before we reach the victim.'

Chapter Five

'What is this colour business all about?' Matt watched Martin clean the scribbles of a previous brainstorming session from the whiteboard adjacent to the one on which the first poem was written. He continued to watch as his boss wrote out the second set of verses in full and then stood to one side so that the three people in the room could read them. DC Cook-Watts chose to read the lines out loud.

It's orange now, a juicy one
but liquid at the core.
It felt delicious when my knife
went in from skin to gore.

He sought me out, he really did
for ridicule and scorn.
My rubbish knots caused me to wish
that I had not been born.

One dragon down and now one perv
and so I can move on.
Quite soon I'll send the other five
to Hell where they belong.

You missed the last one, Martin Phelps,
as everyone has heard.
Miss this one too you will as it
already has occurred.

'Bloody hell!' she concluded. 'I think this one is even more sinister than the last one, but there are a lot of similarities, don't you think?'

'The similarity I'm most concerned about,' voiced Martin, 'is the fact that in both poems the killer is telling us about a crime he has already committed by the time I've read them, and we know that in the case of Miss Rossiter she was stabbed at virtually the same moment I opened the red envelope. I believe we can assume the same thing has happened here. I don't think for one moment I was sent this second poem so that I would have a chance to stop a murder. Most likely someone has already been killed and we can either use the clues in this poem to find out who and where or wait for a murder to be reported.'

Martin rose to his own challenge and suggested that the most important clue in both cases was the colour. 'To begin with we had the red envelope and notepaper, and then we were directed to think of red in the first line of what I will call the red poem. Let's assume that the colour is intended to refer in some way to the location of the crime as we know that the first victim was killed at the Red Dragon Centre. If the colour red had been our only clue it would have been pretty useless as there are possibly dozens of other red-associated locations in and around Cardiff.'

Matt chipped in. 'The Welsh rugby team plays in red so we could have thought of the Millennium Stadium and the Welsh word for red is *coch*, so we may have been directed towards Castell Coch.'

'Yes,' continued Martin. 'We could think of many more possibilities but red was not the only clue we were given. The killer/poet has called his victim a dragon and with the benefit of hindsight those two clues could have taken us to the Red Dragon Centre. So let's look at this second poem to see if there is anything other than the colour orange that may be directing us to the location where I believe a murder has already been committed.'

Matt turned his head away from the whiteboard and stared at Martin. 'The third verse of this poem seems to indicate that if there has been a second murder it may only be number two on a possible list of seven, as he talks about sending another "five to

60

Hell". There's also that personal reference to you, guv, and I hate to say this but we have to consider the possibility that you are one of the other five he mentions.'

'Either that or he is going to make it his business to ensure that I am publically seen to be a failure, in the case of a serial killer with seven trophies and no arrest.' Martin grimaced. 'I must confess the personal element is bugging me, but let's focus on trying to find the location with the vague clues we have.'

'I've been thinking orange,' said Helen. 'There's Orange the mobile phone company, they have a number of shops so that's a possibility, and there's a company called Orange Forestry in Radyr. I only know about them because my neighbour has just had some work done on two ancient trees in her garden. I also know of a place called Orange Grove that is somewhere near St Fagans and I remember going there last year when there had been a spate of burglaries and the local force asked for extra help. Apart from those few I'm struggling to think of any orange related venues.'

Matt nodded. 'The only thing I'm coming up with is the fruit itself in that oranges are fleshy and juicy and maybe we're looking for a place where oranges are sold – and I've seen crates and crates of them piled up in Bessemer Road Market.'

Just as Matt was finishing his sentence the door opened and Sergeant John Evans appeared. 'Guessed I would find you all here and I've come to give you something else to worry about. A woman has just rung in to report the finding of a body and in her words the man has been stabbed with a knife and has bled to death.'

'Where was the body found?' asked Martin.

'It was in one of the smaller units on the Tremorfa Industrial Estate,' Sgt Evans replied. 'According to PC Davies, who is now at the scene, it looks as if the victim has been stabbed twice.' As he had been speaking Evans' eyes had taken in the words of the second poem Martin had written on the whiteboard and was about to ask a question but Martin saved him the bother.

'Yes, sergeant, we have had another so-called poem, but there may be no connection between these new verses and the body that has been discovered this morning.'

Sgt Evans shook his head and replied. 'Oh, but there is, sir, as according to PC Davies the body was found swimming in orange juice. Apparently the company that rents this particular unit produces a range of citrus drinks, and in the area that the body was discovered they were squeezing oranges to make orange juice.'

'No prizes for guessing why our killer chose the orange juice – it's just to fit into his macabre game. He is one very sick bastard,' said Matt. 'What do we think this poor sod did to annoy him?'

'If the killer is to be believed, this victim might be a pervert,' suggested Helen. 'But of course that may be far from the truth.'

'Possibly,' replied Martin. 'However there was some truth in his description of Miss Rossiter as a dragon; certainly a number of the people we interviewed saw her in that light. The sooner we know who the victim is the sooner we can start putting the pieces together. Who is at the scene?' Martin directed his question to Sgt Evans.

'There are four of our lot, and I saw Alex Griffiths and his team heading off in the SOC van before I left the front desk to come up here. Professor Moore has been notified, but as it's the weekend he will go straight from his home to Tremorfa so I suspect he is on his way as we speak.'

'OK, thanks,' said Martin. 'I would appreciate your input at the scene of the crime, John, so would you mind taking Helen in one of the squad cars with you and Matt, and I'll go in my car. No point in blue flashing lights and sirens because the crime has already been committed, as sadly we were in no doubt that it would be.'

Sgt Evans replied. 'I'm happy to help, but I won't be able to leave here for about fifteen minutes as I'm waiting for cover.' He turned to Helen. 'Fancy a coffee while we're waiting?'

Helen left with Sgt Evans and for a while Martin turned his

attention back to the rhymes he had written on the whiteboard. 'Last time we had a clue to the victim's occupation and we believe that she and the killer met as a result of her job. We also believe that she used her position to make the killer do things he disliked, such as playing certain games. Do we have any such clues this time?'

Matt responded. 'Well, here again we are presented with the idea that the victim was unkind to the killer at some time, and we are led to believe that he was subjected to an unbearable level of ridicule and scorn. It was something to do with not being able to tie a knot. The only time in my life that I was ever tasked with learning how to tie knots was when I was in the Cubs. I never made it to the Scouts as I'd become more interested in rugby by then, but I guess you'd learn even more complicated knots as a scout.'

'Come on,' said Martin. 'Let's see what he has left us with this time – it's got to be more than the absolutely nothing he left at his last murder.'

Ten minutes after leaving Cardiff Bay Martin turned off Rover Way and followed the signs to the Tremorfa Industrial Estate. The small unit they were looking for was at the far end and easy to spot because of the number of familiar vehicles parked outside. Three marked squad cars, the SOC white van, and the cream-coloured Lexus belonging to Professor Moore.

'We'll almost certainly be spending most of our day checking CCTV footage,' suggested Martin. 'I would think that every one of these units has their own security cameras and the recordings from all of them will have to be watched.'

PC Davies beckoned to them from the front entrance and they followed him down a corridor flanked by toilets, offices, and a small staff room, then into an enormous cold room where crates upon crates of lemons, limes, grapefruits, and of course oranges were stacked from floor to ceiling.

A short, rather plump woman dressed in white overalls and a white hairnet was leaning against a door on the other side of the cold room and PC Davies introduced her. 'This is Elaine Dixon, she is the lady who found our victim and she is also the person with responsibility for the production process this weekend.'

Martin introduced himself and Matt, and shook hands with the woman who was trembling and had obviously been crying. 'Is there anyone here who could make you a cup of tea or something?' asked Martin. 'I will need to talk to you but first of all I need to see exactly what has happened.' He turned to PC Davies. 'Take Mrs Dixon to the staff room or one of the offices and get someone to make her a drink. How many other members of staff are there?'

Mrs Dixon lifted her head and replied to Martin's question. 'There are only three of us here today. We're getting new equipment installed on Monday and we were just doing a small batch of fresh juice to ensure we had enough to satisfy our customers because we won't be able to restart production until Tuesday. It's normally a five-day working week for us and we use Saturday and Sunday for cleaning and sterilising, but this weekend is a bit different.'

As she spoke the last few words tears streamed down her face and the courage she had been summoning faded. 'Well, more than a bit different,' she sobbed. 'That poor man ... his staring eyes ... and his blood mixed in with the orange juice – I don't think I'll ever be able to close my eyes without seeing him lodged half in and half out of that pulp receiver.'

PC Davies took her arm and guided her in the direction of the staff room while the two detectives went through the door she had been leaning against and walked into a scene that was all too familiar to them.

The SOC officer on the other side of the door ensured that before they actually stepped into the room both Martin and Matt were covered from head to toe with the usual protective garments. Everyone else was already wearing the white uniforms. Not for the first time Martin considered how, as well as protecting the crime scene, the ritual of wearing these clothes seemed psychologically to protect the wearers by creating just that small barrier between them and the evil they were investigating.

Alex acknowledged Martin and suggested he took care, as

the floor towards the middle of the room was very slippery due to the spillage of a mixture of blood and orange juice. 'It's enough to put you off orange juice for life,' he remarked. 'Unfortunately for me it's a very sterile environment, as all the staff must routinely wear hairnets and hats, white coats, overshoes, and latex gloves. The only hope we have is that if we do find any evidence of another human being apart from the victim, it will be that of the killer. So far nothing, not a single fingerprint, and I'm getting a feeling of déjà vu.

'In the circumstances there's not much we can do other than take all the usual pictures, and that's been done. The professor has confirmed that the man is dead, although we were none of us in any doubt, and I get the feeling we are keeping him from somewhere else he would rather be.'

The professor had picked up on the last part of Alex's conversation but spoke to Martin. 'I'm sure we would all rather be somewhere else, but yes, I do have a prior engagement, so as soon as you've seen what you came to see I would like to turn the body over and then get it removed. Unless you want someone else to do the PM it won't be done until after six o'clock, and quite frankly I don't think it will tell us any more than we already know.'

Martin didn't want anyone else to do the post-mortem examination but he knew that the Prof was normally reluctant to say very much at the crime scene and he wanted a bit more information.

He responded. 'I would prefer to have you do the PM, but as I have to wait for that perhaps you could just fill me in on what it is you already know.'

The professor replied in two succinct sentences. 'Two stab wounds. The first was probably fatal and the second unnecessary.'

The body was turned and as suspected the victim's hands were tied behind his back, this time with orange cord but with the same example of a perfectly tied reef knot.

'So, two stab wounds, and hands tied with the relevant colour cord – just like the victim at the Red Dragon Centre. The same killer has struck again, hasn't he?' Martin said.

'I'm the pathologist, not the detective.' The professor muttered the words as carrying his beloved Gladstone bag, he made his way out.

Alex raised his eyes to heaven. 'Thank God for small mercies,' he said and turning to Matt. 'Just imagine having to work with him day in and day out – we should get a gong struck for Mrs Williams, she certainly deserves some sort of recognition.'

Mrs Williams worked with Professor Moore as an assistant in the post-mortem rooms, and was the only person to whom the Prof was consistently civil. She was his right-hand man, so to speak, and he had been heard to say that PMs were murder themselves when she was away. Hardly singing her praises, but coming from the professor such words were tantamount to adoration.

Martin eased his way carefully around some of the stainless steel pipes in the room. The receptacle in which the victim's head and torso had been resting was a circular affair about six feet across and approximately two feet deep. The man's knees had been bent over the edge and his legs draped down the outside at an awkward looking angle, not quite reaching the floor. There was some juice to be seen, but for the most part the stainless steel bowl was full of orange skin and the flesh of the oranges from which most of the juice had been squeezed.

He guessed he was looking at the pulp receiver that Mrs Dixon had mentioned, and she was right about the chilling effect of the victim's protruding eyes and the grotesque combination of blood and orange juice. 'Just check if there's anything in the victim's pockets and then you can remove the body whenever you like,' he told Alex. 'I'll speak to the staff, as what's puzzling me at the moment is what the was victim doing here – he's not part of the establishment, is he?'

'No, according to Will, the young man we spoke to when we arrived, none of the three staff members have ever seen the man before.' Alex spoke as the body was placed on a white sheet on the floor alongside the pulp receiver and he bent down to check the victim's pockets. He handed over a wallet to Martin and started to bag the remaining items that amounted to a set of keys and two till receipts.

'I'll take those,' said Matt indicating the keys. 'I'll take a walk around the outside of the building to see if I can match up any car with them. On the way in I noticed three vehicles apart from ours, but there are three members of staff so they could well be theirs.'

'Check with the staff first,' suggested Alex. 'Will told me that Mrs Dixon is his aunt and so there's a chance they came in the same car.'

Matt nodded and made his way to the staff room and was on a mission to find the car belonging to the set of keys he held.

'No mobile phone?' asked Martin.

'No, that's it.' Alex looked at Martin who had found a debit card, two out-of-date credit cards, three store loyalty cards, and forty-five pounds in notes in the wallet. 'Do I take it from the similarities between this and the Red Dragon murder that this one also came with a poem?'

'Yes, exactly the same pattern as the last time, just a colour change. This time the killer is focusing on the colour orange, but everything else is the same – the envelope containing the poem was addressed to me at the cottage and would appear to be giving us some clues.'

Alex was more than usually concerned as he asked, 'Was there any personal message this time?'

Martin didn't answer directly, mainly because Alex had hit on a point that he would prefer not to think too deeply about. He suggested that they could go over all the details later and scanning the cards found in the wallet he came up with the victim's name.

'Always supposing that this wallet is in the pocket of its rightful owner the name on all the cards is Mr Victor Davies. The bank cards are Barclays so we'll easily be able to find out who he was and where he lived, but I keep coming back to the question of what was he doing here?'

Alex turned his attention to supporting his officers regarding the removal of the body. Martin made his way to the staff room, but stopped at the doorway to listen to the conversation within.

Mrs Dixon had obviously benefitted from her infusion of tea and was giving PC Davies a potted history of the company that traded as Freshly Squeezed.

'It's my daughter's company, you know,' she said. 'Her father and I are very proud of her. She did some market research before setting things up and decided to aim for the upper quartile of the business. Apparently most of the orange juice that the public buy has been heated or cooked and may have additives or even been made from concentrate. It's a huge market and very competitive.

'Karen decided to produce freshly squeezed, unpasteurised juice, so offering a drink with the flavour of the whole fruit and nothing else. The supermarkets take small amounts from us but they are the squeezers when it comes to profit margins and so we deal mainly with speciality food stores. Karen has established a really good customer base in spite of the poor economic conditions.'

Once again tears welled up in Mrs Dixon's eyes, but these were not for the dead man – they were for her daughter – and she stumbled on her next words. 'What's this going to do for her business?'

Without giving her the time to consider that question Martin spoke, introducing himself to her nephew Will and to the stunningly beautiful young woman sitting next to him. Clearly PC Davies had not missed this vision, who looked more Mediterranean than Welsh. He could hardly keep his eyes off her blue-black hair, lightly tanned skin, and dark green eyes.

Will interrupted Martin's introductions. 'Calandra is my cousin from Sicily, she speaks very little English but don't worry because I lived there until I was eleven and I speak the language fluently.' He demonstrated the fact by translating Martin's introduction and receiving a faint smile of gratitude from his cousin.

Mrs Dixon went on to give a fuller explanation of Calandra's involvement. 'Will's father is Sicilian and their family business is citrus fruits, and it may well be that our visits to Sicily over the years was how Karen got her idea for this enterprise. Ironically it's the blood oranges they grow that produce the most delicious orange juice and gives it that rather dark, almost burgundy, colour that our customers love. I don't imagine that any of them will want to buy it after this murder hits the headlines.'

Martin shook his head. He felt a great deal of sympathy for this family's predicament but he needed to focus on the murder, and for the next ten minutes he asked them all questions about their recent activities and where they were all likely to have been when the murder occurred. Normally he would have had to consider them all as possible suspects, but Martin knew that he was looking for the tall, well-built man he had seen on the CCTV of the last crime and none of these people fitted that image.

It was Calandra who suddenly remembered something and looked earnestly at her cousin to translate her recollections. She gesticulated madly as she spoke and Will had to put his arm around her shoulder because she was getting distressed. Finally he nodded to her and told the others what she had been saying.

'She's right,' said Will. 'We all discovered the body at virtually the same time and that was just after we had changed our overshoes because we had worn them outside. We don't normally go outside in them but we heard a really loud bang at the front of the unit and we all rushed out to see what had caused it.'

'Did you find out?' prompted Martin.

Will continued. 'Not really, but we did find a car parked alongside mine and my auntie's car and we assumed it must have backfired or something. If they're busy some of the other units use our parking spaces, but they usually ask and I haven't seen that car before.'

'How long were you all out there?' asked Martin.

'Well we didn't rush back inside,' said Mrs Dixon. 'We were all in early this morning and took advantage of a short break. In fact, Will smoked a cigarette and Cala and I made the most of a few minutes in the sunshine. We were probably outside for about five minutes, certainly no more. We returned via the side entrance so that we could change our shoes, and then walked through together and saw that poor man.'

Having previously witnessed the deadly resolve and accuracy of the killer Martin knew that five minutes would have been more than enough – but what a chance he had taken! At any time any one of the staff could have returned and witnessed the murder. Would the killer have simply run off, or would they now be investigating more than one murder?

Martin thanked the three members of staff for their help and asked PC Davies to ensure they were given all the help they needed with sorting out the aftermath of the crime. Mrs Dixon was telling Martin that her daughter was on her way back from what should have been a well-deserved weekend break in London when Matt came back from the car park.

'Found it!' he proclaimed. 'It's a long time since I opened a car with a key, I'm just used to zapping the remote but there wasn't one. The keys fit a dark green Ford Fiesta, and there is no doubt that the owner is our victim as on the passenger seat I discovered an orange envelope – the same size, shape, and colour as the one you received this morning. It has been sent through the post to the person named on the bank cards, and so we now have the victim's address.'

'DC Cook-Watts and Sgt Evans arrived when I was looking for the car and I asked them to make a start on checking the surrounding units, hope that was OK?'

Martin nodded, walked down the corridor towards his car, and then turned back to Matt who was following behind. 'Did our victim receive a poem as well?' he asked.

Matt replied. 'Not a poem, but a very good reason why he should be at the side door of this unit at a precise time this morning.'

Chapter Six

Less than half an hour later, and with a large cup of coffee almost finished, Martin sat in his office and tried to gather his thoughts into manageable pieces. Failing to do so, he opened his desk drawer and took out a sheet of paper. With his mind all over the place he resorted to a tried and tested way of getting focus and direction.

He drew his three columns headed 'Absolute Facts', 'Facts to be Considered', and 'What Ifs'? As always the discipline worked, and by the time Martin joined the rest of the team for the first briefing on this latest murder, he had at his fingertips all the known facts and had written out lists of possibilities that the team would have to consider.

Incident Room One was a hive of industry and he was pleased to see uniformed officers and their CID colleagues debating the similarities between the two poems and arguing about the possible meanings of some of the lines. This sort of challenging environment was often the key to solving crimes, and in spite of the very high level of noise Martin did nothing to calm things down.

He listened to what was being said, and was quite touched by the number of times that his name was mentioned and how angry most of the officers were that the killer was making these crimes in some way personal to him.

Martin checked his watch and could hardly believe that it was only just coming up to twelve o'clock – no more than three hours since he had picked that orange envelope up from his doormat. His guess at the contents had put him off the breakfast he had planned to enjoy with Shelley, but now he was feeling hungry.

He called the meeting to order and started with a brief recap of the Red Dragon Centre murder, admitting to an unusual lack of progress. 'It now looks as if we are faced with another victim at the hands of the same killer, as we are starting today in an almost identical way to the situation two weeks ago. I must confess that the past two weeks have been amongst the most frustrating of my career. It's difficult to comprehend that with so many potential clues, and even being able to watch the actual murder on CCTV, we are no further forward today than we were then. No knife has been found, we have absolutely no forensic evidence – and this second murder may prove to be equally tormenting.'

Martin went through the drill of allowing his uniformed colleagues to give details of the 999 call and their subsequent actions. He then nodded in Alex's direction and the room was shown the outside of the industrial unit and asked to note the three cars in the car park. 'What you see here is the situation met by us and I have taken the trouble to video the whole of the outside of the building with particular emphasis on possible entrances and exits used by the killer. There is one fire door at the rear but that was closed and so we just have the front and side entrances to consider.

'It's possible to walk around the whole circumference of this unit and the only place where the people from inside can see anyone on the outside is at the front entrance.'

Martin interrupted. 'This killer plans his murders very carefully and goes in and out of the scene without leaving any forensic evidence, but he is still a risk taker.'

'In both cases there were people around and at any time he could literally have been caught in the act. I think he gets a big kick from that.'

Alex nodded and went back to his presentation. 'We went in through the side entrance and although I can't give any scientific evidence I think this is the way the killer entered, although probably via the back of the building and not the front, as we did. There are no footprints and we wouldn't have expected any as it's a gravel-type paving all around. We have picked up fingerprints from the front and side doors but I can't see the killer leaving his prints on anything and I suspect that these prints belong to members of the staff.'

The next images that Alex displayed were of the room in which the body was discovered. After scanning the whole area the camera focused on the body in the position it had been found.

'Gross,' said one of the constables. 'Red and orange can be a strange colour combination at the best of times, and there's something about blood combining with things we eat that's quite disgusting.'

Nobody disagreed and very little else was said as Alex showed the whole process of the management of the body up to the point it was turned and the orange cord revealed. This did cause a ripple of conversation with most people referring to the connections between the two murders.

'We'll come back to all of that in just a moment,' interrupted Martin. 'First I want DS Pryor to tell us about the victim's car.'

Matt got to his feet and referred to the keys that Alex had taken from the victim's pocket. 'As you will remember, from the first images we saw, only three cars were standing in the car park when we arrived and I didn't have a problem finding the one I was looking for. There were three members of staff in the building and two of them had come to work in the same car. They had given me the registration numbers for those two cars so I was left with a Ford Fiesta.'

'There was no remote control for opening the doors, so I risked setting off the alarm and tried the keys in the lock. They worked, and now we know that the victim was the owner of a dark green Ford Fiesta and we presume that he drove himself to the unit. I don't think he would have given the killer a lift – but hell, who knows? This bastard doesn't play by any known rules.'

The constable who had been disgusted by the combination of oranges and blood interrupted. 'Why would the victim want to go there? Was he a member of staff?'

'No,' responded Matt. 'None of the staff had ever seen him

before, but when I opened his car door I discovered a letter which explains why he was there.' Matt held up the envelope contained in a transparent evidence bag and lifted from the table in front of Martin a similar envelope.

The room became lively and the level of conversation got louder and louder as once again the connections were made and opinions were voiced. As before, Martin let the spontaneous discussion run and listened to some of the comments, but before long he banged on the table and got the required response.

With the room now quiet he explained the second envelope Matt had shown, confirming that it had been addressed to him in his official capacity but sent to his home address in the same way the red one had been two weeks ago.

His face was stern as he told his team, 'Everything we think and do from now on must be with the understanding that we are looking for one killer. The most worrying thing is that he has now killed twice but appears to be telling us that he has plans for five more victims, and we can't let that happen. We can't allow a serial killer to get seven scalps on his belt – even this second one is going to cause a public outpouring of disbelief that we are not able to make any arrests, and the press will have a field day.

'They knew far more than we had officially released about the last murder, and I'll take this opportunity to say that I am on a mission to get to the bottom of the leaks that are coming from this building to the media. When I find out – and I *will* find out – who is responsible, that person won't have their job alone to worry about – he or she will be charged with perverting the course of justice.'

Martin looked around the room, knowing that the vast majority would not entertain passing information to the press – but someone was, and he hoped that this public reference to the problem would put a stop to it.

'Back to the business in hand,' he said, and turning to Matt Martin asked him to explain why the victim was in the industrial unit.

Matt responded. 'The envelope I found in the victim's car is exactly the same as the one received by DCI Phelps. Neither is handwritten, and unlike in the good old days, when we could have been looking at identifying an individual typewriter, these envelopes and letters are computer-generated. If the killer is as clever as we think he is he will already have deleted the poems and letters from his system.'

Charlie interrupted. 'He may think he has,' she said. 'Find me the PC or laptop and give it to me and I will make it tell me every key that was ever pressed – there's no such thing as "deleted from the system".'

Matt smiled and told Charlie that as soon as the killer was found his computer would be hers for the taking.

He continued. 'There is no poem in the victim's envelope, just a brief note that very specifically tells him to be at the side entrance of Unit 17, that's the "Freshly Squeezed" unit, at 09.25. It reads:

For the attention of Mr Victor Davies.

If you thought you had got away with your nasty little habits this is to tell you that you have not. Unless you follow these instructions all your Bible-bashing friends will be told what a disgusting pervert you are.

Meet me at the side entrance of Unit 17 on the Tremorfa Industrial Site at 09.25 Saturday morning and I may be able to prevent you having to read about your dirty secrets in the local rag.

Drive to the front, park your car, and walk around the back of the building to the side entrance. Be exactly on time and speak to no one.

'That's it, but there was obviously enough truth in the words to bring Mr Victor Davies to Freshly Squeezed as requested.' Matt looked at Alex, who was waiting to tell the meeting more regarding the car that was now being scrutinised by his team.

'When we moved the car we discovered a spent firework near the back wheel. According to the writing on the case it was a Mega Boom Banger.'

'That's undoubtedly the loud bang that the staff told me about,' said Martin. 'It was enough to ensure all three of them went straight to the front of the building, giving the killer the opportunity to meet the victim at the side door – and he certainly prevented Mr Davies reading anything about himself in the local rag, given that the dead can't read!'

'So we know that Mr Davies arrived at 9.25 and after parking made his way around the back to the side entrance. The killer must have been watching his arrival and waiting to set off that banger as soon as his victim was in place at the side door.'

Martin continued. 'We have already identified him as a risk-taker, but realistically there was almost a one hundred per cent chance that all the staff would respond to the created diversion. As we saw in the Red Dragon Centre the actual killing takes seconds rather than minutes, so the killer wouldn't even have contemplated being interrupted. He was probably in and out of the building within a couple of minutes, leaving no obvious evidence behind and taking the murder weapon with him.'

Matt added a comment. 'This time there are no CCTV cameras for us to scrutinise, as Mrs Dixon told me, with slight embarrassment, that the ones fixed to their building are just dummies. She explained that the cameras are only meant to be a deterrent because they don't keep money on the premises and their equipment is all bolted to the floor and the walls. The most any intruders would get away with would be crates of citrus fruits, and she doubts that anyone would be that desperate to get their five-a-day. There are other units adjacent to Freshly Squeezed and we are currently checking out their security systems.

'As before,' continued Martin, 'we have no idea how the killer arrived at the scene, although this time we will be able to check all the vehicles coming in and out of the main entrance to the industrial estate and determine if there are any without a legitimate reason for being there. There is no barrier on the entrance to the estate, but the security company is based in a small unit at the front entrance and they monitor all the comings and goings. DC Cook-Watts, will you please arrange whatever help you need and get the details of all vehicles driving in and out of the estate this morning, as quickly as possible.' Helen nodded and left the room, taking two of her uniformed ex-colleagues with her.

'We have the address of the deceased on the envelope but it's not an area of Cardiff I know very well. Is anyone able to throw any light on Watch Towers, 52-57 Riverside Road, Ely?' asked Martin.

'Watch Towers?' questioned Alex. 'Isn't that something to do with Jehovah's Witnesses?'

One of the PCs was obviously familiar with the address. 'It may well be,' she said in response to Alex's question. 'But this particular Watch Towers is a block of terraced houses that has been remodelled to provide some sort of sheltered accommodation. To be honest, it's not a very pleasant place, and we've been called out to disturbances there several times.'

There were nods of agreement from some of her colleagues and Matt expressed his surprise. 'I thought sheltered accommodation was for the elderly?'

PC Williams replied, 'I think it is in the main, but this place seems to have attracted more than its fair share of social misfits. Some of the trouble we have been called to sort out has involved members of the staff, who are themselves a bit dubious. I think the place has been on the verge of being closed on a number of occasions.'

Martin thanked her for her input and added, 'So Mr Davies is unlikely to have a loving family, and he must at some time have treated our killer very badly to have possibly merited such a brutal end. Our man obviously knew his victims, but I wonder if they knew one another – perhaps Davies was also a teacher, although that is not alluded to in the poem this time.'

'What is suggested is that the victim is some sort of pervert and we can quite easily check out the official sex offenders register, but of course he may only be a pervert in the eyes of the killer. Following this briefing DS Pryor and I will visit Watch Towers and see what we can find out. Meanwhile, does anyone have any suggestions regarding the lines of the poem that relate to the tying of knots?' Martin had opened the floodgates and almost everyone in the room had an idea to put forward.

Matt started the ball rolling. 'Probably the first knots we learn to tie are the laces in our shoes, although thinking of my nieces even their trainers and school shoes have Velcro fastenings. We don't think our killer is a young man so when he was growing up laces would have been the norm.'

It was surprising how often knots featured in people's lives, and ideas ranged from learning to knit to the notion of a couple 'tying the knot' when getting married. However the majority of people came up with Cubs, Brownies, Scouts, and Guides, and as the killer was a man he would only have been eligible for two of those. Girls could be members of a scout troop these days but that wouldn't have been the case when the killer was a member.

Seven of the people in the room had memories of being a cub and then a boy scout and explained how there were a few basic knots you had to be able to tie before you were allowed to go camping with the troop. There were even badges you could win for mastering more advanced types of knots such as a sheepshank and a half-hitch. For most of the seven it was a few minutes involving a pleasant trip down memory lane, but two officers had different memories and PC Wilding voiced his with a fair degree of venom.

'I was hopeless at tying knots, and boy was it an issue. My team was the Badgers, and my team leader got me transferred to the Moles because he wanted everyone in the Badgers to be good at everything. It sounds something and nothing now, but at the time I was devastated and I left soon after that.'

Martin nodded with a lot of sympathy, as bullying of any kind was high on his list of things he hated. 'It's possible that the killer was either a cub or a scout and that his team leader or even the scoutmaster gave him a hard time – "sought him out for ridicule and scorn" according to the poem. My money would be on it being the scoutmaster, as in my mind that fits more with what I believe the age gap is between the victim and the killer. I would guess that Mr Davies was in his seventies and my gut feeling is that our killer is in his fifties.'

'So what are we thinking?' asked Alex. 'We have some man in his late fifties, possibly older, who is now looking back over his life and killing the people who hacked him off at various key points. First of all it was one of his primary school teachers and today we have possibly got his scoutmaster. Who would be next as he was growing up – possibly the first girl who dumped him?'

Martin admitted he had been thinking along those lines. 'In doing so we are both jumping the gun because, at the moment, we don't know if Miss Rossiter ever taught our killer or if Mr Davies ever had any connection with the Scout movement.'

'The net is just too wide at the moment,' he continued. 'What we do know is that during the course of her teaching days Miss Rossiter taught just over a thousand children. We are making our way through the names that were on the papers we collected from her house. It is beginning to look more and more as if these were not her regular pupils. Their work is either outstanding and she was encouraging them further or poor and she was giving them extra tuition. We have picked up on one unusual name and traced it to a man who has reason to remember Miss Rossiter favourably.'

'He remembers being given extra English lessons at Miss Rossiter's home because she deemed that he was exceptionally gifted. It seems she was right on that score, because he has just returned from a tour of America where he had been enlightening them on the works of Shakespeare.

'His name made it easy for us to find him, but in some cases we only have a first name to work with. The school in which Miss Rossiter worked is cooperating with DC Cook-Watts but some of the children she taught at home could have come from anywhere – there would be no records of them.'

Martin rubbed the sides of his face and tried to free himself from an uncharacteristic mood of depression. He had a bad feeling about this case and he forced his mind to focus away from the fact that the killer had known both his victims and also knew him. Now wasn't the time to be having these thoughts – they were for a more private time – but he knew they would have to be addressed and soon.

The briefing had come to a natural end and Martin checked that everyone knew what had to be done before the next session, and he set that for six o'clock. 'By then we will have the PM results, and hopefully something from the security cameras that DC Cook-Watts is checking. Uniform are continuing to look around the area and interview people from the adjacent units, they may have some news by then, and DS Pryor and I will be back from Watch Towers.'

'When the news breaks of this second murder we will have headlines indicating that a serial killer is on the rampage in our city and speculations about his next victim. God knows how but we are going to have to keep one step ahead of the press. I would like to say one step ahead of the killer, but there is no doubt in my mind that he has a masterplan and unless we can put a stop to it there are five other names on his hit list.'

Chapter Seven

On the way to Ely it was Matt who voiced the concerns that Martin had been pondering earlier. 'The two victims clearly had a profound effect upon our killer, but it's quite possible that they barely remembered him – if at all. It must be like that when someone has had a long career in, say, nursing. The nurse would have met thousands of people, and would probably only remember a handful, but if the point of contact had been a matter of life or death the patients and their relatives would be likely to remember the nurse.'

Matt then got around to what he was really thinking. 'I suspect that over the years and especially when you were in uniform, you made countless arrests that you can't even remember – but I guess that the criminals all remember you.'

Martin nodded. 'I know where you're going with this, and yes, I must have been a thorn in the flesh of many criminals. If this man is working his way through his life cycle and killing off his perceived tormentors then I could be one of them. He obviously knows me, as is witnessed by the letters being sent to my home and the direct mention of my name in the poems. It's the knowing my home address bit that doesn't fit with the theory that he's someone I've dealt with professionally, as I can't think of a single case where anyone I arrested knew where I lived.'

'You take care, guv,' replied Matt. 'This one definitely knows where you live, and to be honest we're all a bit concerned for your safety.'

'Don't worry,' said Martin with all the enthusiasm he could muster. 'I get the feeling that this bastard is more out to get me in terms of damaging my reputation as a detective rather than actually killing me. Nevertheless, thank you for your concern, Matt. You can rest assured that I will be taking care.'

'It's on the right, just over there,' said Matt as Martin turned the car into a side road. 'PC Williams was right when she told me that the houses on either side of Watch Towers are boarded up.'

Martin pulled his car into the kerbside and both men got out and looked at the outside of the building. It was in serious need of some TLC and it looked as if all the litter that had been dropped in the street had settled in an untidy collection at the side of the front door.

'If I ended up in a place like this,' said Matt, 'I think I might even be grateful if someone finished me off – maybe not in such a violent way as was used on Mr Davies but, bloody hell, no self-respecting person would want to live here!

'PC Williams said that if we got no response from the buzzer labelled "Administration" we should bang on the window nearest the front door in the hope of waking up one of the attendants.'

Martin had already pressed the buzzer once and was now leaning on it with no apparent response. Just as Matt was about to pound on the window they both heard a woman's voice echoing down the corridor with anything but dulcet tones.

'If you boys don't get your fingers off that buzzer I'll do something to you that will make sure you never father any kids – enough is enough and you are really pissing me off now.'

The voice could have come from a grizzled old dockworker, and so both men were taken aback when a petite young woman, probably less than twenty years of age, opened the door. She looked a mess, with her poorly applied eye makeup smeared across her face and her dyed blonde hair showing signs of dark roots. When she saw the two detectives she stopped shouting and quickly fastened the top two buttons of her blouse that, up until then, had left absolutely nothing to the imagination.

Without giving her the chance to open her mouth again Martin showed her his warrant card and introduced himself and

82

Matt.

She obviously didn't have a quiet voice as even now she bellowed. 'OMG, I thought it was those little buggers from the end house. They lean on that buzzer at all hours of the day and night – especially when they know I'm busy.'

Martin wondered exactly what she had been 'busy' doing but he kept his thoughts to himself and just asked her if a Mr Victor Davies was one of the residents.

'Vile Vic, yes, he is one of ours but he's not here. I wouldn't normally know if he was in or out, but I saw him going out this morning. He had this envelope in his hand. Made me think, 'cos yesterday, for the first time since he's been here, he had a letter.

'At first I thought it must be his birthday because it was one of those coloured envelopes, you know, they usually come with a card that matches, but it was more official-looking because the name and address weren't handwritten. My boyfriend wanted me to open it but I told him one of the attendants was sacked for doing that so I just took it to Vic's room. He doesn't like me calling him Vic so I do it just to annoy the man. He's a real creep.'

She was still addressing Martin and Matt as if they were both profoundly deaf and they were all still standing on the doorstep.

'Would it be possible to speak to you inside?' asked Martin. 'We have some questions and we will need to see Mr Davies' room.'

She made no attempt to let them in but showing his impatience Matt took a step towards her and she had no option other than to move out of the way. The first door along a short stretch of corridor had originally been labelled "ADMINISTRATION" using stick-on gold letters but some letters were missing and others moved so that it now read "A MINI ST ATION".

From inside the room a man's raspy voice shouted, 'Get your arse back in here, Lucy – I'm not paying for half a job.'

'You can't just barge in there!' yelled Lucy, but her words fell on deaf ears as Matt was already in the room. He had heard the man shouting and so knew there would be someone inside, but the elderly man sitting in the chair without his trousers, and in a state of semi-arousal, was a bit of a shock.

It was also a shock for the man, who quickly used his discarded pants to hide his dignity.

Martin and Matt were left in no doubt about what Lucy had been busy doing when the buzzer called her away and Matt was not prepared to hide his disgust. 'What's this?' he asked looking around the room. 'The administration office for Watch Towers or your own private knocking shop?'

'It's nothing like that. Joe is one of the residents and I was just helping him with a little problem.' For the first time the level of Lucy's voice was within the realms of normality and she looked a bit shaken.

Matt shook his head. 'But not out of the goodness of your heart, as you're getting paid for your services if what Joe said is true.'

'Of course it's not bloody true,' shouted Lucy with renewed volume. 'Joe's an idiot and most of the time he doesn't know what day it is – he's grateful to have me to talk to a couple of times a week, aren't you, Joe?'

Matt looked at the man who had struggled into his trousers and was now standing at the side of the chair with his head bowed. A mixture of anger and pity grew inside Matt as he recognised that this man was not old as he had originally thought, but just looked very downtrodden by life. Joe obviously didn't know what to do next, and so Matt suggested he should return to his room and he shuffled off with a grateful but vacant expression on his face.

Martin turned to Lucy. 'Do you have a similar twice a week therapy session with Mr Davies?' he asked sarcastically.

'What! Are you mad? I wouldn't go nowhere near that perv – and anyway he would be more interested in my boyfriend than me. He's been done for it you know – at least that's what I heard. It was years ago but he got away with it 'cos none of the boys would speak out and their mothers couldn't prove nothing.'

Even with a bit of prompting there wasn't anything more that Lucy and her double negatives could tell them about Mr Davies, and the only paperwork available on the residents was a wooden box file where they picked up his full name, date of birth, doctor's contact details, previous address, and next of kin.

The next of kin was recorded as a Mr Thomas Davies with an address in Swindon, and alongside his telephone number was a message written in red ink, 'To be contacted only on the death of the resident and at no other time.'

Well, he would be contacted now, that was for certain, but it could wait until they got back to Goleudy. Martin held his hand out towards Lucy and asked for the key to Victor's room. She started to quote the rules regarding staff going into residents' rooms in their absence but Martin had had enough of her deciding how best to use the system to her own advantage. 'This is a murder investigation,' he said bluntly. 'The keys please.'

'What murder? Who's been murdered?' Lucy wasn't upset by the suggestion of a murder, and if anything she was excited and she shouted even louder than before.

Martin insisted she stay in the office and the two men made their way to Victor Davies' room. In the corridor Matt put his hands over his ears. 'What a woman,' he said. 'She doesn't speak at all – every word is a shout and the sound of her voice is still booming around my brain. Here it is, Room 11.'

An A4 sheet of paper was stuck to the door, and the message written on it in perfect copperplate stated quite unambiguously that the resident of this room did not want to be disturbed.

The room was bigger than Martin had expected, and was in the form of a bedsit, with just one internal door leading to a very small toilet and shower room. Although the décor was shabby the room was immaculately tidy and the bedsheets at the end nearest the window sported perfect hospital corners. There was one armchair and a smallish television standing on a high table. The only other furniture was a bedside table, a freestanding wardrobe and a plain wooden upright chair placed alongside a chest of drawers. It looked as if the latter was used as a desk as the calligraphy pens and ink used to write the notice on the door were set out at the back in regimental style.

Along one wall was a counter with built-in cupboards below and on the top was a microwave oven, a kettle, a toaster, and a small fridge just big enough to take a couple of pints of milk and one or two other items, but there was actually nothing in it. Matt opened the cupboards and there was nothing in them either – not even a tin of beans or a jar of coffee. But then there wasn't a cup, plate, spoon, or frying pan either.

'It looks as if no one lives here,' said Matt. 'Even if he used to eat out every day he surely would have wanted the occasional cup of tea or a mug of coffee, wouldn't he?'

'There's a carrier bag from the Red Cross charity shop on the floor of the wardrobe and it's full of trousers and sweaters, but there's nothing hanging up, and not a thing in the way of shoes or socks anywhere.'

Martin continued opening the drawers in the desk and came across some papers. He thumbed through them but there was nothing recent and the only thing that vaguely caught his interest was a map and some directions to a campsite.

'We'll take this lot back with us,' he told Matt. 'Although I don't relish the prospect we will have to speak again to the not-so-lovely Lucy before we go.'

Matt cringed and locking the door behind them he pocketed the key. 'I'll hang on to this,' he said. 'I'll get uniformed officers to call in twice a day for the foreseeable future – that should put a stop to Lucy's antics until the relevant officials see fit to rehouse these God-forsaken residents.'

Martin made the session with Lucy as short and to the point as he could and he answered none of her questions other than to say he had every reason to believe that it was Mr Davies who had been murdered. She said she had never been in Mr Davies' room, as no one was allowed in, and all the staff had to do was to check once a day that he was still alive.

The only relevant piece of information she was able to give came via something she had learned from her boyfriend. 'Robby says that if he passes Big Bites Café on his way to see me Vic is always sitting in the seat nearest the door and staring through the window. He's never with nobody and always sits in the same seat but as I said before the man is a creep – or at least he was a creep – I still can't believe he has been murdered. Bloody hell! How?'

Martin ignored the question and after putting the papers from Mr Davies' room into the boot he left his car outside Watch Towers and walked with Matt in the direction they had been given for the café. It was less than five minutes away, and large white writing on the front windows advertised a 'fit for a king breakfast with toast and coffee for just £3.99'.

Although it was way past breakfast time this still seemed to be the meal of choice for the dozen or so men who were sitting in groups of three of more. It immediately struck Martin that a table with just one chair and situated near the door was vacant and he visualised the man whose body he had seen earlier sitting there.

As the two detectives entered the café an almost instant hush fell and not for the first time Martin wondered if he had 'police officer' tattooed across his forehead. The silence became almost palpable as he took out his warrant card and introduced himself and Matt to a grossly overweight man with long black hair tied back in a ponytail.

'I'm Lee Simms and I own this place. What may I do for you?' the man asked Martin. 'I take it you haven't come to sample my cooking, even though this lot will vouch for it being excellent value – especially the breakfast. Isn't that right, boys?' He waved his arm in an all-embracing way towards his customers and got a few nods and some muted response. It was clear that none of his regular customers wanted to join in his banter: they were all much more interested to find out what the detectives wanted, as it obviously wasn't the well-advertised breakfast.

Knowing that his every word was being listened to, Martin asked Mr Simms if he knew anything about a man who was possibly a regular customer and who normally sat in one of the window seats.

Simms immediately pointed to the single chair that Martin had noticed. 'That's where he usually sits,' said Lee. 'He's been coming here for a long time. Every single day, rain or shine. The only day we don't open is Christmas Day and I don't know what he does then.

'That's the strange thing. I can tell you more than you would care to know about all my other regulars but the man you must be talking about is an unknown entity. I began chatting to him in my usual way when he first started coming here, but he basically ignored me and everyone else.

'Just before you arrived we were all talking about him because he hasn't been in today. We all call him 'Daily' because none of us know his real name. He has the full breakfast every day, but he does vary the time he comes in so I was still expecting to see him. Has something happened to him?'

For the moment Martin did not respond to the question but turned away from Lee Simms and asked the customers if they were able to help. With his mouth stuffed full of toast and sausage one of the younger customers attempted to speak. 'My mother helps out in the Red Cross charity shop.' He washed his food down with a few gulps of coffee before continuing. 'She saw him in here once when she came to give me some cash and she told me later that he gets all his clothes from the Red Cross.'

'I know where he lives,' volunteered a customer who was sitting on an extra chair at the corner of a table meant for four people. 'It's in that hell-hole, Watch Towers. I live in the next street and I've seen him going in there a few times. What's happened to him?'

This time Martin felt obliged to give a formal response and he chose his words carefully. 'The man we are all talking about is a Mr Victor Davies. He was found dead this morning and all I can say at the moment is that we are treating his death as suspicious.'

Before they were faced with the inevitable barrage of questions Martin and Matt made for the door and after walking for ten minutes arrived at a small group of shops at the end of which was the Red Cross charity shop. It is quite often impossible to tell if two people are related by looking at them, but the woman sorting through a recently deposited bag of donations just had to be the mother of the boy who had spoken in the café.

Martin approached her and as he did so he introduced himself and Matt. Then he smiled as he said. 'Unless I am very much mistaken we have just been talking to your son in the Big Bites Café.'

In spite of the fact that Martin had smiled the woman still jumped to the wrong conclusion.

'What's he done now?' she asked. 'Everyone says he's the spitting image of me but that won't stop his father going mental if he has got himself into any more trouble.' Martin quickly reassured her. 'He's not in any trouble that I know of – in fact he was very helpful and that's why we are here. He told us that a man we know to be Mr Victor Davies used this shop on a regular basis and we wondered if you could tell us anything about him.'

The woman looked puzzled. 'I don't think I know anyone called Victor Davies – why did our Paul say I did?'

Matt joined the conversation and told the woman what little he and Martin knew about Victor. He was able to give her a general description and tell her his age but it was when he added that Mr Davies was in the café every day and lived in Watch Towers that the penny dropped.

'Oh, you mean the man the boys call Daily. Yes, he does come here, and that bag of clothes over there is waiting for him to pick up. I know his sizes in everything and I have taken to putting stuff to one side if I think it will be of use to him. I'm not sure why I bother because I never get a word of thanks. We've all come to the conclusion that he never washes any of his clothes and just picks up something from here each week and gets rid of what he has been wearing. Of course we don't know that for sure, but we only ever see him dressed in what he bought from us the last time. Not that there's anything wrong with that, is there?'

Matt shook his head. The woman was rambling on but it was not unusual for people to do this when confronted by someone official. He looked at Martin who nodded his head, second-guessing why Matt was seeking his approval.

'I am sorry to have to tell you but Mr Davies was found dead this morning and there is unfortunately no doubt that his death was not through natural causes. So we are trying to put together a picture of the man and his lifestyle and hoping that someone will be able to tell us some more about him – for example, did he have any enemies?'

Paul's mother gasped and called to her colleague who was in the back room using a rather vicious-looking steamer to get the creases out of the donated clothes before they were offered for sale. 'Vi, come here.' With no response she tried again and this time loud enough to be heard over the hissing of the steam.

'What is it, Brenda?' said Vi, coming into the shop with her face red from the heat of the back room. 'Are these two men causing trouble?'

Somewhat embarrassed Brenda explained that the two men were detectives, and that the man who her son called Daily had probably been murdered.

'Bloody hell!' exclaimed Vi. 'I don't think I've ever known anyone who was murdered – are you sure?'

Martin nodded but didn't want to get into a discussion regarding the death of Mr Davies, he wanted to know a bit more about his life and asked Vi if she knew anything about the man.

'He never told us anything about himself and the only time I ever got to know anything was on the one occasion he was in the shop when Mrs Ryan, the vicar's wife brought in a load of bric-a-brac that they didn't sell at the church fête. They obviously recognised one another instantly but neither of them was pleased by the meeting and Mr Davies quickly took his bag of clothes and left.'

Vi looked a bit sheepish about her next words and she apologised in advance.

'I know I was being nosy,' she said, 'but it's not often that

90

Mrs Ryan is rattled and I had to know what had caused it. She wasn't very forthcoming and told me several times that she was not one to gossip but from what I could gather Mr Davies had at one time been very involved with the church and was even the scoutmaster, but something went wrong and she thought he had left the area. That's why she was surprised when she saw him – and she certainly wasn't pleased to see him,'

Martin and Matt exchanged a knowing glance and Martin sought confirmation regarding what had been said. 'Are you sure he was the scoutmaster?'

'Well, no,' responded Vi. 'I only know what the vicar's wife told me but her husband is the vicar of St Stephen's church so if it's important you could go there and ask her. In any case they'll probably know more about Mr Davies than we do.'

Martin thanked the two women for their help and he and Matt walked back to the car. As they returned, passing the café, they saw that business was brisk, confirming the idea that there is no such thing as bad publicity.

They rounded the corner leading to Watch Towers, only to find the place inundated with the press and television cameras.

Lucy's makeup was freshly applied and she posed for photographs on the doorstep with a young man, presumably Robby. They were both lapping up the attention. Martin's first thoughts of a leak from somewhere within the force were soon quashed as he overheard one of the local journalists giving a thumbs up to Lucy's boyfriend and arranging to see him in the pub later.

As soon as they came into sight Martin and Matt were surrounded and it became a bit of a street fight as questions were simultaneously fired at them from every direction. Earlier in the day a press release had been issued from Goleudy but it had not given out the name of the murdered man. With the information they had now undoubtedly received from the duo on the doorstep the media were putting two and two together and demanding a total of five at the very least.

It was interesting to hear that they had done their homework on Mr Davies, and Max Richards, a local reporter well known to Martin, pushed his way to the front of the crowd to boast about his knowledge.

'Afternoon, DCI Phelps – having a busy time are we? It's usually a sad occasion when someone is knocked off but there won't be too many people crying at this one's funeral. It was long before your time, but there was a lot of talk about the way he used his position as scoutmaster to satisfy his passion for young boys – the kids wouldn't speak out, though, and so nothing was proven. We thought your old boss DCI Austin would get him but he didn't take the case. Shame really because we all know what lengths he would go to in order to get the results he wanted.'

Martin certainly knew, but he chose to ignore the comments about his ex-senior officer, although he couldn't ignore the next question from the same reporter. 'We have to sit on some of the information we have been given for the moment but it is leading us to believe that the murder in the Red Dragon Centre two weeks ago and this one today is the work of the same killer. Are we right?'

'You may well be,' responded Martin curtly. 'However, as you are only too keen to remind me, we have as yet not been able to bring the killer of Mary Rossiter to justice and so we don't know who he is.'

He was interrupted as a microphone was almost thrust up his nose and a strident middle-aged woman challenged him.

'It's much worse than that, isn't it?' she questioned. 'According to our sources you haven't got a single lead or scrap of evidence so it looks as if that killer has got away scot-free. Is it going to be the same this time? Is this killer likely to go for a third victim or maybe there will be more. What do you think DCI Phelps? – you're supposed to be the clever one!'

Martin could cheerfully have rammed her microphone down her throat but his response was straight out of the 'dealing with the press' text book. 'We are still working hard to solve the murder of Mary Rossiter and will be putting in the same degree of effort in this case. You can all rest assured in the knowledge that the killer will be found. Now, if you will allow me, I will get back to my team who are putting the pieces together even as we speak.'

The mob was not going to allow the two detectives to get away that easily and one reporter asked Martin if he thought he was up to the job. Another asked if there was likely to be a third murder and this triggered a series of related questions.

'Have we got a serial killer on the loose?'

'How is he choosing his victims?'

'Any chance you will catch him before he kills again?'

'What does Superintendent Bryant think of your poor performance? – it won't do much for the excellent crime detection figures he's always ready to push down our throats.'

Matt elbowed his way towards the car, making room for Martin to follow, but they both knew the press would not be satisfied. Question after question was followed by accusations of poor performance and even incompetence. These accusations were not general – they were without exception aimed at DCI Phelps, and both men were relieved when Martin was able to start up his engine and they drove off.

Matt looked back over his shoulder and shook his head. Since he had worked with Martin he had been aware of the positive relationship between his boss and the media. Today there was very little sign of that, in fact quite the opposite. It felt as if that pack back there were being deliberately encouraged to have a go at Martin personally – just as the killer was doing in the poems.

Chapter Eight

'We've got to eat at some time, guv,' said Matt as the car skirted the edge of the city and they were heading back towards Cardiff Bay. 'It's Saturday and there's no Iris to serve us hot food back at base, so there'll only be sandwiches. I feel like something a bit more substantial – what about you?'

The encounter with the men and women of the press had left Martin feeling deflated but he recognised that he was probably also being affected by a low blood sugar level and so eating would be a sensible option. He would have to do something, anything to shake off this unfamiliar dip in his spirits.

'Well, Shelley's planning to raid the local deli and rustle up an evening meal, but I can't see us getting away before eight and that's being optimistic. It's a quarter past four now and the briefing is set for six so yes, let's get something to eat.'

Matt responded. 'Take a left at the end of this stretch and almost immediately on the right is The Cat and Fiddle. My sister Beth takes her lot there for the occasional after-school treat as she's trying to wean them off McDonalds, and at least the pub offers an alternative to fries. I've been with them a couple of times and for pub food it's more than OK.'

Martin pulled into the car park and he thought it was quite busy but then it was Saturday so possibly families were out and about. As Matt had indicated, the menu was basically what one would expect in a pub, but there were one or two exceptions. Welsh lamb in a redcurrant sauce served with seasonal vegetables was the one that took Martin's eye, and Matt plumped for the homemade corned-beef pie with the same side order as Martin.

'I could murder a pint,' said Matt, 'but I don't think it'll go down well with the team if we return smelling like a brewery.'

'That's unlikely to be the case after one beer,' replied Martin. 'If I wasn't driving I would definitely go for it, so order me a J2O and get yourself a beer. Please make sure the J2O is apple and mango, though; I don't think I could face one of the orange ones today.'

Matt gave a wry smile and went to the bar to place their order. Martin watched his sergeant smiling and talking to the barmaid, knowing that it was no more than a superficial friendly gesture. He had probably been chatting up barmaids all his drinking life but Martin was hearing more and more hints dropped about the way in which Matt's relationship with Sarah was becoming serious.

Although it hadn't been his fault, Martin still felt some responsibility for the knife injury Matt had received several months earlier while they were apprehending a killer. It had meant the end of his rugby playing, but Sarah had recently introduced him to watersports, and Martin had noticed a few days ago that the back of Matt's 4x4 was now full of wet suits, body-boards, and pieces of surfing equipment. Maybe one of these days Martin would invite Matt and Sarah to his cottage and they could test the surf at Llantwit Major. However, Shelley was the only one he wanted to share the cottage with for now. Simply thinking about her lifted his mood ten-fold, and that was before the food had elevated his blood sugar.

'That was really good,' he said to Matt as they drove out of the car park and were heading back to Goleudy. 'Much better than I would have expected, but I bet the excellent waitress service was more to do with you giving her your little boy lost look than her normal dedication to customer service.'

'Back to business now, Matt. See if you can find out if there have been any developments – anything I need to know ahead of the team meeting at six.'

For the rest of the time it took them to return to Goleudy, Martin focused totally on his driving, as the roads were suddenly very busy, while Matt used his mobile to contact various team members, making a few notes regarding their progress.

By the time they pulled into the office car park it was twenty past five and Martin said he was going to see if Professor Moore had anything to tell them. 'Rather than have you come with me, I'd prefer you to do some checking up and ensuring that everyone is prepared for this briefing. Please let there be something we can work on – surely the killer will have made a mistake somewhere along the line.'

The two men parted company, and after putting on the mandatory disposable clothes and overshoes Martin entered the main PM room and watched for a few moments as the Prof and Mrs Williams continued a well-rehearsed routine. Mrs Williams had noticed Martin, and waited for a convenient moment before letting the professor know they had a visitor.

'As you can see,' the professor said bluntly, 'we have sluiced off the orange peel and opened him up. There is nothing inherent that would have taken him to meet his maker at the moment. As before the knife wound, from a thrust below his ribs and in an upward direction, is the reason we have him on the slab. It's almost a carbon copy of the woman we did two weeks ago and they are around about the same age.'

Martin interrupted. 'No need to concern yourself with estimating his age – this time we know the identity of the victim and we have a date of birth.'

The Prof continued. 'Well, as I said, it's that one single stab wound that did the damage, so the killer was either lucky both times or he has had a lot of practice. What I don't understand is why, in each case, he bothered with the second stabbing. With both victims the wound to the neck is superficial – and it's not as if he's gone for the carotid artery; if anything it rather looks as if he has avoided it.'

'Well, my own view is that nothing this killer does has got anything to do with luck – but I take your point about him possibly having had plenty of practice. Is there any sign that the victim struggled with his attacker?' asked Martin.

'No, there's nothing at all. No bruising anywhere on the

body, and he either didn't see the knife coming or just accepted his fate as there are no defence wounds on his hands or arms. Personal hygiene was not high on this man's agenda, but he was neither obese nor undernourished and the only other thing I have noted is that his skin and organs were not well-hydrated. I can't really offer an explanation for that and in any event it's not germane to his murder.

'Sorry, DCI Phelps, but I can't be of any more help. What's left for me now is the routine brain examination, but I don't expect to find that he died of a cerebral tumour. If you will forgive me I will skip the scheduled meeting, as to be perfectly honest my input will be surplus to requirements on this occasion.'

Martin made his way to the changing room door and called back over his shoulder. 'Your input is always valued by the team as well, you know, but I'm happy to relay the results of the PM – as you say, they speak for themselves.'

A quick check of his watch told Martin that it was already five minutes to six so he went straight to Incident Room One. On the way he thought about what the Prof had said regarding Mr Davies' general health and wondered if, with the addition of a couple of glasses of water a day, the daily consumption of one 'fit for a king breakfast' and nothing else could be the answer to the country's obesity problems. He couldn't imagine eating just one meal a day, though, and certainly not the same meal as yesterday and every day before that, stretching back for years. What strange lives some people led.

Most of the chairs were already full when Martin walked into the room and as had been the case at their earlier session it was the two poems that were attracting the most attention.

A young PC was very cynical. 'Even if we had been given these poems days or weeks before the murders were committed, we still couldn't have prevented them. Just look at what we are considering to be clues – every one of them only makes sense with the hindsight we now have.'

There was a lot of debate but in the final analysis no one disagreed.

Martin called for the briefing to start and did a five-minute recap on what had been seen and discussed at the earlier session. 'OK let me start the ball rolling by saying that I have just left Prof. Moore and rather as we had suspected he can confirm exactly the same cause of death for Victor Davies as was recorded for Mary Rossiter. Just to remind you all, we are talking about fatal damage caused to major blood vessels near the heart as a result of a long sharp knife being plunged into the chest, below the ribs in an upward direction and with considerable force.'

'According to the prof. death would have been swift with most of the haemorrhage being internal although inevitably some blood loss around the site of the stabbing. In both cases a second knife wound was inflicted in the neck but it's possible the victims were already dead by then. If the killer had gone for the carotid artery in the neck there would have been a bloodbath and so the Prof thinks it was deliberately missed and he is not able to offer any scientific rationale for that second stabbing.'

'What does this information, together with what is written in the poems, tell us about the killer – anyone got any ideas?'

Martin looked around the room. It was Alex who started the suggestions that then came rolling in thick and fast.

'He knows what he's doing with that knife. I have a fair understanding of human anatomy but I'm not sure I would hit the right spot once, never mind twice in succession.' Other comments followed.

'He's making some sort of point – pardon the pun – with the second killing.'

'This killer is on a mission to wipe out people who have offended him and has perfected the art of doing it.'

'He's good at what he is doing so we need to stop him before he does any more.'

'Yes, but he's already threatened to do some more killing so how do we stop him?'

'I don't like the fact that he's playing games with us and thinks he's one clever bastard.'

'He appears to know you, sir – and that's a big, big worry.'

'He most definitely has a masterplan and that apparently involves another five murders. God forbid!'

Almost everyone in the room had a comment to make and Martin allowed them to continue until there nothing new was being said and then summarised.

'OK, we know the exact time of the first murder and the time within minutes of the second one. They both happened on a Saturday morning. We also know that the killer knew both his victims and so they were not randomly chosen.

'The first one was a teacher, Miss Mary Rossiter, and it is likely that she either taught the killer at Penbryn Primary School or that he was one of her private pupils. The poem and things we have learned from other sources confirm that she was a strict disciplinarian, hence the reference to the dragon and I suspect the choosing of the Red Dragon Centre for the crime.

'What most of you will not know is that during our investigations this afternoon Matt and I discovered that the second victim, Mr Victor Davies, was, many years ago, a scoutmaster.'

This revelation caused an outbreak of general discussion as the obvious links between boy scouts and knots were made.

Martin continued. 'What links the second victim to Freshly Squeezed is not immediately obvious. Maybe it's just a venue the killer came up with to fit in with his macabre game – who knows?'

'We have some knowledge of what the killer looks like. He's well built, and an inch or two under six feet.'

'Would now be a good time to come in?' DC Cook-Watts asked her boss. 'We have had a bit of a breakthrough with the CCTV tapes from the entrance of the Tremorfa Industrial Estate.'

'Feel free,' Martin replied.

Helen continued. 'As you know, we spent time with the security staff – and they were able to identify every vehicle that went in and out during the timescale we gave them – one hour before and one hour after the murder. We were disappointed when, with the exception of the victim's car, all the cars, vans, and lorries were deemed to belong to owners or employees known to security and said to have a legitimate right to be there.'

'Nevertheless we spotted a total of seventeen cars and vans and two lorries, and started to go through the process of interviewing the drivers, some of whom were still on site and we got an early break. The fourth person we interviewed, a Mr Steve Lewis, gave a lift to a man he picked up at the far end of the approach road to the estate. The timing fits very well, as there are less than ten minutes between Mr Lewis' van and the green Ford Fiesta coming through the main entrance.'

'Mr Lewis was able to tell us that the man he picked up was very specific about where he wanted to be dropped off and took us to the exact spot. It's only two units away from Freshly Squeezed and, surprise, surprise, in a camera black spot. I asked Mr Lewis if he would normally have driven to this part of the estate, and he said he wouldn't as his unit is much further over but the man he picked up had asked him to detour, so he did.'

'When I asked him if he was always so obliging he laughed and said no, but there had been something in the authority of the man's voice that made him do as he was told – that's what he said.'

Martin looked pleased and asked a few questions about Mr Lewis and whether or not he knew the man he had given a lift to.

Helen responded. 'He says he's never seen the man before and I'm afraid that's where our luck runs out, as the description Mr Lewis was able to give us is pretty hopeless. Yes, the man was the about the same height and build as our killer, and he wore the same type of headgear we saw in the Red Dragon tapes, but the only other thing he was sure about was that the man was clean-shaven, definitely no beard or moustache. He couldn't remember the shape of his face, the colour of his eyes, nothing, except that he lacked facial hair!'

'That's better than nothing,' said Martin. 'What about the voice? You said Mr Lewis was in some way influenced by the man's voice.'

'Yes, I pushed him on that, and he said the man spoke like someone who was used to giving orders and having them obeyed. He was a bit embarrassed that he had been so compliant and said it wasn't like him to do what he was asked to do without question. Anyway, Mr Lewis is being extremely cooperative and is currently in the identification suite with our photo-fit staff to see if they can jog his memory.'

'Well done.' Martin thanked Helen and the officers who had worked with her, and then asked Sgt Evans if he had any progress to report.

'Nothing really from our end, and we've spoken to everyone who was working this morning in the units surrounding Freshly Squeezed. A lot of the units aren't operational at the weekends, and two such units have CCTV cameras. We've located the owners of those two and they are on their way to Tremorfa to give us access to their tapes. The other surrounding units have a variety of cameras – two scan their entrances, five are fixed, and the rest are dummies. We've been through them all but not one person is seen walking, and the only vehicles correspond with what DC Cook-Watts has scrutinised. We will of course look at the other two tapes when we get them but looking at the angles of their cameras I don't hold out much hope.'

'I wish I could put my finger on it,' continued Sgt Evans. 'There is something about the build and stance of this killer that, coupled with what we have been told about his voice, is ringing a vague bell.'

Martin looked up sharply, as he held a great deal of store by John Evans' intuition. His 'copper's nose', as it was sometimes referred to, had proved to be on the right track many times.

'Stick with it, John,' said Martin. 'If you can think of anyone who even vaguely resembles the limited description we have, just let me know.'

Sgt Evans nodded and finished his report. 'The area has been thoroughly searched for any sign of blood or a weapon, but we've come up with nothing, so it looks as if, like before, the killer has taken any evidence home with him.'

'Talking about him going home,' said Martin, 'do we know

if he thumbed a lift out of the Estate?'

Helen Cook-Watts responded. 'We looked at the tapes for a two-hour slot after the murder and the drivers have been identified, but we haven't finished interviewing all of them as yet. So far, no one gave anyone a lift – and there's no sign of anyone walking out.'

Matt offered a couple of suggestions. 'We know the only way in and out by vehicle is via the main entrance, but maybe there's another exit for pedestrians. The other possibility is something I think you thought of when we were looking for the killer after the first murder, sir. You wondered if he was still in the area and getting some sort of kick watching us trying to figure things out.'

Helen responded to the first of Matt's suggestions. 'According to the security staff the steel fencing around the estate is almost ten feet high and isn't broken at any point. One of their duties is to check it every day and at 8.30 this morning there were no problems reported.'

'So, either he was given a lift by one of the drivers not yet interviewed, or he has waited and watched and walked out later.'

Martin turned to Helen. 'Continue checking those exit CCTV cameras, there has to be some sign of him leaving and it may be a lot later than we have so far considered. Is there anything else? What about you, Alex?'

Alex expressed his profound frustration. 'I can't ever remember a situation when we had so little forensic evidence to bring to these sessions. The detailed analysis of the scenes of both crimes have produced absolutely nothing to show that the killer was ever there, other than the two similarly dispatched victims.

'We've crawled all over Miss Rossiter's car and the surrounding parking bay with nothing to show for it, and the area in which Mr Davies' body was found is more sterile than most operating theatres. There's not a fingerprint or a footprint anywhere – nothing whatsoever for us to work on.'

Martin sensed and shared his colleagues feeling of

disappointment, but he was determined not to show it and he rallied the troops. 'Disheartening, yes, but we are building up a profile of the killer, and we now have a witness who's seen his face and heard his voice and that's one hundred per cent improvement on the last time.'

At Martin's request Matt filled everyone in on what they had discovered earlier about Mr Davies and especially the rumours of possible improper relationships, when he was a scoutmaster, between him and some of the boys. He explained that although it was still part of local gossip nothing was ever proven at the time and all checks revealed that Mr Davies had no official stain on his character.

Martin turned to Alex. 'We now have three pieces of correspondence from our killer, all sent through the post: the letter that Matt found in Mr Davies' car and the two poems sent to my home address. Do they give us anything to go on?'

Alex replied. 'Well, from what we've seen of this man we wouldn't have expected fingerprints, and he knows enough about using computers to have generated the envelopes and the contents electronically. Interestingly, his printer isn't the most common ink jet variety that most people have at home, it's a high-specification laser printer.

'The coloured paper and matching envelopes are not exactly run of the mill either, but not that difficult to get hold of either online or from craft shops like Hobbycraft or Paperchase.

'I get the feeling that this man either knows first-hand about forensic detection methods or watches a lot of television crime series. He used water to wet the gum on the stamps, so no saliva for a possible DNA match.'

Helen interrupted. 'I didn't think you had to lick stamps now – I thought you just peeled them off a book and stuck them on the envelope.'

'Not if you buy a sheet of stamps from the Post Office,' Alex replied. 'We can see that these are torn from a sheet because the stamp on the envelope sent to Martin today is missing a tiny piece from the bottom right-hand corner. That tiny piece is to be found on the bottom left-hand corner of the stamp on Mr Davies' orange envelope. Confirmation, if it was needed, that both letters were sent by the same person using postage stamps taken from the same sheet of stamps.'

'All three letters were sent first class before the respective killings, Davies' on the Thursday and both of Martin's on the Friday. Despite the bad press Royal Mail gets from time to time, there's almost a one hundred per cent certainty that they would be received on the Saturday morning – and they were.'

Martin nodded. 'Let's turn our attention to the contents of the three envelopes and first of all the two poems. I don't want to go over what we have already covered, but is there anything new that we should be considering?'

Helen responded. 'When we looked at the second poem earlier, we didn't know that Mr Davies had been a scoutmaster, and so now the lines about knots make perfect sense. The killer may also be making some sort of sick posthumous gesture by tying his victim's hands behind their backs using reef knots. Mr Davies would have been in no position to ridicule his efforts this time.'

Martin agreed. 'There's plenty for everyone to be doing, so let's get on with it. Helen, go back to those CCTV cameras. Matt, get the ball rolling regarding the Boy Scout angle. Take John Evans with you and pay a visit to the vicar of St Stephens and his wife – I suspect they are the "Bible-bashing friends" referred to in the letter sent to Mr Davies. If they can tell us the period when Mr Davies was the scoutmaster it will give us a more accurate take on the killer's age, as if my memory serves you need to be a certain age before you can join a scout troop.'

'Scouting is a huge organisation; there must be some sort of central register that we can access, and maybe get the names of the boys who enrolled during the time Mr Davies was leading the troop. Let's get hold of those names if we can and compare them with the names we have on the exercise books from Miss Rossiter's house, and from her school. Even if we only match first names it could help with the identification of this killer.

'Before you all go I want us to think ahead. If this killer's plan is to systematically kill off people whom he believes have caused him pain then who do you imagine would be next? It sounds a bit defeatist to be considering his next murder rather than solving the first two, but I think that's the only way we are going to catch him – by trying to anticipate his next move.'

Matt made a few suggestions. 'Well, so far we have someone who upset him when he was just in primary school, so he would have been no more than ten or eleven years of age, and he was perhaps in his early teens when he was a boy scout. After that the thing on the mind of most young men would be looking for love, or at the very least sex, so perhaps his next potential victim will be someone who treated him badly in the relationship department.'

'That doesn't even help us to know if the next victim on his list is male or female as we don't know his sexual orientation. The person we are thinking about could be one of his loves that let him down, or maybe someone who stole someone he loved from him. As I said, it doesn't even give us a clue as to whether we are looking at a man or a woman. Generally speaking, when we're growing up we tend to be involved with people roughly the same age as us. So if we are on the right track with our thinking the next victim could be quite a bit younger than the first two.'

Helen intervened. 'Do we have any way of predicting what colour he would use next? He obviously has five others planned, and probably has five more poems already written with murder venues arranged to fit his wacky colour codes.'

'Miss Rossiter was a primary school teacher and red is a primary colour – but orange isn't, more's the pity, or we'd only have to consider red, yellow, and blue. Sorry, boss, I'm rambling – there is no clue in what we know so far that could give us an inkling of the next colour.'

'Rambling is good.' Martin was not going to stop anyone considering whatever popped into his or her head. 'I suggest you all get a good night's sleep and tomorrow we start in earnest at what will be just the plain hard slog of going through every bit of information and seeking out records from years ago. The identity of this killer is our main focus, and before I leave I will speak to Mr Lewis to see if our photo-fit staff have been able to jog his memory.'

The room cleared quickly. Martin remembered that it was a Saturday night and most people had homes and families to get home to. He shouted out a big 'thank you, everyone'. Matt and Helen remained but Martin quickly told them he was happy to see Mr Lewis without them, and left them to clear up a few ends as he made his way to the identification suite.

Mr Lewis looked tired and was rubbing his eyes as Martin joined him in one of the pods used by the identification team. The little rooms were soundproofed, as their business was not just building up an image of someone's face – it was about voice, facial expressions, habits, and a whole raft of other things that made identifications possible.

Martin introduced himself, apologising that things were taking so long, and thanked Mr Lewis for his help.

Mr Lewis smiled. 'My tiredness is nothing to do with this, it's because we've got a young baby and a good night's sleep is a thing of the past. However, I would be more motivated if I knew what this is all about. I obviously gave a lift to a man that you desperately want to speak to but no one has yet told me why.'

Martin explained that it was possible that the man he had picked up had committed a murder soon after he was dropped off.

'Jesus Christ!' Mr Lewis yelled. 'He could have murdered me – bloody hell, what would Kim have done without me to help with the sleepless nights? Was I in serious danger of being killed?'

Martin was quick to reassure him that the killer had planned the murder and was out to kill someone specific, not just anyone at random. He explained that the CID believed the murder to be linked to the one two weeks ago at the Red Dragon Centre.

'I read about that,' said Mr Lewis. 'Some balls that killer must have, to stab someone in broad daylight and with so many people around. Seriously, you think I gave that animal a lift in my van?'

Martin told him that it was highly probable and emphasised why it was so important that Mr Lewis think of anything that could help with the killer's identification.

Emma, the girl working with Mr Lewis, praised his efforts so far and updated Martin on their progress.

'At first, Mr Lewis told us that he could remember nothing other than that the man was quite tall and well built, but he has surprised himself with the number of other details we now have to offer.'

Martin was shown a computer-generated image of a man with an estimated height of five feet eleven inches. From the recollections of Mr Lewis the weight had been fixed at fifteen and a half stone, and the image was 'dressed' in black jeans and a high-necked navy sweater. Although Martin said nothing he knew how closely this image resembled the one they had from the Red Dragon tapes.

Emma explained that she had been unable to put in some features, such as the nose and eyes, because in spite of many attempts there was nothing that Mr Lewis could remember.

'This is probably because the man wore a baseball hat and it came down well over his eyes,' she told Martin. As you can see, Mr Lewis has suggested that it had a larger-than-normal rounded peak, and he is fairly certain it was black.'

'It was,' confirmed Mr Lewis, 'and I'm certain about his sports bag being navy blue. What I'm not certain about is what we have done with the shape of the face and the mouth. It's more of a gut feeling I have about the man been square-jawed with thin lips, and I would hate to mislead, but I do know he barely opened his mouth when he spoke.'

Martin reassured Mr Lewis that he was not misleading anyone and asked about the killer's voice.

'As I told the lady detective earlier, the thing I most remember about his voice is its authoritative tone. Normally if someone asked me to go out of my way to drop them off, I would suggest a point on my route and that would be that. This guy told me exactly where he wanted to be dropped and that's where I dropped him off – I'm still scratching my head over that!'

'Did he shout?' asked Martin. 'Did you feel as if you were being threatened?'

'No, not threatened exactly, and as I said he barely opened his mouth when he spoke, but it was if he was used to being obeyed and for some reason I didn't argue with him. All he said was, 'Drop me off at unit 17, will you, mate,' but it wasn't so much a request as a demand.'

Emma commented on the killer's accent. 'We've run a number of voice tapes using the actual words that he used and I am in no doubt that this man has a definite Cardiff accent – Mr Lewis recognised it when, using our equipment, the general Welsh element was lowered and the Cardiff accent was increased.

'When we've finished I will be able to give you the image we've come up with and a tape of what we believe the killer sounds like normally. It's possible, of course, that he tried to disguise his voice, but we find that certain elements, such as a fundamental local accent, are difficult to hide.'

After thanking Emma and Mr Lewis, Martin headed for his car, and twenty-five minutes later he was approaching his cottage. It wasn't dark but the daylight was fading and Martin could see some candles flickering in his lounge. He shook off the feeling of violation that the letters had brought to his home. Shelley was waiting for him and with maximum resolve he put the two murders behind him until tomorrow.

Chapter Nine

It was Friday September 23rd, and getting towards the end of a month of warm sunshine, when the weather suddenly changed and autumn arrived almost instantly. Rain and high winds had invaded in the early hours of the morning, and by the time most people were awake the gutters were full of leaves.

Martin walked down the path of his cottage but didn't get straight into his car. He allowed the wind that was coming in off the sea to blow his short dark brown hair in every direction. The rain felt good on his face and he wished that the elements could wash away the last few weeks of his professional life.

It was almost three weeks since the murder at the Red Dragon Centre of retired schoolmistress Mary Rossiter, and almost a week since Victor Davies, an ex-scoutmaster, had been stabbed in a similar fashion on the premises of a company that produced orange juice. The colours red and orange were part of the key to solving the murders, as were the links between the victims and their murderer and these clues had been exhibited in the poems sent by the killer to Martin.

Martin needed a clear head and all his wits about him this morning, as a major press conference and public appeal was being staged and it was not something he was looking forward to. Contrary to his normal experience, the last week had seen the press turn on him personally and he had been slated for the lack of progress.

It was not through lack of trying, as Martin and his team had explored every aspect of the victims' lives and had cross-referenced names of people they may have mutually known. They were working from the basis that the killer had a personal grudge with each of his victims, and the horrifying thing was that they had every reason to believe that he had five more victims lined up. This possibility had been deliberately kept from the public for fear of widespread panic.

In spite of every attempt to keep certain aspects of the murders out of the public domain, the press had some knowledge of the poems and now labelled the killer as 'The Bard'. Martin was certain that this would be pleasing the man and he was also certain that a major part of the satisfaction this butcher was getting related to the fact that he was in the public spotlight.

Well, there would be plenty of publicity today, and Martin's boss Superintendent Bryant had expressed an interest in attending the press conference, much to Martin's dismay. He was one of the people giving Martin a hard time, and he constantly told Martin that DCI Austin would, one way or another, have had things sewn up by now. It was the 'one way or another' element that Martin would have worried about if Austin was still around. He knew that his ex-boss may well have stitched up a suspect rather than solving the case legitimately.

Martin suddenly realised that the rain was becoming more of a downpour and he jumped into his car and headed for Goleudy. He knew that the whole team were dispirited with the lack of any solid evidence, and he made up his mind to raise their spirits. Today would soon be over, one way or another, and perhaps if he offered to get the first round in at one of the local pubs after work they would all be inclined to join him.

It was barely eight o'clock when he arrived at his office, but looking out through the window he could see armies of the press congregated in the street outside. The press conference was set for eight thirty and there was also to be re-enactments of the two murders in an attempt to jog memories. Martin knew that this would bring in hundreds and possibly thousands of phone calls, with the likelihood that none of them would be any use, but just occasionally something was of help and so the process was considered necessary. He would have liked to be able to say that his officers were too busy to get involved with this exercise but in truth they were all at a virtual standstill.

Matt had obviously seen him come in and after knocking the door with his foot he walked in with two cups of coffee.

He put the coffee on the desk and joined Martin at the window. 'I see you've spotted the wolves circling. I made the mistake of coming through the front entrance about ten minutes ago and I was almost mobbed.'

'Why did you come in that way?' asked Martin.

'Sarah dropped me off. Three of my nieces have got an inset day so there's no school for them and their parents couldn't get time off work. Sarah has a couple of days off and has agreed to take them to Folly Farm, but it's a bit of a squeeze in her car so I've lent her mine.' Matt always spoke fondly of his nieces but Martin noticed something special in his tone as he spoke of Sarah.

'Getting serious, is it?' he teased.

'We're taking it slowly, but not such a slow start as you and Shelley had – from what I remember, that was very much at snail's pace.'

Martin laughed as he recalled the truth in what Matt had said, and he wished they could spend their morning talking about the two women who had recently transformed both their lives – instead they were having to face a baying media.

No knock this time but the door opened and Superintendent Bryant, buttons shining brilliantly, came into the office. 'I wouldn't have thought you would have time for personal chit-chat,' he accused. 'Where is DC Cook-Watts, I presume she is attending the press conference?'

'Good morning, sir,' said Martin gritting his teeth. 'It was not my intention to involve DC Cook-Watts as I thought you, me, and DS Pryor would be enough.'

'We probably will be more than enough, but you need to start thinking more politically, and the involvement of a woman is what the public are coming to expect. I'm always questioned about the predominately IC1 make-up of the police force – as if I alone am responsible – and I have recently been challenged about the scarcity of women at senior levels, too.' Martin cringed as he thought of Helen's reaction to being included in something just to tick a box.

The superintendent continued. 'It's time we were downstairs. I'll sit in the middle, make the necessary formal introductions, and provide the background, then you can give an update and field any questions.' He marched off and Martin picked up some papers from his desk and followed behind with Matt in tow.

Martin had attended lots of press conferences in the large purpose-designed room on the ground floor, but he had never before walked into this level of sound. The room was crammed, with every chair taken and the sides and the central aisle packed with photographers and people holding various pieces of electronic equipment. Everyone was hopelessly attempting to make themselves heard, and it took Matt several loud taps on his microphone before the volume of heated noise diminished and a relative calm ensued.

The three men had seated themselves at the front of the room in the preordained order and as Matt gave one particularly loud rap on the mic the superintendent rose to his feet and the audience fell quiet.

He began speaking in his practised public voice that sounded false and patronising, and Martin inwardly cringed. 'Good morning, ladies and gentlemen, we are most grateful that you are able to take time from your busy schedules to be with us this morning.'

If the super was angling for mutual respect he was instantly disappointed.

'We wouldn't have missed it for the world,' shouted one woman and her comment was followed by others that soon made it clear that the press were there more on a mission to hang Martin out to dry than help solve two murders.

The mood was indeed hostile, and Matt banged on the microphone again. He also shouted for quiet – and when Matt shouted he could be heard above anything.

'We will get nowhere if every one of our sentences is followed by this sort of juvenile barracking – so make up your

114

minds, either curb it now, or we knock this session on the head before it's even started.'

The majority of the reporters wanted the full story and the opportunity to ask questions, so quiet and order followed Matt's outburst. Instead of getting straight down to business the superintendent persevered with the speech he had planned and formally introduced himself, Martin, and Matt.

'We know who you all are – we want to know what you are doing.' The same woman as before interrupted, but this time she was silenced by her associates, although Martin sensed that the majority felt the same way she did and wanted answers, not the pompous utterances of a senior officer.

The plan had been for Superintendent Bryant to give the background to the two murders and for Martin to continue, but the two interruptions and the obviously hostile atmosphere caused the super to bottle out and he immediately handed the session over to Martin.

No one listening would have guessed that Martin had been placed on the back foot. He got to his feet and speaking with clarity and authority, and without mincing his words, he described the two murders. He gave details of both the victims and their possible connections with the killer. It had been decided before the conference not to withhold many details and to let the press have almost everything that the CID had. The rationale for that decision was based on the fact that the press was already getting some inside help on a number of aspects, but in the absence of a complete picture they were filling in the gaps themselves.

The strategy was working and it was becoming apparent that the audience had never anticipated this level of disclosure, nor such an honest appraisal of the progress to date.

After describing the murders in detail, Martin went on to confirm that the CID had received poems with clues about the murders, but that they had not been received in time to prevent them happening. He also ratified that, as had been printed in the newspapers, he was mentioned in each of the poems. What he did not tell the press was that the poems had been sent to his home address. This piece of information appeared not to have reached them and it was the one thing he wanted to keep out of their hands.

The room was now really quiet as Martin went on to describe the way in which colours were being used by the killer. He even told them that each of the victims had been discovered with their hands tied behind their backs, with the appropriate colour cord and each with a perfectly executed reef knot.

He had now been speaking for more than twenty minutes and was suddenly amused by the look of naked admiration he was getting from Superintendent Bryant. He had to restrain himself from laughing, especially as he saw that Matt had picked up on the situation.

Martin was pleased with his own performance but was not complacent because he knew this was the only part of the press conference he could control – the questions and answers session would be a different ball game.

He concluded by reminding everyone of the re-enactments that were scheduled for 10 a.m. and then sat down.

As anticipated, the room erupted and questions were fired from every direction, but Martin said nothing and it soon became obvious that none of the questions would be answered unless the audience got themselves into some sort of order.

The woman who had previously interrupted was about to shout out a question, but she was silenced by Laura Cummings, one of the local television crime reporters. Martin remembered Ms Cummings as someone who only attended the high-profile conferences and who was usually extremely well briefed.

She was, as always, immaculately dressed and looked even better in the flesh than she did in front of the television cameras. She flashed Martin a disarming smile as she spoke. 'Nice one, DCI Phelps, that took us all a bit by surprise – but what a pity you didn't feel able to share this information at an earlier point in the investigation. So why now?'

Martin got back onto his feet. 'You have enough experience to know that one of the biggest issues when we release murder details early on is the well-known phenomenon of copycat killings – it's always something we have to consider very carefully. The exercise we've got planned for later will give the public much more information than we usually release, and there may be someone out there sufficiently deranged to want to copy it, but we now consider that to be a calculated risk. As I have shared with you, we are unfortunately light on hard evidence – so any help will be greatly appreciated.'

Although everyone was desperate to ask their own questions, Ms Cummings didn't allow anyone else to get a word in. She asked Martin to tell her more about the poems. 'Why don't you release the poems in full?' she suggested. 'Or are there still things you are keeping from us – like the possibility the killer is telling you he has more victims in his sights!'

Martin swallowed hard. He didn't want the public being told that someone who had already killed two seemingly upright members of the community had five more victims already identified. He gave the stock answer. 'It's not a question of keeping things from you, but more a matter of not causing unnecessary public concern.'

Before Martin could complete the rest of his explanation, the determined female reporter shot down Ms Cummings and managed to get in her third interruption.

'Who are you to say what unnecessary public concern is? If you know the killer intends to stab to death even more victims then you should tell us. You have no right to withhold such information. Who do you think you are?'

With considerable effort Martin managed to keep his cool and after tapping the microphone a couple of times he answered her questions.

'I know exactly who I am and I have sufficient experience to be able to judge what information to release in the best interest of the public. If you had listened to what I had said earlier you would realise that both victims were known to the killer and that he is not going around randomly stabbing people.'

Another journalist joined in. 'But you do have reason to believe that there will be other victims, don't you?'

Martin knew better than to simply lie and he told the

audience that if he had anything to do with it there would be no more killings.

'Not doing a very good job so far, are you?' This time a question came from the back of the room and from someone Martin had never seen before – probably a reporter from one of the nationals.

Martin responded calmly. 'I can assure you that the team here at Goleudy are working around the clock in an effort to bring the killer to justice, so please don't judge us until the job is done.'

It was always the case that in a press conference everyone in the audience had their own agenda and barely listened to the questions posed by others. As if to prove that fact a woman standing in the aisle draped with cables asked a seemingly random question.

'So are you expecting the next murder to be on Saturday the first of October?'

For a moment the room fell silent as everyone, including Martin, wondered about the basis of the question.

'Sorry,' he said. 'I'm not sure I understand where you are coming from, would you like to explain?'

Enjoying the spotlight she answered. 'Both murders were on a Saturday morning, the first on the third and the next on the seventeenth of September. So it stands to reason that the next will be on the first of October, making them all two weeks apart.'

Martin was horrified by the speed at which the majority of the members of the media jumped on to this suggestion, although there were others who like him where shaking their heads in disbelief.

'I think you are entering into the realms of probability forecasting, but in order for that to make any sense we would need more than two dates. At this moment in time the dates of the two murders give us no scientific equation for identifying the next date. It could well be that our killer intends to kill on the third and the seventeenth of each month or even on the first two Saturdays in September each year. If there is going to be a

118

regular pattern then we need at least three dates for any form of probabilistic forecast.

'So, to answer your question more directly, I am not anticipating a third murder on October the first, although there is equally no scientific reason for me to rule it out.'

No longer wanting to be in the spotlight, the journalist glared at Martin and wished she had never asked the question.

'What about the issue that the killer knows you personally?' asked someone in the middle of the room.

Martin responded. 'I am mentioned in both the poems, but I have no idea in what capacity I have met the killer, if at all, and that may only become clear when we find out who he is.'

Martin could now see that the voice from the middle of the room belonged to Mike Hiscock, a journalist from one of the smaller local papers.

Mike lifted his head above the crowd and continued. 'Those of us who are local know that over the years you have put away a large number of lowlifes – do you think this killer is one of them and that you will be one of his targets?'

Martin managed a strained smile that got nowhere near his eyes. 'Yes, of course, I have considered that possibility, but it's not one I want to dwell on.'

The press conference so far had gone much better than Martin had anticipated, but it was starting to degenerate, and ad hoc questions were being drowned by people voicing their own suggestions as the possible answers. Criticism about lack of progress and general and personal blame was being thrown in the direction of the three officers sitting at the front. The superintendent was getting noticeably fidgety and Martin looked at his watch before calling time on the proceedings.

'We've been here for the best part of an hour, and I know most of you will want to follow the events set to start at 10 a.m. so shall we call it a day?'

It was a rhetorical question and inside a minute the three men made their way from the front of the room and were walking back up the stairs in the direction of Martin's office.

Superintendent Bryant was the first to speak. 'I thought we

handled that very well and we managed to hide what is after all a distinct lack of progress. I've got a superintendents' meeting at the Dyfed Powys HQ at twelve so I'll be off. Keep me informed.'

Instead of reprimanding his sergeant for disrespect, Martin chose to ignore the face Matt pulled as Bryant walked away.

Moreover he wholeheartedly agreed with Matt's next words. '"We handled that very well" – what's with that "we"! It was you who turned what could have been a very messy session into what I would mark as being a victory for our team. His input was pathetic, but he did give me a laugh at one point when I thought he had turned to hero-worshipping you. You had the journalists in the palm of your hand, and I think the super was there too.'

Martin laughed as he remembered that moment. 'Well, the whole thing was much better than I had anticipated, but now I need some food. I thought we were going to be torn apart and I had no appetite for breakfast, but now I'm starving.'

Matt never needed any encouragement when food was mentioned, but he looked at his watch anxiously. 'It's ten minutes to ten, but Helen's covering the re-enactments so we don't need to be there. What I'm more concerned about is there's usually nothing left in the dining room by now, so you may have to work your magic on Iris.'

They hurried towards the staff cafe where Iris was supervising the clearing away of the breakfast items and preparing for the lunchtime menu. She was one of the most enthusiastic supervisors that Martin had ever met, and she treated all the CID staff and uniformed officers as if they were part of her own family. She did have her favourites, though, and everyone knew that Martin was one of them. She also had an invisible antennae and always seemed to know if they had been to a murder scene, or to a nasty PM or a difficult press conference.

She greeted the officers. 'I bet you're glad to see the back of that lot with their cameras and questions – made you hungry, have they?'

120

'Too true,' answered Martin, 'but it looks as if we are a bit late for breakfast.'

'What about a few rashers of bacon with some scrambled egg and toast?' she asked.

Martin gave her the thumbs up and found a seat while Matt went in search of the coffee.

His heart gave a jump as he looked around the room to where three tables had been pushed together and spotted Shelley sitting at the central one surrounded by fourteen men and four women. He remembered that she was leading an intensive course for workplace health and safety officers, and the people surrounding Shelley would be the designated officers for their police stations in various parts of Wales.

They looked as if they were having a good time and Martin compared the atmosphere of her group to the bored expressions he remembered from when he had attended health and safety courses. She had told him that there were to be major changes in some of the legislation from next year, and he knew that she was working hard to ensure she would make her revised course entertaining. Only Shelley could make health and safety law exciting, he thought, as feeling inexplicably proud he turned away from the group and focused his attention on the coffee Matt had chosen, and then on the feast that Iris brought to the table.

Even then his thoughts returned to Shelley and their last weekend at the cottage that had cruelly ended with the receipt of the orange envelope and the subsequent discovery of the second body. This weekend Shelley had to be with her diabetic father but tonight they had both been invited to dinner with Alex and Charlie and he knew that would be the tonic he needed.

The late breakfast with the help of occasional cups of coffee sustained him throughout the day and just after five o'clock he remembered his morning thought of inviting the team for a drink. Most people were pleased to be asked but declined the offer in favour of getting home at a reasonable hour but Matt was happy to accept along with Helen, Sgt Evans, and five other officers.

It was a quarter to six by the time they had all walked the short distance to one of the bars in Mermaid Quay and were looking out across a stretch of grey murky water.

'What a difference a week makes,' said PC Davies as he pointed towards the outside seating area. 'This time last week I was here with my partner and we were sitting on those seats in baking hot sunshine and now look at it.'

Sgt Evans was downing his first pint in the happy knowledge that his daughter had agreed to pick him up at seven o'clock. A similarly blessed Matt had already swallowed his first pint and was looking for a refill. 'Sarah has my car, so I qualify for an automatic lift home tonight – it doesn't happen very often so I'm making the most of it.'

Martin was a bit peeved to be the only one not indulging in the Friday night alcoholic escape but he would make up for it later. He had to drive to the cottage after this session, so couldn't risk a drink, but Shelley had agreed to pick him up and take him to their evening with Charlie and Alex. She was taking her father out tomorrow morning and didn't mind not drinking. Everyone's attention was suddenly caught by the images on the large television screen as the news programme *Wales Tonight* broadcast images of the re-enactment of the Red Dragon Centre murder followed by the one at the Tremorfa Industrial Estate.

The actor they had chosen certainly fitted the bill, and it was almost as if the producers had seen the actual murder tapes – with two exceptions. This pretend murder didn't demonstrate the level of force that had been used by the real criminal, and he didn't walk in quite the same marching fashion, but overall it was a good effort.

The times of the murders were emphasised, and the public asked to consider whether they were anywhere near the scenes of the crimes at these times. It seemed as if the presenter was finishing the appeal when she issued dedicated phone numbers to be used by anyone who could give any information. She appeared to have been prompted as she added. 'The killer has been buying lengths of coloured cord, certainly red and orange.

He has also purchased coloured paper and matching envelopes, again of red and orange. If you know anyone who may have been doing this it is worth notifying the police using that some number.'

Sgt Evans let out an almighty groan and it was one in which his colleagues joined him.

'That will do it,' he said. 'We will now have every person who does any form of art or crafts hauled into the police station for questioning. Whose bright idea was it to stick that at the end of the appeal? Even without that the phones will be red-hot with the usual cranks wanting their five minutes of fame, but with that addition they'll be ringing nonstop.'

The group was only too pleased when without warning the television channel was changed, and Sky Sports advertised a rugby league match between Huddersfield and Leeds due to kick off at 8 p.m.

PC Davies expressed an interest. 'The Giants and the Rhinos, that should be a good game. My other half is from Huddersfield and we went to the Galpharm Stadium last time we were there.'

The conversation turned from work to discussing the relative merits of rugby union and rugby league, and when he was happy that the group had left the week behind and were happily plunging in to the weekend Martin took his leave.

Chapter Ten

'What's it to be?' asked Charlie. 'Beer, wine, or some of the really hard stuff.'

Martin grinned. 'After a few weeks from hell I could easily finish off Alex's birthday present, but bringing it and drinking it doesn't seem quite right and anyway I'm really thirsty, so make mine a beer please.'

Alex had unwrapped the bottle of Jack Daniels that Shelley had handed over to him with a kiss and he was laughing at the rather rude verse on the card they had bought for his birthday.

'There's nothing wrong with my libido, thank you very much,' he told his guests. 'So the aging man on the front of this card with a bottle of Viagra pills isn't even a pale reflection of me – and what's more I can prove it.'

As if on cue Charlie came from the kitchen and manoeuvred her wheelchair so that she could hand around some special nibbles.

'Do you remember when Iris did those theme days in the staff café?' she asked. 'The first one was with Welsh cuisine and she had some Peri Las cheese.'

'Yes,' said Shelley. 'You raved on about it.'

'Well, this is it, and that there is the walnut bread we always have with it – what do you think?'

Charlie watched as Shelley ripped off a chunk of the walnut bread and spread it with the soft, creamy blue cheese.

'You're right,' she said. 'It really is delicious, here, try some, Martin.'

Taking a large bite, Martin nodded his approval and told Charlie. 'You have great taste in food, and I know from past experience that your cooking is fantastic. I don't know how Alex manages to stay in shape. If I lived here I would be putting on the pounds at the rate of knots.'

Martin wished he had not used the word 'knots', even if it did refer to a different type, and he quickly pushed thoughts of coloured rope to the back of his mind.

'Talking about piling in the pounds'' said Alex, 'let me introduce you to someone who will soon have a legitimate reason to do so.' He knelt down beside Charlie and took her hand. 'However, sometime around the 6th April 2011 she will return to her current stunning shape and we will have either a baby daughter or son.'

Alex grinned from ear to ear and Martin suddenly realised that the head of SOC had been giving him hints for a couple of weeks but the penny hadn't dropped – not surprising really given what had been happening.

There were hugs all around and Charlie shed a few tears. 'Don't mind me,' she explained. 'I've never done crying in my life, but at the moment just anything sends me into floods of tears. It's got to be a hormonal thing but it's stupid – so irrational!'

Shelley hugged her friend and asked how she was feeling. 'Well, as I just mentioned, I seem to have no control over my emotions, and even the waterworks come on for soppy television ads – and the other thing is an overwhelming feeling of tiredness. Not all the time, but if I just sit back in my chair and close my eyes you can guarantee that I'll be asleep within a matter of minutes.

'Yesterday, I closed my eyes in the post office and the man next to me in the queue had to wake me up for my turn at the counter. I was so embarrassed. I knew about morning sickness but I've had none. Maybe everyone feels shattered in the first trimester of pregnancy but it's easier for me to drop off when I'm shopping because I just have to lean back in the wheelchair and I'm off with the fairies.'

Shelley laughed at the thought of the other shoppers seeing Charlie asleep and knew there would be a mixed reaction. In her experience some people still found it difficult to cope with anyone in a wheelchair, and the 'does he take sugar?' mentality still existed – and to a larger extent than most people imagine.

Charlie had an amazing sense of humour and had told Shelley countless stories of how she'd turned the tables on people who treated her as if she was invisible, thick, deaf, dumb, or someone with two heads. She stayed constantly cheerful and was so full of life even though it had dealt her a cruel blow – she would make a wonderful mum.

'Need any help in the kitchen?' Shelley asked.

'All sorted,' was the reply. 'I've kept it simple in case I nodded off when I should have been pan-watching. Alex, everything is ready and it'll be much quicker if you carry things through to the dining room.'

Charlie's idea of keeping things simple was to serve chicken breasts stuffed with mozzarella cheese and wrapped in Parma ham. She had cooked them slowly in a homemade tomato, olive oil, and basil sauce, and as they were served the cheese oozed from the chicken. In the centre of the table on a very large platter was an array of roast vegetables. According to Charlie she had just roughly cut peppers, courgettes, aubergines, red onions, chestnut mushrooms, and baby new potatoes, liberally sprinkled them with olive oil, seasoned them, added a few herbs and popped them in the oven. They looked stunning and everyone tucked in as the four friends looked forward to a few hours when the conversation would embrace music, sport, current affairs even touching on politics and anything but murder. Normally Charlie would have opened a couple of bottles of wine for her and Shelley to share, but she wasn't going to jeopardise her baby's health and so the women shared a six pack of non-alcoholic ginger beer, it being something that Charlie had fancied at the deli. By the end of the evening it was difficult to know which group had been drinking the alcohol. All four of them were in the sort of high spirits that come not from drinking, but from the perfect enjoyment of an evening spent with good friends.

Charlie had managed to keep awake and, as always, was the

life and soul of the party, but Alex suddenly noticed that his wife looked tired – and when he realised that it was past midnight he suggested it was time for bed. The evening had flown by and, with promises of a repeat performance for Charlie's birthday in November, they said their goodbyes.

As Shelley drove towards the coast she glanced at Martin who seemed to have caught Charlie's 'falling asleep in an instant' bug, although his exhaustion had more to do with Alex needing help to get to the bottom of the Jack Daniels. He was pretty drunk and would probably remember nothing of his journey home or being stripped off and put to bed by his girlfriend – and the latter he would regret.

He also would never know that Shelley had not left him immediately but had waited until 2 a.m. just to ensure he was safe and unlikely to vomit. He realised she had considered the possibility because there was a large plastic bowl by his bedside when he woke up just after seven, and a note alongside it that read:

Sleep well my love. I wish I could stay but my dad will need me later and I suspect you will be nursing an almighty big hangover. Take some paracetamol and drink plenty of water! I love you.

After reading the note he pulled the covers back over his head. The last thing he could remember was toasting the good news of the baby with Alex for the nth time. No wonder he felt like the proverbial and wondered if he shut his eyes tightly he could get back to sleeping it off.

It was not to be, because as his brain got in to even the lowest of gears, the world of work and murder and clues and press conferences crowded in – and this morning they were making even less sense than they had done yesterday.

Shelley's advice was taken, and after a couple of painkillers and three pints of water he started to feel marginally less fuzzy. His mouth was so dry, his skin felt tight, and he ached in the way one does at the start of a bout of flu. To think that there are

128

some people who punish themselves like this every weekend with their episodes of binge drinking, Martin thought. He vowed 'never again', but like the regular revellers, he didn't mean it.

He cleaned his teeth for the second time and then with superhuman effort he took a hot and then frigid shower. It was worth it, as his headache had all but disappeared, and he transferred his attention to some fresh coffee and even managed a piece of toast. It had been a good evening and it had been just what he needed to give him some breathing space and if being hung-over was the price to pay it was worth it.

He drew back the curtains in the lounge and saw that it was still raining, and he wondered how he was going to spend the day. No Shelley, and no chance of doing anything in the garden, so maybe he would just read a novel. He would have to do something, or else his mind would be back on the job and there would be no chance of any respite.

His landline rang and Martin could see immediately that it was Shelley. 'Good morning, my guardian angel,' he said. 'I hope I didn't give you too much trouble last night?'

Shelley replied. 'You sound a hell of a lot better than I was expecting you to – seriously, I'm amazed, I wondered if you would even answer the phone; thinking you'd still be out of it. Do you know that you and Alex finished off that bottle of whisky we bought him for his birthday – and you'd already had a couple of beers before that?'

Martin winced at the very thought of it and then told Shelley that although he couldn't remember the details what she said came as no surprise. He added. 'I wonder how Alex is feeling this morning but it's really good news about the baby. Do you think she'll be all right?'

Martin knew that Shelley was one of the few people that Charlie spoke to regarding her spinal injury and he was pleased to hear her reply.

'When they were talking about getting married Charlie spoke to obstetricians about her chances of getting pregnant and carrying a baby to full term. They were extremely optimistic on

129

both those counts but there is a very high possibility that she will need a Caesarean section – still, she's not worried about that.

'Sorry I can't chat any longer – my dad wants his breakfast and so it's insulin time. I only rang to check you're OK.'

'I'm more than OK, thanks to my chauffeur, and some woman who stripped me naked and put me to bed. I love you, Shelley Edwards. Have a good day and I'll see you tomorrow.'

'I love you too, you drunken old sod.'

'Hey, less of the old!' replied Martin as he replaced the receiver and went in search of something to read.

The day had a definite autumnal feel and Martin pulled on a sweater before going upstairs to the room his aunt used to sleep in. He browsed through the bookshelves that had, in the main, been untouched since she died. The last thing he wanted was a crime novel; that would be far too real. He chose a nineteenth-century classic and sprawled on top of his aunt's old bed. He was soon in a very different world to the present, though not a better one. *The Adventures of Huckleberry Finn* took a first-hand look at entrenched racism, intolerance of anyone different, and even feudal killings. Martin wondered if society had learned anything over the past century. He came across little notes that Aunt Pat had made placed between some of the pages and found himself agreeing with most of her comments.

Martin heard a vehicle pull up at the entrance to the cottages and with a sinking feeling he saw that it was a Royal Mail van. For the past three weeks he had dreaded the post arriving. He strained his eyes to see what the postman was carrying.

There was no sign of a coloured envelope and he began to breathe more easily, but he had to answer the door as one of his letters was too big for the small letterbox that he was always intending to replace.

The postman greeted him with a smile and a good-natured complaint about the weather. He handed Martin an A4-size white envelope and two letters. One was clearly a bank statement and the other his personal mobile phone bill. All were addressed to 'Mr Martin Phelps' – not a 'DCI' or a coloured envelope in sight. Martin thanked the postman and heaved a huge sigh of relief.

Lulled into a false sense of security, he opened the large white envelope and got a sickening shock. Inside was a yellow envelope, formally addressed to 'Detective Chief Inspector Martin Phelps'. Martin knew that his worst fears were about to be realised.

He didn't open the yellow envelope, just picked up a jacket and headed for his car. On the way down the path he called Matt and in less than half an hour they were both in Incident Room One, reading the latest poem and debating the possible consequences.

Now it's yellow, yellow, yellow
have you not got it yet?
Still working on the other two
on that I'll take a bet.

He stole away the one I loved
drove off without a thought.
The bitch will not be laughing now
as his last breaths are caught.

Two down but they were easy prey
this one will be more fun.
It may need more than just a knife
and so I'll take a gun.

It's time for action, Martin Phelps
so time, I'll give you more,
With this one done I calculate
the number left is four.

'Well, it's certainly the same man,' said Matt. 'It couldn't possibly be a copycat, we haven't let the press know that the previous envelopes were sent to your home. This bastard thinks he's clever – he'd know you'd be looking out for another coloured envelope.'

'We have been, of course,' replied Martin. 'The sorting office on Penarth Road has been on standby, ready to alert us day or night if a coloured envelope addressed to me at the cottage came through their doors.

'We should have second-guessed that he'd switch to another means of getting his poetry through. Get on the phone to the sorting office, Matt – I want to know when any letter or parcel addressed to me, in whatever capacity, is received by them. I don't want to wait until it's delivered, I want every piece of my mail as soon as they get it. I don't just want stuff that is addressed to the cottage – I want anything that they receive addressed to me at home, at work, or anywhere else. Will they be able to do that?'

'They've been only too pleased to help so far, but their systems are totally automated and as I understand it they use the postcode, not the name, as the key factor – but I'll get on to them straight away.' Matt walked towards the door and Martin called after him.

'Will you also make sure that our traffic division knows that if they get a call from us to pick up anything from the sorting office it must become their top priority.'

'Will do,' replied Matt. 'I've just heard Helen's voice and the rest of the team are either here or on their way in. Where do you want us?'

Martin replied. 'Here, and as quickly as possible. This evil bastard says he has given us some time but he alone knows what he means by that. Get everyone rounded up and we'll start a session in five minutes.'

Using the last of the smaller whiteboards Martin did as before and wrote the poem out so that everyone could see it. He then moved the boards around so that all three poems stood side by side in the order that they had been received.

He was dealing with only the third serial killer of his career. The first one had been when he was a newcomer to CID. Martin had never been satisfied with the outcome of that case, the conviction of a young man with mental health problems for the murder of three prostitutes working around Cardiff Central bus station. It still concerned him that the crucial evidence, which had been missed initially, suddenly turned up in the man's flat when the investigation looked to be on the point of failure.

Those three women had been left with their throats cut, so knives had been used by that killer too, but it now looked as if the poetry writer was thinking of stepping things up a notch and using a gun. Martin worried for the safety of both the public and his officers, but for the moment there was no way he could protect them because he had no idea where or when the third murder would be committed. He prayed that somehow it could be prevented.

The team assembled and Sgt Evans confirmed everyone's belief that no serious crime had been reported that morning. 'We've sent officers out to one domestic disturbance and two minor RTAs and that's about it, but I'm sure things will change as the day goes on.'

'OK,' said Martin. 'You can all see the third poem and it comes close to our speculation last week as to who the third victim would be. We thought it could be someone the killer had been in a relationship with, or someone who had caused a break-up between him and someone he loved. It seems to be the latter, as described in the second verse.

'I have no doubt that the killer will strike again today, even though the last verse suggests he's going to give us more time. He's still playing games. The colour is our only real clue as to where the murder will be carried out, and we now know how tenuous that clue can be. It's only with hindsight that we know that the second victim was to be found in a place that squeezed oranges – we would never had guessed that, would we?'

DC Cook-Watts answered Martin's question. 'No, I don't think we would have but now that we know the colour clues are likely to be cryptic we will have to do some lateral thinking.'

'Let's do it, then,' suggested Martin. 'Someone's life may depend upon us coming up with a venue linked to the colour yellow, so what have we got?'

Various members of CID and uniformed officers offered

133

suggestions.

'There's the Big Yellow self-storage company.'

'Yellow Brick Road – they do hypnotherapy for all sorts of things.'

'There's something called the Yellow Card Centre at the University Hospital of Wales but I don't think it's a public place. It's somewhere where doctors and nurses report adverse drugs reactions and other things – so maybe not a sensible suggestion.'

Martin interrupted. 'I'm not looking for sensible suggestions – just call out anything that comes into your mind regarding the colour yellow.'

'A place where they squeeze lemons.'

'Cardiff Yellow Pages.'

'The Woodville pub in Cathays gives you a discount if you sign up to their yellow card scheme.'

'Double yellow lines.'

'The Primrose garden centre in Rookwood. Primroses are yellow.'

'The three yellow ellipses at the Cardiff Bay barrage.'

'The Yellow Kangaroo in Elm Street.'

The suggestions dried up but Martin had managed to write all of them on the space beneath the yellow poem.

'There are probably many more that we have not considered and from what we've so far seen of the twisted mind of our killer the venue could just be somewhere where a yellow bus passed through last week. But we can't just hang around doing nothing and if this colour yellow is the only slender clue we have let's continue to work on it.

'Are there any places amongst those that have been suggested that we think would be attractive to our killer? He's no shrinking violet – he's not averse to killing in a public place and seems to thrive on taking calculated risks. If we could put ourselves in his shoes, where would we choose to be sure of getting away with this third murder? Are there any common denominators between the first two? Come on everybody, think, time is of the essence.'

Sgt Evans suggested two similarities. 'You would usually travel to both sites by car, although the killer may have parked his some distance from where he did the killing. He used places where access wasn't that difficult. There are just public barriers at the Red Dragon Centre, and only limited monitoring at the Tremorfa Industrial Estate, so I think that rules out Big Yellow Self Storage because you need codes and swipe cards to get access to that building.'

'Good thinking,' said Martin and he rubbed Big Yellow off his list. 'I'm also going to wipe off "double yellow lines" as that's an impossible thought – where in Cardiff are there *not* yellow lines of one sort or another? I can't see this clever swine using the same type of venue twice and so "a place where they squeeze lemons" is also coming off the list.'

Matt suggested 'Cardiff Yellow Pages' be removed as none of them could even guess where it was produced. There was no science or even any obvious rationale to the process but doing nothing was not an option. He looked at what was left and asked Martin what he intended to do next.

Martin replied. 'There is one other I want to remove and that's the "Yellow Card Centre". The hospital is an extremely busy place and parking can be a nightmare, so there'd be no guarantee that a potential victim would turn up at a specified time. If I were the killer planning my next homicide I would see that venue as providing too many opportunities for error.'

Everyone agreed, and Matt added, 'So we are left with five possible venues based on the suggestions we've come up with but if you asked another group of twenty or more people you could be looking at an entirely different set of yellow places.'

'I don't disagree,' said Martin. 'Yes, they would probably come up with some we haven't thought of but we all know Cardiff very well and I think the five places we've come down to are distinct possibilities. It's now ten past ten and we've heard nothing regarding a third strike from our killer so for some reason he is giving us more time – we were actually at the scenes of crimes for the other two before this time on the respective Saturday mornings.'

'Perhaps he wants to be caught,' suggested Helen. 'It has been known.'

'Maybe,' responded Martin. 'Let's not forget that he is taunting us with the fact that even if he is successful today there are still four people he plans to kill.'

'What are the three yellow ellipses?' asked Helen.

'What would I do without my nieces and their homework projects?' laughed Matt. 'It's a piece of public art by a Swiss guy called Felice Varini. *3 Ellipses for 3 Locks*. Basically, it's three yellow strips painted on the locks, the gates, and the outer sea wall. It was designed to highlight the main working parts of the barrage, and if you walk around the area it just looks like splashes of yellow paint, but it's much more than that. The whole project is very clever, we found a spot where the so-called "anamorphic illusion" can be seen in its entirety ... but, anyway, I won't spoil it – you should all go and see for yourselves.'

'Remind me to put your nieces on the payroll,' said Martin, smiling. 'Could you see the killer stabbing someone there?'

Matt though for a moment then replied. 'Yes, I would say that as a murder spot it's a contender.'

'OK,' said Martin. 'So this is what we do. We work through the other four suggested sites and we form a group decision about the feasibility of a murder at each. If we decide a venue is likely to interest the killer we act on it immediately. Having decided the barrage is a possibility I would like you, Sgt Evans, to get officers to that area as quickly as possible. Ensure they all have a description of the man we are looking for and it is likely that he will be wearing the same headgear and carrying the same canvas bag. You will need to ensure that all your officers are issued with protective vests, and something we haven't yet spoken about this morning is the threat in the poem of him using of a gun. I want this man caught, but not at the expense of any of our officers or random members of the public.

'We know he is in control when carrying out a planned execution, but we have no idea how he will act if cornered. He could turn his knife on any one of us or any member of the public. We just don't know, so no heroics, please.'

Sgt Evans nodded, and with three constables in tow he left to action the first of potentially five operations.

Who suggested Yellow Brick Road?' asked Martin.

One of the PCs raised a hand. 'They specialise in hypnotherapy, and something called Neuro-Linguistic Programming, NLP. They're based in Roath, and I know about it because my sister went there for treatment to help her lose weight, see. She lost just over three stone, so no medals for guessing she thinks it's fantastic.'

'Yes, but would our killer think it a fantastic place for his third murder? What about access?'

'Well, it's on The Parade in Roath, guv, so there is street parking – though on a Saturday morning it would be busy.' Looking around, Martin could see a number of people shaking their heads, but in his view it was bizarre enough to be considered by the killer.

He asked the PC to chase after Sgt Evans and arrange for officers to be stationed in and around the area adjacent to Yellow Brick Road, and then turned his attention to the three remaining venues.

'Would The Woodville be operational at this time of the day?' asked Martin.

Matt replied. 'I very much doubt it. I just Googled their website and they don't open until 11.30 on a Saturday.'

'I was going to say let's skip that one, but remembering that the killer is giving us extra time today maybe 11.30 is on the cards.' Martin thought for a moment. 'We'll just put that one on the back-burner and take a better look at the remaining two – the Primrose Garden Centre and The Yellow Kangaroo.

'I've been to that garden centre twice, and it ticks all the boxes in terms of easy access and the yellow link could obviously refer to the name but also to the unusual display system they have. Unlike most garden centres they don't display their plants and flowers in groups of the various species, but they group together all the different species and market them by colour – it's very effective.'

Matt thought that such an idea would appeal to the killer, and suggested that he and DC Cook-Watts check that one out.

'Yes, do that,' said Martin. 'As I said before, I want you all back here safe and sound at the end of the day. I would prefer that you were seen as live cowards rather than dead heroes, so remember the colour yellow and don't be afraid to hide behind it.

'Before you disappear, what about The Yellow Kangaroo? I don't think we can rule it out, so I'll take whoever can be spared and have a look at that option myself.'

Matt said what everyone else was thinking. 'You insisted that we take extra care, so remember to apply the same rules to yourself. We have every reason to believe that you are somewhere in this bastard's sights so the rules are even more applicable to you.'

Inwardly Martin knew that this element of the case was not going to go away, but he managed a wry smile and suggested that everyone get to wherever they were going as quickly as possible. The room emptied, with the exception of PC Lyons, who had been chosen to accompany the DCI. The constable was typically Welsh – standing at about five feet eight, with coal-black hair and a heavy accent, unsurprising given that he hailed from the ex-mining village of Treorchy in the Rhondda.

'What do you think, sir? Is it likely we will find this bloke before he kills again?' he asked Martin.

'God only knows,' was the reply. 'If we do, I'll start believing in divine intervention, because there must be dozens more places we could be considering. Come on, we need to get kitted out before we go.'

Matt and Helen were in Matt's 4x4 heading for the garden centre, and the windscreen wipers were having to work hard to push away a heavy downpour. Helen wriggled uncomfortably in the passenger seat and adjusted her jacket. 'These things,' she complained, pointing at her stab vest. 'They were never designed for those of us who have boobs. This one was definitely designed by a man, and not one who had ever had any intimate knowledge of women!'

Matt laughed and navigated the next roundabout. It was an easy route; all he had to do was follow the A4119, and after fifteen minutes they were almost at their destination.

It was Helen who first spotted a high level of police activity, as ahead she could see two sets of blue flashing lights and then they were overtaken by an emergency rapid response vehicle heading in the same direction as they were.

'Looks as if there's been an accident,' she volunteered, and Matt nodded. The mini ambulance turned off the road and into the side road that went past Rookwood Hospital.

'That's the road we need to take,' said Matt. 'It looks as if we're indulging in a spot of ambulance-chasing.'

Helen smiled but a moment later the smile disappeared from her face. Just past the hospital on the right-hand side was the long driveway that led to the car park of the Primrose Garden Centre. In there were only four cars in the car park, standing in puddles of water.

It was their blue flashing lights that told Matt and Helen their chosen venue had 'hit the jackpot', and that they were in all probability too late to prevent a third murder ...

Chapter Eleven

'Are you psychic?' asked a police constable who had just got out of the squad car that had passed them a few minutes before. 'We've only just got here ourselves and it's usually a while before CID join us at the scene of a crime.'

'Let me guess at the crime,' replied Matt. 'The victim is a man, probably in his late fifties; he's been stabbed twice, and his body has been found in the area of the garden centre where the displays of yellow flowers are set out.'

'Bloody hell!' replied the constable. 'You *are* psychic! But you're wrong about the victim having been stabbed twice – it's more like half a dozen times from the information we've been given.'

Matt phoned Martin and caught him just leaving the squad car near the The Yellow Kangaroo.

'We've found the victim and yes, I'm afraid it is a victim, but it doesn't sound as if our killer had it all his own way this time. We don't have the two stab wounds as before; this time I'm told there are multiple injuries, so let's hope he has panicked and left some bits of himself behind. Alex and the Prof have apparently been sent for, so see you here as soon as.'

Matt and Helen made their way to the entrance of the building and walked through aisles of garden products, following wooden signs leading to the 'Colours of Creation' plants section.

Matt recalled Martin's earlier description of how the plants were displayed according to colour and he had to agree that it was very impressive to see. They walked past the red section, where dahlias, carnations, Peruvian lilies, and numerous other red flowers were artistically displayed, flooding the senses with the intensity of their combined colours. Next to the reds was a white display, and the purity of the prominently displayed roses was quite sensational. Here, though, the pleasure ended and horror struck – perhaps even more than a murder scene usually did, because it was such a beautiful place.

As expected, the body was lying in the most mood-lifting section, where brilliant sunshine colours still tried desperately to mask what had been dumped in their midst. Undisturbed, the mini sunflowers on the upper edges of this section still held their heads towards the sun, though there was no sun today.

Matt didn't know if the central display was filled with pansies or viola, or even a mixture of both, but they all looked as if they had little yellow faces and he seemed to see expressions of bewilderment on each one of them.

Spread over most of this display, with his face touching many of those tiny yellow faces, was the body of a man. His blood had spread and was in danger of upstaging the red section, so much of it had been spilled.

Helen noticed the paramedic standing near the body. 'No chance that he's still alive, is there?'

'No chance whatsoever,' replied the paramedic. 'I checked for a pulse, but I wasn't surprised to find none and so that's really all I have done. It's obviously not an accident or natural causes so I was careful not to disturb anything. The officers that were here earlier have got my number and as there's absolutely nothing I can do, I'll be off.'

They thanked him and moved in to get a closer look at the body. The victim's hands had been tied behind his back with yellow cord, but not with the usual reef knot. This was a botched job in more ways than one, but unfortunately the killer's ultimate aim had still been achieved.

Martin had recovered very well from the over-indulgence of the previous night but was reminded of it as soon as he clapped eyes on Alex. They pulled into the garden centre car park within seconds of one another, and close on their heels was Professor Dafydd Moore.

'What have we got here?' asked the professor. 'Is it the red and orange man or do we have another killer on the loose?'

Martin briefed the pair of them with the information Matt had given him over the phone. He also told them about the latest poem, how yellow was the colour of murder this time and how close they had got to working out the venue for this killing.

'Oh, really bad luck, old boy,' said the Prof. 'You were on the right track, so ten out of ten for effort and for some impressive lateral thinking.'

Coming from the professor the words were praise indeed but they were soon followed up by his more familiar moaning. 'Trust this brute to pick a garden centre, did someone tell him I am allergic to pollen? I took some cetirizine hydrochloride as soon as I got the call to come here, but no amount of antihistamine will stop the red, itchy eyes and runny nose that will be my fate within the next couple of hours. Come along, let's get on with it – the sooner I get away from here the better.'

Alex hung back and helped his team get some of their tools from the SOC van. Normally Alex would have driven the vehicle himself, but he was concerned that his blood alcohol levels could still be an issue. He had drunk more than Martin last night and hadn't reached the point of being able to eat anything this morning. What wasn't an issue was his ability to do the job, and like clockwork he and his team began the task that was expected of them.

A few minutes later the 'Colours of Creation' section was cordoned off and all SOC personnel were clad in their white suits. It looked as if aliens had landed and were picking over the remains of a human who had been sacrificed for their scientific interest.

Martin took in the details and then left the experts to do their job. 'Did anyone see anything?' he asked Matt.

'The officers who were on the scene first have ensured that no one has left since their arrival. There are a handful of customers plus the staff and the manager in the coffee shop waiting to be interviewed, but I have been told that nobody actually saw the murder.'

Calling the place they arrived at a 'coffee shop' was stretching it a bit. It was one corner of the main building sectioned off with some wooden trellis. There were just four round wrought-iron tables with matching chairs – and a number of very shocked faces.

As the two detectives approached a tall young man got to his feet. 'I'm Tim,' he said. 'Tim Jones, the manager, and you must be the CID men we were told to wait for.'

Martin nodded and made the formal introductions, not just to Tim but for the benefit of everyone. 'You must all feel shaken by what you know has happened here and we won't keep you longer than we have to. Just in case there is any doubt, I will tell you that a man has been murdered on the premises and we would like to speak to you all before you leave.'

Martin had already scanned the group. There was nobody who even came close to resembling his vision of the killer, but hopefully someone had seen something.

The first to speak was an elderly man who was sitting with a much younger woman and a teenage girl.

'Chief Inspector,' he addressed Martin, 'I was with my daughter and my granddaughter and we were at the tills when the alarm was raised, so none of us saw anything. Can we go now?'

The man's voice was shaking slightly and Martin saw that his daughter was squeezing her father's hand tightly.

Matt pulled from his jacket pocket the photo-kit image of the killer that lacked facial detail but gave a reasonable overall impression.

'While you were here, did you see anyone who looked like this man? He is tall and well-built and was probably wearing a dark hat with a brim, something like the baseball cap you see here.'

The man and his companions all shook their heads. Martin told them they could leave after giving their names and contact details to the PC who had been sitting with the group in the café.

Meanwhile, Matt had been showing the image of the killer to

the remaining customers and two women had started arguing between themselves.

'I definitely saw someone looking like that when we were trying to decide what weed killer to buy.'

'Are you sure?' asked Matt.

'Yes, I am.'

'No, she's not,' countered the other woman.

'Ladies, this is very important, just think for a minute and try to decide who saw what and when.' Matt stared at the two women. He judged that they were in their early forties. Both were good-looking women; one a blonde, the other a brunette who was greying fast.

The blonde was the one who doubted her friend's suggestion that she had seen such a man in the garden centre, and after thinking for a moment she thumped the table. 'I've got it,' she said. 'We *did* see a man fitting that description but it wasn't here. Don't you remember, Laura, it was about half a mile away? You were driving and there was a car at the side of the road not far from a bend, and you said it was a stupid place to park. There was a man walking away from the car and in this direction and I would say that he fits this image perfectly.'

'She's right,' said Laura. 'But then she usually is – don't let the bottle-blonde image fool you, Meg is a bit of an egghead.'

Matt was getting excited. This MO fitted the other two murders, where it was likely that the killer had left his car some distance away and walked to meet his victim.

'Can you describe the car?' he asked Meg.

'Wrong one this time, sergeant,' said Meg. 'I may be the brainbox in this relationship, but when it comes to cars there is nothing that Laura misses.'

Matt prayed that she would be proven to be correct and on this occasion his prayers were answered.

Laura grinned and gave Matt the information he wanted. 'It was a BMW 525i SE Saloon and the manufacturers call the colour "space grey". I couldn't, by looking at it, tell you if it was manual or automatic or what fuel it used, but I guess it was registered in Wales sometime in the middle of 2008.'

Impressed by the woman's ability to rattle off that level of detail about a car she had probably only seen for a few seconds, he probed a bit further. 'No chance you remember the numberplate?'

Laura laughed. 'It's cars that interest me, not their plates, but I can tell you it was a letter C to start. As we both know, all that tells us is that it was registered in Wales, so it's probably not much help.'

'Well,' said Matt, 'that C certainly helps us narrow it down a bit.'

Martin had dismissed all the remaining customers before Matt told him the good news about the car. The two women had not been able to add any more detail to the description of the killer, as Laura had been looking at the car as well as concentrating on the bend and neither of them had seen his face.

'Take Helen with you,' said Martin to Matt. 'Get these ladies to show you exactly where they saw that car parked, and then ask around if anyone saw him – and especially if anyone saw him going back to the vehicle. This time it's highly unlikely that he would have got away without taking some of the victim's blood with him.'

With only the members of staff left to speak to, Martin made quick work of the interviews and returned to the crime scene. He had been disappointed to hear that there were no security cameras anywhere. According to the manager it was something they had talked about, but the business was not in a position to afford the initial outlay on even a modest system. None of the staff had seen or heard anything, but there were only three of them all together. The one who had discovered the body was still shaking from the experience but she swore that she had not seen the killer at any time.

Alex was directing operations and Martin noticed that the Prof had already left.

'He said he couldn't remain any longer in this pollen-infested environment, but he's free to do the PM just as soon as we can get the body moved. At least this time we have some things to work with, as it looks as if the victim fought back.

146

There are defence wounds on his arms and hands, and blood on his hands and under his nails. There are also three partial shoe prints where it looks as if the killer has stepped in some of his victim's blood and carried it towards the end of this section.'

'The first one is the whole of the front part of a shoe, my guess a trainer, but the second one is just the toe section and the third one little more than a smudge. Still, it's something, and it demonstrates that the killer walked away in the direction of the public toilet. He may even have used the toilet to wash off any obvious blood. There is only one toilet here, and some of my staff are in there now looking for any traces of our killer. This was something I could have done without this morning, but it's certainly the best cure for a hangover – I haven't even had time to think of my poor aching head for the past couple of hours.'

'We have the victim's wallet,' Alex continued. 'It was in his back pocket and stuffed full of £20 notes, several hundred pounds' worth. He was clearly a "cash only" man, as there's no sign of credit or debit cards to be found. His car keys led us to a black Vauxhall Corsa parked at the very edge of the car park, and I've given the registration number to Matt for him to check out. There is no other way of identifying the body, as there's nothing on the man or in his car to give us a clue. I guess I was hoping for a yellow envelope but there was nothing. Come to think of it, we still don't know how the killer got Miss Rossiter to go to her execution point, do we?'

'No,' replied Martin. 'It could simply be that he knew both of them well enough to just pick up the phone. I don't really see that as a possibility but we don't actually know.

'I'm making my way back to Goleudy,' he continued. 'At least this time we all have something to work on. We may have had some luck with the killer's car but I'll fill you in with all of that later. My suggestion for an initial brief is 3 p.m. Will that give you time to finish here, get the body back, and for the Prof to do the PM?'

'Moving the body is our next job,' replied Alex. 'I know the Prof has gone to pick up Mrs Williams so no doubt they will be waiting for it. We won't be finished here for some considerable time, but I'll be able to make a three o'clock session and then come back.'

Martin walked to the car park and instinctively looked for his Alfa Romeo, but seeing PC Lyons he remembered that the officer had been driving him to The Yellow Kangaroo when Matt had called him.

On the way back Lyons was a useful sounding board. He said nothing and listened to Martin untangling the details of this third murder. The journey only took just over fifteen minutes, but it gave Martin the time he needed to get his thoughts in order and he was grateful for the unusual luxury of a chauffeur.

What he was not grateful for was the presence of Superintendent Bryant, who was getting out of his car when PC Lyons pulled into the staff car park.

The superintendent had heard the squad car coming to a halt and as soon as he saw Martin in the passenger seat he stopped and waited for him.

'Good afternoon, sir,' said Martin. 'We must stop meeting at weekends, it can't be doing your handicap much good.'

Today the super was not dressed in the designer golf clothes of three weeks ago, and he was in no mood for Martin's banter. In fact he looked more angry than Martin had ever seen him look and the DCI was about to find out why. 'As it so happens, the rain is the reason there is no golf today, but in any case one of my golfing partners told me there has been another murder. Why is it that I have to learn about these things from friends at the club and not through the correct chain of command? Do you know how unbelievably stupid that makes me look, DCI Phelps?'

Martin had other things to think of and was inclined to tell the super that his sensitivities were not high on the team's agenda but he bit his lip. He was more interested in who had told his superior officer about the murder and when. He asked. 'The murder is hardly public knowledge, so how come people at the golf club are so well-informed?'

'I don't like your tone, DCI Phelps, and if you think things like a murder can be kept quiet while you and your second-rate team chase their tails, well, think again. One of our members lives in Rookwood, and he saw all the police activity at the garden centre and rang me.'

Martin hardly heard the end of Superintendent Bryant's sentence as he was incensed by the suggestion that his team was considered to be second-rate and he made no bones about saying so. 'Say what you like about me, I'm only too aware of how you think I match up to some of your previous DCIs, but don't you dare accuse my team of being second-rate. They have worked day and night for the past three weeks and came tantalisingly close to preventing a murder today. I won't have a bad bloody word said against any one of them – not from you or anyone else – do you hear me?'

The superintendent was incandescent with rage. 'Do I hear you? What do you mean, do *I* hear *you*? Do you realise who you are talking to? If you weren't in the middle of a triple murder investigation I would suspend you for insubordination.'

'Feel free,' said Martin. 'While you're at it, bring back one of your old cronies and let's see if some of their slipshod methods work as well today as they did all those years ago. I think you'll find that time's moved on – it's scientific evidence and proper detective work that solves crimes nowadays, not brute force and witness manipulation.'

The two men faced one another, both their tempers coming to a boil, and then almost simultaneously they realised that PC Lyons had not felt able to walk past them, and had heard every word of their heated exchange. He stood there sheepishly, sincerely wishing he hadn't been present.

Martin came to his rescue. 'Thanks for bringing me back,' he said in a voice that was now calm. 'I would be grateful if you could ensure that everyone knows about the 3 p.m. briefing. I'm expecting all personnel who have had anything to do with any of the murders to be there, so contact people at home or wherever but bring them all in. We've got a lot to talk about.'

Grateful for the opportunity to get away, PC Lyons moved quickly up the steps at the back of the car park and left the two CID officers to face one another.

The superintendent was the first to speak. 'I will take advice on this,' he said. 'Not only have you shown complete disrespect for a senior officer, but you have done so in the presence of someone who is a mere PC.'

Martin looked at Bryant in total disbelief. How on earth was he supposed to have any respect for someone who referred to the very foundation of the police force as a 'mere PC'?

He forced down the anger he was feeling and went for the moral high ground. 'I look forward to the results of the advice you get regarding my conduct, but for now I have work to do so if you'll please excuse me … *sir.*'

Martin turned on his heels and followed the direction that PC Lyons had taken. He wondered if Superintendent Bryant would follow him but he heard a car door slam and the sound of an engine starting up. He sighed with relief. His spat with the super was possibly years overdue and he knew there would be consequences, but for now he really did have work to do.

Does losing your temper make you hungry? All Martin knew was that he was suddenly starving and he made his way to the staff café. As it was Saturday there were none of the usual tempting smells of Iris' cooking, but to be fair to her she did fill the vending machines every Friday evening and there was a good choice of sandwiches and wraps available. Martin chose one labelled 'Croque Monsieur' and blasted it for a couple of minutes in the microwave, while he used a different vending machine and managed to get a cup of strong black coffee.

The cheese and ham toastie had an exciting foreign name but Martin thought that it didn't quite live up to the ones enjoyed by Aunt Pat and himself when they had sampled a genuine Croque Monsieur at one of the pavement cafes in Paris. Still, it filled the gap in his stomach, and he was tempted to go for another one when Matt and Helen walked in.

'I'm not sure why,' said Matt, 'but I always feel a bit guilty doing such mundane things as eating when some poor sod has been murdered.'

'We've all got to eat,' said Helen, 'but I know what you mean. It makes it even worse for me if I start to think that somewhere out there could be a family waiting for a husband or a father to come home and we know that it isn't going to happen.'

Martin picked up on what Helen had said. 'Have we had any joy identifying the owner of the Vauxhall Corsa?'

Matt nodded. 'The details are waiting for us upstairs, but we thought we'd grab a bite to eat first and then be fit to get stuck in for the rest of the day.'

Martin couldn't argue with Matt's thinking as it mirrored his own. He decided to supplement what he had already eaten with a ham salad sandwich and a packet of shortbread biscuits and finally felt satisfied. Helen and Matt, armed with a variety of sandwiches from the vending machine, brought over another cup of coffee for him and they all sat eating, drinking, and catching up on the past hour or so.

Helen began. 'Meg and Laura took us to the spot where they had seen the killer's car parked, and it's now cordoned off and has a police presence as Alex wants to check it out in more detail later. We knocked doors in the immediate vicinity but the only person who saw anything was a nine-year-old girl. Her mother told us that it is only over the past two months that the daughter Molly has been allowed to take their dog out for a walk on her own. Today the girl had only been gone ten minutes when her mother heard her return.'

'At first the mother, Mrs Pearson, thought her daughter had come back because of the rain but she knew different when she found her daughter crying in the kitchen. It apparently took some time before the daughter would tell her mother why she was upset. Eventually she said that she had seen a man crossing the road and coming towards her and he had blood over his clothes. She said the he saw she had noticed him and he kicked her dog.'

Matt interjected. 'We spoke to Molly and she was more upset about the man's treatment of her dog than the sight of the blood but she was absolutely certain it was blood. She told us it was just like when she had a nose bleed and it all gushed out.

'The timing fits perfectly but unfortunately she isn't able to

151

tell us anything new. She can confirm that he was wearing a black baseball cap and carrying some sort of bag but nothing else. For a nine-year-old she was very sensible, and absolutely adamant that she had not seen his face. She said she wouldn't even want to see the face of a man who kicked animals, and that was when she started crying again.'

'He's the animal,' commented Helen. 'It makes me feel furious when I think how close we got to stopping him today.'

Martin nodded in agreement. 'Yes, but there's still every chance that we will catch him this time, and at least we will be able to put a stop to his killing spree and hopefully stop four more deaths. Things have obviously not gone according to his carefully crafted plan, and my guess is that he will be really rattled by that.'

'You must have loads of work to do and I want to see how the Prof is getting on with the PM, so let's make the most of the nearest thing we have had to a real breakthrough since these killings began.'

They parted company and for the next hour Martin immersed himself in the post-mortem examination. The professor made every ounce of the dead man's body talk, and when Martin left the laboratories to begin the three o'clock briefing it was with the knowledge that this time the Prof's input into the meeting would be anything but surplus to requirements.

PC Lyons had certainly done as requested, and when Martin walked into the incident room at 3 p.m. he was the last to arrive. There was a different atmosphere to the sessions following the previous two murders, as this time there was more for the officers to work on and Martin enhanced the mood.

'First of all, my thanks to those of you who were involved in this morning's session when we actually did come up with the Primrose Garden Centre as one of the possible locations for this murder. Unfortunately the killer beat us to it but what it does mean is that we are getting inside the mind of this evil bastard.

'Professor Moore and Alex Griffiths will tell us more about what is likely to have happened, but first of all, Matt, I'd like you to tell us what you have found out about the victim.'

'Well, there has not been a formal identification yet, but a set of car keys was found in his pocket belonging to the Vauxhall Corsa in the car park of the garden centre. There was no form of identification found on the body or in the car, but the car's registered to a Mr Arthur Taylor with an address in Danescourt, Llandaff.'

'DC Cook-Watts and I have just come back from there, but unfortunately Mr Taylor moved away about three months ago. His former neighbour's description of him fits our victim very well, as he does have some pretty distinguishing features. She describes him as being about my height and with very bushy eyebrows, but most significantly she describes two small fire-breathing dragon tattoos, one on each of his forearms.

'The people who now live in his old address were at work but the neighbour we spoke to, a Mrs Jenkins, had obviously been quite friendly with Mr Taylor and his wife. So there is a wife, but apparently no children. Mrs Jenkins told us that she had been surprised at the couple's decision to move and put it down to some nuisance calls they had been getting. They just told her they wanted to get away from Cardiff and she has no forwarding address. She doesn't think the move is permanent because they haven't sold their house, they're just renting it on a month-by-month basis to the couple who are living there at the moment.

'The woman also told us that Mr Taylor was ill and was getting treatment for something serious, probably cancer, but she wasn't sure.'

Helen added. 'The neighbour told us that in spite of his health problems Mr Taylor always tried to be cheerful. He was a car dealer before he retired and he always joked that his wife had come to him to buy a car and left with more than she, or her boyfriend at the time, had bargained for.'

Martin jumped on this sentence and moving to the boards on which the poems were written he underlined in red the lines 'He stole away the one I loved, drove off without a thought.'

He spoke quietly. 'I can't believe it's going to be that easy.

The victim was a car dealer. Mrs Taylor could originally have been the girlfriend of the killer but then met Mr Taylor, who drove her off in one of his cars leaving our killer with one hell of a grudge to harbour. So what are we saying – find Mrs Taylor, ask her who her boyfriend was when she met Mr Taylor, and de facto we have the killer? There is no way this twisted maniac is going to make it that simple for us.'

Matt anticipated Martin's next question. 'Everyone outside this room is working on the job of finding Mrs Taylor, but the time it takes will depend on how keen the couple were to hide their tracks. I suspect it was the killer who made those phone calls that drove them away in the first place so they will not have wanted to be found – but obviously Mr Taylor was!'

'Let's take a look at the crime scene,' said Martin, indicating to Alex that his input was needed next.

Alex showed the general layout of the garden centre and then the specific area where the body was discovered sprawled amongst the dainty yellow flowers.

'The most significant difference between this murder scene and the other two is the amount of blood we see here and the disturbance that has been caused.' He pointed out a number of breakages and the flattening of some wooden trellis as clear signs of a struggle.

'We were able to see immediately that there were many more than just the two stab wounds we have come to expect, but I know the Prof will want to tell us about those later so I won't steal his thunder. The significant piece of evidence from my point of view is this partial shoe print that may eventually be helpful in securing a conviction but for now just tells us in which direction the killer left the building. There was nothing to show he had used the toilet that he must have passed on his way out and in any event a young girl has told us that he was still covered in blood when she saw him.'

Matt interrupted. 'Yes, and if the weather hadn't changed this morning he would probably have been seen by a lot more people, talk about the luck of the devil.'

Alex went on to explain that the yellow cord looked as if it had been tied in a hurry and was a granny knot instead of the expected reef knot. He was disappointed to report that as before the killer had left behind no fingerprints and must have taken a very blood-stained knife away with him. It certainly hadn't been found at the garden centre.

The professor was the next on his feet and this time he had a lot more to bring to the investigation and was in his element as the audience became more and more engrossed in his findings.

He pointed to an abdominal wound. 'This is the incision with which the killer would have been expecting to kill his victim. The knife has been thrust into the body in the same part of the anatomy as with the other two victims, and we could well have expected the same result, but let me tell you why we didn't get it.

'Compare the first two victims with this one. They were slightly built, and you'll remember the sunshine of the past weeks when we were all wearing lightweight clothes. Today's victim has a lot more adipose tissue and a great deal of it is deposited around his waist. Coupled with that, he was wearing a moderately heavy raincoat, and those two things made the journey of the knife through his body much less predictable.

'With the killer not hitting his target immediately, the victim had a bit of an opportunity to fight back and it looks as if our man lost control.'

The Prof showed seven other stab wounds on the body and this time there were two attempts at the neck. He added. 'That's where all this blood came from, because this time he did slash the carotid artery and in my opinion that would have been the fatal wound.

'There is blood under the nails of the victim but underneath the blood there are tiny bits of black fibre. I believe that the blood will be the victim's own and the fibres will be from the killer's jacket so I don't think he left any of his DNA behind, just minute particles of his sleeve.

'Even if Mr Taylor had not been butchered in the way we see here, he would still not have been around to open his Christmas presents. He had advanced carcinoma of the pancreas and it looks as if he was receiving radiotherapy treatment. If he has a wife waiting for him to come home I suspect she will raise the alarm early. Even without the intervention of the killer she would have good reason to think her husband could have been found dead somewhere.'

'Life's a bitch,' said Matt. 'You mean to say that this poor sod was suffering from some incurable form of cancer, was driven out of his home, and ended up getting stabbed to death. From what we know it's more than likely that the killer knew his victim had cancer – he needn't have bothered killing Mr Taylor, he could have just let nature take her course.'

'That would involve a certain degree of humanity,' said Martin. 'This killer wouldn't know the meaning of that word. He wasn't going to let Mr Taylor get away with stealing his girlfriend, and he was not going to let Mother Nature steal his opportunity to carry out a murder he has thought about for years. He's the sick one!'

Chapter Twelve

It was five hours since he had murdered Arthur Taylor, and if things had gone according to plan he would now be sitting in his rented accommodation and switching from channel to channel to see the best coverage of his handiwork. He couldn't make up his mind if the actual killing was the best part of the process, or if it was watching the aftermath from the comfort of his armchair. Or maybe it was the years of planning, watching his identified victims from a distance as he worked out their part in his killing game.

This time things hadn't gone as he had anticipated because he had been surprised by the physical strength of his intended victim. He had known that Taylor was terminally ill and had read on the internet all about cancer of the pancreas and the relevant treatments. He'd expected the bastard, who had stolen his one and only love, to be weakened by the disease and the debilitating therapy.

Taylor had always been a big man and was something of a fatty twenty-six years ago when he and Carol had first met. That was one of the things the killer couldn't understand. How could the woman he had been living with for three years possibly have preferred an overweight, brainless moron to someone who was, in his own eyes at least, a respected member of the community, and who kept himself in good shape.

What really rankled then, and had over the years poured ever more poison into the killer's mind, was the fact that he had been instrumental in their meeting. It was he who had suggested that Carol should upgrade her car for her birthday, and had sent her to look at models he had picked out for her in a dealership on Hadfield Road.

He had loved Carol more than he had ever believed he was capable of doing, but he knew that their relationship was on the rocks and that she was likely to leave. He saw the gift of a car, barely second-hand, as delaying the inevitable. Although he loved her there was little else in the world he even liked and he was by nature a ruthless man – or as Carol's mother was known to call him, 'a nasty piece of work'. He had done well in his chosen career and was used to getting his own way, and so he expected the same in his private life.

There was no woman who had been put on this earth who was going to make a fool of him and get away with it, and Carol would soon know that she had been foolish to try. She would not even be afforded the bittersweet memories of having nursed her husband through the last days of their life together. She would soon be told that her beloved Arthur had been stabbed to death amongst the pansies and that would be a laughing point for anyone who had ever bought a defective used car from her second-hand husband.

It was when he heard that Carol had actually married the moron and become Mrs Taylor that he had vowed to get his revenge, and now he had done just that. But unlike his first two murders this one had not left him with the sweet taste of success. He knew he had panicked when he forced his knife into Taylor's body and it felt so different from the other two. It hadn't hit the spot and instead of the life draining from Arthur's eyes it was as if a light had been turned on.

The killer looked at the sleeves of his showerproof jacket and could see the marks left by Arthur's nails as he had clawed at them, had even attempted to take the knife. He knew that fibres of his jacket would be found under his victim's nails but he had prevented Arthur from getting his nails anywhere near his face so he was sure none of his own DNA had been left behind.

The fibres from the jacket would keep the police busy, but they would soon find out that the jacket was one of thousands sold on market stalls all over the country and they would have no way of connecting this particular one to him. He had been

158

worried that the shambles of this killing would put the rest of his plans in jeopardy, but he was now returning to his more logical and ruthless way of thinking and he believed he had nothing to fear.

Nevertheless, he couldn't prevent his mind from jumping all over the place and it settled for a moment on the woman he was planning to be his next victim. He remembered how, several years ago when he had been drinking alone in his club, he had overheard some of the committee members chatting and laughing. He had listened with distain to their juvenile banter but the proverbial red mist had descended when he realised that he was the subject of their petty amusement.

The woman who was next on his list had not been with the group that day, but she had obviously told them that he was pretty useless on the golf course and that being rubbish at golf was not his only handicap.

He had memories of leaving the club that day and contemplating suicide. He still couldn't figure why, in his usual bullish way, he had not challenged the gossipers, but it was quite likely that he was at that time suffering from chronic depression and the conversation he had overheard tipped his balance.

Before he had even got home from the club all thoughts of self-harm had vanished and a germ of an idea was hatching. Like many men who turn out to be bullies, he had painful memories of being bullied himself, and that evening he had sat down and made a list of the people who had, in one way or another, really pissed him off at various times of his life.

It had given him a new focus and for the first time in many years he felt as if he was once again the kingpin, as he was now in control of these people's lives and they didn't even know it. He contemplated getting a gun and simply putting bullets in their heads, but what would be the fun in that? It would all be over with far too quickly.

After compiling a list of seven people, he had circled the fifth name with a red pen. The name of Detective Chief Inspector Martin Phelps. How the killer regretted the day their paths had crossed, and he fretted upon how different his life would have turned out if Phelps had asked fewer questions. Phelps would be the centre of whatever plan he put in place to annihilate his tormentors. He spent months, following the hatching of his plan, deciding on how he would murder this man who had caused him so much grief.

Eventually he decided that killing the DCI first would be too good for him, and came up with the idea that killing Phelps' illustrious career would be more painful to the man. Once Phelps knew what it was like to be a public failure the killer would be only too happy to put him out of his misery.

The killer was not in a hurry and subscribed to the theory that revenge is a dish best served cold. He had an imaginative and agile brain and jotted down, alongside the names on his list, a few adjectives that in some way related to each of them.

For some inexplicable reason colours kept on cropping up, such as red when he thought of Miss Rossiter as a dragon, the greens of the golf club, and the uniforms of the boys in blue. His evil mind soon put those innocent colours into a definite pattern and for the next two years he meticulously worked out every detail of his plan. It was not until he was completely ready and his plan had been checked and rechecked that he began his evil programme of killing by colours.

He would make a fool of Phelps – that would be one of his prime objectives – and the idea of sending personal clues in the form of poems appealed to the killer's warped sense of humour. He knew where Martin lived. He even knew that the cottage in Llantwit Major had been left to Phelps by his Aunt Pat. He knew enough about the nature of Martin Phelps to believe that receiving such poisonous mail at his beloved home address would be sickening to the play-it-by-the-book detective.

He had no trouble remembering why he hated the people on his list, and although he had been just seven years old when he was in Miss Rossiter's class at Penbryn Primary School he could still recall her voice. She had always seemed to be singling him out for attention and although the killer had been a big boy even then, he had also been anything but confident.

He'd struggled with maths and in one of her classes she had made him give the answer to the sum of seven and nine. He had mistakenly given the answer as fifteen and she had gone ballistic.

Still traumatised by the memory, he shuddered as he recalled being hauled out of his seat and positioned in front of a class full of giggling children. As he stood there, feeling totally let down by some kids he had considered to be his friends, something else had let him down. It was his bladder – and to the sound of Miss Rossiter's voice pouring yet more scorn on his head he had run from the classroom leaving a warm puddle of urine behind.

Children can be very cruel, and instead of curbing the way in which the killer was teased by his classmates Miss Rossiter seemed to encourage it. She had her pets, they were always the kids who did well, and there were a few others who, like the killer, were open targets. Inevitably the teacher's misfits grouped together and the killer remembered how he had learned that there is safety in numbers and a single swot was no match for a gang of Miss Rossiter's duffers.

Maybe he should be grateful to his teacher, as she had sent him down a road where he learned that lying and manipulating others could in fact be rewarding. It was a skill he honed well, and used to further his career, but it was her repeated humiliation of him that made Miss Rossiter number one on his list.

It hadn't been difficult to track her down and organise her killing at the Red Dragon Centre. He simply made a phone call and told her that her remarkable achievements concerning the value she had added to the lives of children was going to be recognised. He posed as someone who needed to speak to her possibly being a recipient in the Queen's birthday honours list, and had given her an exact time and place for their meeting.

He laughed as he remembered her surprise at the venue but it had been easy to convince her of the need for secrecy and she had agreed not to tell anyone about the fact she had been approached for fear of upsetting 'Her Majesty'. What a vain, pompous woman – but what a shock she had received when the killer had approached her car, not with news of a gong from the Queen but with a long sharp knife and a suggestion that she could now wet *her* pants.

Tracking down Mr Davies hadn't been that difficult, as the killer still had lots of contacts and could easily manipulate many of them. It took just three phone calls and the threat of revealing someone's involvement in a scam before he got the Watch Towers address of his second victim.

The killer's initiation to sex had been when he was just eleven years old, and it had not been as a result of a quick, innocent fumble with one of the girls in his class.

It had been courtesy of the sickening attention paid to him by Mr Davies, who had been one of the scoutmasters at the killer's first camping holiday. He had been surprised when Mr Davies had offered him a place in his own tent and had suggested helping with the problems the killer was having with tying knots, as it was something the scoutmaster usually taunted him about. He remembered the looks on some of the boys' faces as he lauded this over them. One of them even tried to dissuade him from taking up Mr Davies' offer, but the killer had put that down to sheer jealousy because the other boy hadn't been chosen by the scoutmaster himself.

By the following morning the killer knew exactly what he had been chosen for, and he still felt sick as he remembered how his young body had been violated. He understood the knowing glances that were exchanged between some of the scouts and wondered how many of them had suffered Mr Davies' uniquely disgusting take on a lesson in tying knots.

Mr Davies had told him that no one would believe him if he said anything and so the killer joined the other 'special' boy scouts in a vile conspiracy of silence.

Getting Victor Davies to turn up for his own execution really had been as simple as sending him the letter. Although there had been a lot of gossip about possible abuse of his position in the scout troop, nothing had ever been proven, and he would do anything to ensure that the full depths of his perverted

162

behaviour were not discovered.

Mr Davies had not even recognised the killer when he joined him at the side entrance of Freshly Squeezed, but he understood the knife that was pointed in the direction of his heart. A heart that was already beating fast as a result of hearing an almighty great bang from the front of the building, just before the killer had arrived.

Within seconds he had been introduced to his own 'liquidator' and left in no doubt about what was going to happen to him. As the knife entered his body, Victor Davies was told that the killer regretted not being able to cause him as much suffering as others had endured by being the victims of his grotesque sexual perversions. Davies accepted his fate without a struggle, and it was a bit of a disappointment to the murderer to realise that his victim might even have been grateful to be out of the picture for good.

The killer continued to recall bits and pieces from the last three weeks, and from the darkest archives of his life. He firmly believed that his recent actions gave him the moral high ground. He was championing the cause of all the others who had suffered by the hands of his victims. These people deserved to die.

He had a sudden urge to get home, and he looked down at his hands as they rested on the steering wheel. The sleeves of his jacket were stained with blood but his hands were clean, both physically and psychologically. He had stuffed a pair of latex gloves that were thickly coated with blood into an empty cardboard coffee cup, and he was struggling to agree with himself on the next course of action.

He knew that he couldn't yet risk going back to his flat for fear of one of his prying neighbours catching sight of his blood-stained clothing. It was bad enough that some pathetic little girl with her scruffy mongrel had spotted it earlier and he half wished now that he had silenced the girl and her bedraggled pet. He convinced himself that there was no way that anyone would be interested in the imagination of a kid, especially if she had gone home and told her mother that Count Dracula had kicked her dog.

The killer was unaware that the two women he had seen driving past him as he walked towards the garden centre had been instrumental in helping the police make contact with the young girl. If he had been aware he would most likely have added three more names to his hit list.

He thought again about why he had not enjoyed this killing. He remembered how after he had made that first upward thrust with his knife Arthur had stared him in the face and managed to knee him in the groin. It had been painful, but not enough to stop him, and he managed to release the knife and randomly stabbed at whatever part of the body his knife made contact with. Although the two men had not seen each other for many years Arthur knew his attacker and realised he would be unlikely to overcome him in an ordinary fight, not to mention one where his assailant had a knife.

However he fought back with every ounce of his being and clawed at the waxy material of the killer's jacket. Unfortunately for Arthur all efforts to make contact with his attacker's face were thwarted, and when a final stab wound to the neck found the carotid artery his fight was all over.

The killer spoke aloud and reprimanded himself. 'You made a bloody fucking mess of that. You should have used a longer, sharper knife, but no matter, the job has been done. What matters now is getting the other four sorted.'

He pondered what DCI Phelps would be doing at that very moment and allowed himself a mental pat on the back. For the past three weeks he had read every inch of newspaper coverage and listened to and watched every item of radio and television reporting on the first two murders and he knew that Phelps was getting a hard time – just as planned. It would be even worse for the detective when this latest murder came to light and the killer's mood lightened at that prospect.

Perhaps they would have another re-enactment. He had enjoyed the other two and had personally attended both of them. It had been one of the biggest laughs of his life. At the very moment the news presenter was making a public appeal for help in identifying the killer he had been standing just a few feet from her and she had actually spoken to him. She had given out a description that fitted the man looking straight at her but she had failed to notice his presence – what an idiot!

He turned on his car radio and catching the news he received instant gratification. The newscaster was expressing the public outrage that another of the so-called 'Bard murders' had occurred, and this time at a popular garden centre in Rookwood. It was explained that the victim had not yet been formally identified and that more information would be made available at the next full news session.

It was the last sentence of the brief report that made the killer sit up and take notice.

The reporter said that the police had reason to believe that the killer drove a grey BMW 525i SE Saloon and asked for the public's cooperation in tracking down the vehicle.

The killer froze, and it was almost as if he expected members of the public to instantly start thumping on the doors of his car. He looked around, but he had driven to a piece of wasteland about a mile from his home and there was not a soul in sight. However he knew instantly that he would have to do something about his car, as he suspected that it was likely anyone grey BMW would be stopped.

There was no chance he could just leave it, though, as within minutes of it being found the registration number would bring the police to his door. Even if he took the bloodstained gloves with him he knew enough about modern-day forensics to realise that some evidence of his latest victim's blood might be found in the car. In any case there was no chance he could walk from there to his flat in his current bloodstained state.

How in the fucking name of hell did the police know the exact make and colour of his car? It had to be something to do with that kid walking her dog. She must have watched him get back into the car – but then he was sure he had seen her disappear around the corner before he started up the engine. His first instincts, to stick the knife into her and her mongrel, had been right, and he thought what an idiot he had been not to do as he usually did and follow his gut instincts.

During all the time he had planned his killing game the thought of getting caught had never been seriously considered, but he was intelligent enough to know that it was now on the cards.

'Not before I finish off what I set out to do,' he told himself. 'No one is going to be able to stop me, it's just a question of moving the planned timescale and getting the job finished.'

His only plan in terms of dates for the murders had been to make sure they would all happen on a Saturday, simply to cause as much disruption to DCI Phelps and his team as possible. Now the killer would have to set aside that objective, as he thought about the possibility of killing the remaining four people quickly, before he was discovered. He had an exit plan, but he didn't really want to spend the rest of his life in some remote corner of Poland – and certainly not before he had fulfilled his mission.

He looked at the rain that was now easing off and remembered that a forecast he had heard earlier was promising a return to fine weather within a day or so. That would make it easier to keep to his game plan and kill in the order of the colours he had planned. If it stayed wet he would have to jump to his blue victim – namely DCI Phelps.

He didn't want to think too much about the reasons he had for wanting to get rid of Phelps. There was no moral high ground to be taken in that particular case. It was one hundred per cent personal.

It was getting darker. The rain had almost completely stopped, and the killer brought his focus sharply back to the here and now. He would give himself another ten minutes or so and then drive back to his flat. He knew that his neighbours went out quite early on a Saturday night, so he would soon be able to risk going home. After all, even murderers had human needs, and right now he needed a pee – and was relaxed enough to be considering the bacon and eggs that had become part of his post-killing ritual.

Less than a quarter of an hour later he had driven the car to his home and locked it in the garage. Luck had been with him and he'd been able to get inside without being seen. He wouldn't be using the car again for a very long time and would see about hiring one tomorrow.

He stripped off for a shower and bagged all his clothes with the intention of getting rid of them the following day. The television provided some more information and he saw with dismay a reporter standing on the very spot where he had parked his car before walking to the kill. To add to the killer's frustration, there was a very brief interview with Martin Phelps in which he looked far from embarrassed by the case's lack of progress.

Facing the cameras with confidence, Phelps expressed his regret that there had been another killing, but told the public that he and his team were very close to solving the crimes and putting away one of the most deranged killers he had ever had the misfortune to come across.

In conclusion, Phelps had said, 'Whoever you are and wherever you are, we are now in a position to put a stop to your macabre games and to ensure that you will soon be paying the price for your actions.'

The killer made a fist and thrust it under Martin's face as the news item faded and he was left with his fist aimed at the image of a brick wall. He yelled at the screen. 'Laying down the gauntlet are you, DCI Phelps? Well, let's see how your public image holds up after next Tuesday.'

Picking up his house phone the killer punched in a number and after five rings heard a woman's voice. He told her who was calling and received a less than hospitable response.

'Yes, I know it's been a long time, and I know we parted on less than favourable terms, but the truth is that I would like to make amends and I wondered if you would consider a round of golf. The weather is set to clear up over the next couple of days and it should be perfect for eighteen holes by Tuesday morning.'

Before the woman had a chance to reply he played his trump card. 'I would prefer not to say anything to your friends about the trouble you were in some years ago. I just want to make my way back into favour at the club, and if you help me do that I will help you keep your criminal record a secret.'

There was silence initially at the other end of the line and then some expletives that were not very ladylike and were accompanied by accusations of blackmail.

The killer just laughed. 'Call it whatever you like. I think you and I could make a good team on and off the greens, but the decision is yours. Do you want to risk letting everyone know what crime you were arrested for back in 1997, or shall we tee off in the first available slot on Tuesday morning?'

Chapter Thirteen

It was almost midnight and Martin, Matt, and Helen were the only people left in Incident Room One. They were surrounded by the various pieces of information that had been gathered over the past three weeks, and Helen was putting the last touches to a whiteboard on which she was building up a picture of the killer.

An image from the CCTV tapes of the Red Dragon Centre had given her a central outline, and she had added what had amounted to just small snippets from the memories of witnesses at each of the murders. In isolation, their evidence was sparse, but it was coming together and she stood back to admire her handiwork.

'I think we should go to the press with this,' she suggested to Martin. 'We now know we are looking for a well-built man, not far off six foot, who has a marching gait – but that's not too obvious until you really start looking at it. He has been seen on at least three occasions wearing a black baseball cap with a wide brim and we know the exact make and colour of his car. That's a lot more than we had for the last public appeal and should jog someone's memory.'

Martin nodded but at the same time he looked at Matt who was in danger of swallowing his own head with the size of his yawn. 'Come on, let's call it a day and pick it up again in the morning. You both look shattered and I know I am. So let's all go home and try to get some sleep.'

Martin took one last look around the room when the others had left. He had an itch that he seemed to be incapable of scratching. Sgt Evans had said that there was something about the killer, something about his voice and the way he moved, that rang a bell, and that was a feeling that Martin had also experienced since the start of this investigation. He made a mental note to speak to John Evans the following day and switched off the lights.

It seemed more like ten minutes than ten hours when he was back in the same place but this time surrounded by the whole team.

'Let's forget about the first two murders for the time being and concentrate all our efforts on what happened yesterday. The killer was lucky to get away with his plan because Matt and Helen were on their way to cover the garden centre as one of our identified possible sites for this murder.'

Matt shook his head. 'It's so bloody frustrating. If we had been fifteen minutes earlier, maybe less than that, we might have prevented it – or at least caught the killer fleeing the scene.'

Martin continued. 'We have still not had the victim formally identified but we are in no doubt that he was a Mr Arthur Taylor. He had left his car in the car park and we traced his registration number to an address in Danescourt. There was no one at the house and according to the neighbours Mr Taylor and his wife moved away some months ago, but none of the people we spoke to, nor the DVLA, have a forwarding address.

'The small dragons tattooed on his forearms are exactly as described by one of the neighbours and we have heard from the PM result of yesterday that the victim was being treated for pancreatic cancer and didn't have long to live anyway. It surely won't be long before his wife reports him missing – I'm just surprised that she hasn't done so already.'

Matt interrupted. 'It's normal for us to wait until someone has been missing longer than a day before taking any action, and if the person is a non-vulnerable adult it could be longer than that. Hundreds of people leave their homes every day and never come back – it would be impossible to follow them all up. Many just come back the next day.

'As for where they moved to, well, that could be anywhere, and they obviously didn't want their new whereabouts known.' Matt was showing an unusually high level of frustration. 'Mr and Mrs Taylor could have left the country, we have no way of knowing at the moment. We may be able to find out but it will take time.'

Martin spoke firmly. 'The killer was able to make contact with Mr Taylor and persuade him to turn up at a specified time to the Primrose Garden Centre. If he was able to find the Taylors then we should be able to. What have we got?'

Martin answered his own question. 'We have a name, a known previous address, a detailed description that includes some significant identifiers, and a man who had a life-threatening medical condition. I phoned the professor last night to get some more information on that last one and he said he would talk to colleagues at the Velindre Hospital.

'Velindre treats cancer patients not just from Cardiff but from the whole of south-east Wales. The Prof seemed to think that even if Mr Taylor had moved out of the area he could have chosen to continue to be treated at Velindre if his programme had already been established there. They would surely have an up-to-date record of his address and the Prof will let us know if he gets anything.'

Sgt Evans spoke. 'We have used the national network to pick up on any missing person reports. Although there may be little action taken straight away there will always be a missing person's form completed and I suspect there will be only one report giving details of dragon tattoos to match those on our victim's arms. We will get notification immediately if any report does contain that sort of detail.'

'Thanks for that,' said Martin. 'While you're on your feet, did you give any more thought to what you said about having some vague recollection about certain aspects of the killer?'

Evans shook his head. 'No, but it's still nagging at me, and I've even woken up a few times almost feeling that I know who it is, but I can't get beyond that – it's still just a feeling.'

Martin said that he was having the same sort of feeling.

'Perhaps we are both thinking of someone we have come across during one of the many investigations we have jointly been involved in over the years.'

'Well, there are plenty of those,' replied Sgt Evans. 'I've been, through personal choice, at the same rank since you returned from Swansea to join the CID here as a DS. A lot of water has gone under the bridge since then, and we must have been together for countless arrests – it's something that relates to someone we have investigated, I'm sure, and it will come to me.'

'Keep thinking,' Martin encouraged him, and then added. 'Let's think a bit more specifically about the killer, Matt, take us through the evidence given by the two women at the café and the young girl.

'Well, thanks to a woman who has an amazing knowledge of cars, we're able to give you the details you see on the board here. Her friend remembered exactly where they had seen the killer leave his car, and they were both able to identify him from the image we showed them. Unfortunately, though, neither of them saw his face in any detail.

'DC Cook-Watts and I knocked on doors surrounding the spot they identified and came across a schoolgirl who had seen the killer while out walking her dog. She was able to tell us the man had blood on his clothes, and he had obviously seen her looking at him because the bastard kicked her dog. The only additional information we got from the girl was that the man was wearing what she called "trainer boots" and she said that one had blood all over the toe. I think that fits in with what Alex found at the scene.'

Alex spoke to confirm this. 'We found some partial footprints. All three came from the same shoe, the right one, and the little girl confirmed that it was the right shoe that was bloody. It doesn't help us identify the killer though, and it will only serve as evidence if we eventually find the shoe in his possession.'

Martin thought for a while and then opened up his thoughts for comment. 'The killer has now struck three times, and we have been told through the medium of his poetry that all his victims are known to him. We know that one was a teacher, one was a scoutmaster, and yesterday's victim was a car salesman. Here is where we have to do some more boring investigative work.'

'Helen, I want you to find out everything you can about the three victims. We already have shedloads of information on the first two, but I want you to cross-reference until you're blue in the face. The killer knew all of them, so how many people would have been in that position, and don't forget me. How many people who knew Miss Rossiter, Mr Davies, and Mr Taylor also know me? It's a tall order but something more efficiently done by a small group of people – do your best.'

'Matt, do whatever you can with the information we have on the car. Find out who every grey BMW with a Cardiff registration plate belongs to and chase up their details. If any one of them was anywhere in South Wales yesterday I want to know about it.' Martin paused and then continued.

'The details of the killer's car were read out by one of the television presenters last night, so the killer will probably be aware that we have a lead on his car. I think that means that we have seen the last of the BMW, and if I were in his shoes I would be looking to use a different vehicle. If he doesn't have access to another vehicle he may consider hiring one.'

'OK,' said Matt. 'What you are asking for regarding car owners is not going to be a five-minute job – it could take days or even weeks to complete. Even then we may have to contend with cars that have been stolen, or owners who've sold cars on without completing the correct documentation.'

Martin replied. 'I know all of that, but it has to be done so let's just hope we get an early break.'

Matt nodded. 'Picking up on anyone who hires a vehicle over the next few days will be easier, provided of course that the killer goes to a registered car hire company. I'll get calls out to all of them within a fifty-mile radius and ensure we are notified of any customer meeting our killer's description. We will need to receive that information while the customer is still on their premises, having the paperwork processed.'

'We won't want the killer being alerted to our interest so we will have to ensure that the car hire companies are discreet, but that exercise is also going to be time-consuming and potentially unproductive.'

Matt was aware that he was sounding negative and tried to end on a positive note. 'At least we've all got things to do, and it marks an end to the navel-gazing of the past three weeks. We will get this killer, and we must all be on a mission to ensure that it's before he kills again, so any volunteers please – there's lots of phoning and legwork on offer.'

There was no shortage of officers willing to help Matt, and the numbers in the room dwindled down to a mere handful. Charlie signalled her desire to be included and on the way out was explaining how she could bring high-tech support to the exercise.

Martin watched Charlie wheel her way out and thought how well she looked. The news of her pregnancy was not yet common knowledge as she and Alex wanted to keep their secret between themselves and just a few good friends for a bit longer.

Alex noticed Martin watching Charlie and he smiled and said quietly. 'Looks good on it, doesn't she? I didn't think she could be more beautiful than she was on the day I married her, but now look at her. I'm sure everyone must recognise her radiance for what it is.'

Martin nodded his agreement. He had never seriously thought about having children of his own and had, to a certain extent, been put off the idea by the over enthusiasm of his ex-wife – but now there was Shelley. There was no doubt that the love and excitement that oozed out of Alex and Charlie was contagious, so maybe it was worth thinking about. He pulled himself together sharply, not just because he realised that he and Shelley hadn't even spoken about having a family, but also because he had murder to think about.

Some distance from Goleudy was a woman whose mood itself was murderous. Connie Jackson was feeling anxious and her usual haughty attitude was nowhere to be seen. She stared out of the window of her large detached house in Cyncoed and prayed for rain, but the wind had blown away the clouds and for the moment it was looking like a return to summer.

The phone call of yesterday had rattled her and was threatening to turn her well-ordered world upside down. She adored her lifestyle and luckily for her she still had a small fortune with which to indulge herself. Connie admitted to being over forty, but stopped well short of her real age of fifty-three years. To be fair to her, she did look younger than her age, but she was beginning to find it more and more of a struggle to sustain the gap between fantasy and reality.

Swimming and regular sessions at the gym kept her figure where she wanted it to be, and she thought disdainfully of some of the women she knew who seemed content to let everything be taken over by the pull of gravity. An excellent hairdresser, with a price tag to match his expertise, kept her hair the colour of a true ash blonde. Her wardrobe was classic and her jewellery simple but expensive. Connie's biggest let down was when she opened her mouth.

For the first twelve years of her life she had lived in the East End of London, but when her parents divorced she had moved to West Wales. As a teenager she was ridiculed for her Cockney accent and did her best to mimic the accents she heard around her. The result was an unmitigated disaster, but she got by because of her amazing figure and classic good looks.

She was only eighteen when she met and married Stefano Giordano, an Italian who was the first person ever to enjoy Connie's harsh accent. He had twin business ventures in Milan and Cardiff and his companies thrived and provided the couple with every possible creature comfort. Connie quickly learned to enjoy the good things in life, but she was young and easily bored and her experiments with pills at parties soon turned into a much harder habit that was still with her.

In 1997 her husband had died of a massive coronary. She had other memories of 1997, as yesterday's phone call had reminded her. How did that bastard know about her conviction for possession of class A drugs? Her very expensive barrister had assured her, at the time, that it would be buried and that none of her friends would ever get to hear about it.

Connie was unaware that the man who had called her yesterday was the killer that she had just been hearing about on the news. She just knew him as a member of the golf club who some years ago had taken an unwelcome fancy to her, and who had seemed to think they would make a good couple.

She had been in the running for becoming the first female president of the club at that time and didn't want to upset any of the members who were eligible to vote. So for the sake of a peaceful life she had endured a few rounds of golf with him, but when he had made it plain that he wanted her as more than just a golfing partner she had unceremoniously dumped him.

He had not taken rejection well and continued to boast to members of the club that they were an item. In order to quash this line of gossip she remembered telling some of the committee members that he was useless on the golf course and even more pathetic on a personal level. Thinking back, she realised that the day she had spoken so scathingly about him was the last day she had seen him. He hadn't been to the club for years, so why the sudden interest in a round of golf – and with her of all people?

She moved from the window and poured herself a very large glass of brandy. She drank the first mouthful of the neat spirit without batting an eyelid. How would she cope with the proposed round of golf planned for Tuesday morning? The bastard sounded serious about letting people know of her past conviction, and it couldn't be happening at a worse time for her.

Her current houseguest was a distant relative of her late husband and he was loaded. Her husband had left her very well provided for, but that was over ten years ago and last year she had been forced to partially mortgage the house for the first time to top up her capital. There was still something like a million in equity left, but with no income and expensive outgoings it wouldn't last for ever – she had seen how quickly money disappeared.

Roberto was obviously interested in her, but he knew nothing of her addiction and she suspected that if he even got a whisper he would be on the first plane back to Milan. She would make sure he never found out, or at least not until after they were married. Even Connie's closest friends were unaware of her cocaine habit, and until the noxious phone call of yesterday she firmly believed that the only people who did know were two dealers in Cardiff.

Since that horrendous time when she had been stopped for a minor traffic offence and the police had found cocaine in her car, Connie had been a model addict. It was unlucky for her that the incident had occurred during a 'Get Tough on Drugs' campaign.

She regretted that her husband had been made aware of her arrest but it was he who had hired an expensive legal team and kept things out of the public eye. The stress of the whole episode undoubtedly exacerbated an underlying heart condition and he had died before the end of what Connie called her *annus horribilis*.

Since her husband's death Connie had attracted the attention of a number of men, but until Roberto there had been no one she had seriously considered. The Italian family of which her late husband and Roberto were members was keen to see her settle for another member of their clan, if only to ensure that the property once owned by Stefano stayed with them. Not that the family needed more money or equity, it was more a point of honour that no one outside the family should get what Stefano had worked hard to achieve.

There had been several hopeful admirers at the golf club, and she knew she had led some of them on but not the one who had phoned her yesterday. She wondered how some people got to be members – there were a number of ex-cons and undesirables mingled in with others who claimed to be pillars of the community. Probably the only thing anyone really needed to get membership was the ability to pay for the privilege.

The day was passing very slowly and there was still tomorrow to endure before she could get that round of golf over

177

and find out exactly what was behind this sudden blast from the past. Connie felt strung up and knew what would sort her out, but with Roberto walking about upstairs she couldn't risk it. Her hand hovered over the bottle of brandy, but she must have been more uptight than even she realised because she knocked the bottle over and it smashed against the legs of a circular marble table. She swore and bent down to pick up the broken bottle, but cut her hand on a shard of glass, and quite out of character she burst into tears.

Having heard the sound of breaking glass Roberto had come downstairs and was now cradling her in his arms.

'*Cucciola mia*,' he said tenderly. 'What is the matter? Why are you crying over a broken bottle of cognac? It is not important, I will get you another. Please don't cry.'

Connie felt very stupid and didn't want Roberto to see her with a blotchy face and smudged makeup. She was having trouble holding herself together and she knew what she had to do. Gently removing herself from his arms, she made the excuse of wanting the bathroom and made her way to the one room that was her own private domain.

Within ten minutes she was back in the lounge with freshly applied makeup, feeling much in control of the situation. Only someone who knew what to look for would have picked up on her dilated pupils and slightly runny nose, but Roberto was just pleased to see her back to her normal upbeat self.

'Sorry about that,' she said. 'I don't know when I last cried, and I don't think it had anything to do with the brandy – it was just one of those things. You can put it down to me being a silly woman,' she laughed.

Roberto kissed her and in her state of post-cocaine euphoria she responded with an enthusiasm that took him by surprise. But he was a red-blooded Italian, and he wasn't complaining as giggling like school children they raced up the stairs and landed in a heap on his bed.

Two hours later he confessed that he was feeling hungry, and went in search of something to satisfy his other appetite. It was usual for Connie not to want anything to eat after feeding her habit and she chose instead to take a long shower.

She believed that the past few hours had sealed her relationship with Roberto and that it would not be long before he popped the question. Even more reason for her to be worried by the possible intentions of Tuesday's golf partner. Why had he contacted her? Why now? The biggest question of all was: what did he really want? Not to put things right between them, she was sure of that, and not just to ask her to help him ease his way back into the club either. He could do that without her. She knew for certain that there were a number of his old colleagues who were still members, and a few of them had risen to the dizzy heights of the committee.

Even after the weekend, there was still Monday to get through before her questions would be answered. Part of her wanted a return to the torrential rain of a few days ago so that the game would have to be called off but realistically she knew that it would just result in the inevitability of a reschedule. That would mean waiting even longer to find out what he really wanted.

Perhaps he thought that, having found out about her drugs problem, he could blackmail her into having a relationship with him. Perhaps he just wanted to see her humiliated as she was forced to walk around the club with everyone thinking he was her new partner on and off the course. Perhaps, perhaps, perhaps. Connie contemplated the most bizarre possibilities, but at no time did she consider the thought that her caller just wanted to get close enough to kill her …

She had to get out of the house. She had to find something to take her thoughts off that man and the awful places he was sending her mind. There was no better way she knew than some serious retail therapy and kissing a somewhat bemused Roberto on the top of his head she headed for Cardiff to join the throngs of other Sunday shoppers and to lose herself in the crowds.

Roberto watched her walk towards her car and settled his mind to the fact that he would never understand British women. One minute they were giving a man everything he could possibly want, and the next minute they were going shopping!

He picked up the phone as he watched her drive away and then called Milan. Like all good Italian boys he would have to talk to Mama before taking the first steps towards asking Connie to be his future wife.

That marriage would not happen if the killer had anything to do with it, and unlike Connie he was far from being at a loose end. Between now and Tuesday morning he intended to start the ball rolling, so that by the end of next week all the names on his list would need referring to in the past tense.

Connie was the next on his list and with gloved hands he put a sheet of green paper into an envelope already addressed to Detective Chief Inspector Martin Phelps at his home in Llantwit Major. Written on the paper was the fourth poem, and on his table was a short length of green cord that in his mind was an essential piece of his manic, homicidal game-plan.

Normally he would have put a stamp on the envelope and then waited until the particular Friday he had scheduled before posting it. That had been the original game plan but since the last murder he knew that things had changed, and that the police would be gathering information that would soon lead them to him.

He thought back at how easy it had been to get his victims to do what he told them. Taylor hadn't queried the man who had phoned him from the Primrose Garden Centre to tell him his wife had won a garden makeover. He had told the killer that she was always doing competitions and was quite good at them, having won two holidays, several sums of money, a mountain bike, and endless hampers and gift sets. But then the killer already knew all that.

He had told Arthur that wherever possible the makeover team liked to surprise the prizewinner by getting help from someone who knew that person well, to keep the win a secret and help with the design.

Part of the prize was to be a weekend break and the actual garden makeover would happen when the winner was away. Arthur said they would like the weekend break but as they were not currently living in their own home the makeover team would not be disturbed and could go there at any time,

Arthur was thrilled to be involved and was looking forward to seeing Carol's face when she saw her prize-winning garden. It was good that he was getting a say in the design and he would ensure that it was as maintenance free as possible. That way when she was back at their home in Danescourt and he was no longer around, she would be able to cope with it.

The nice man from the garden centre had told him that their car park was being resurfaced and that they had an arrangement with the local hospital for customers to use their car park to avoid getting clamped on the double yellow lines that were all along the main road. What he hadn't taken into account was the fact that Arthur was not really up to walking far and so had decided to drive nearer to the garden centre car park and take a chance on parking.

As Arthur had approached the garden centre he had been surprised to see a few cars parked in their car park and no sign of any resurfacing. He wondered if they had been forced to reschedule because of the poor weather conditions. Thinking no more about it, he made his way to the plant section which was the planned rendezvous site, expecting to claim his wife's prize – not to lose his life …

As the killer had entered the garden centre on foot he hadn't walked near the car park and had not seen Arthur's car. If he had done he would have rethought his plans. If the brainless idiot had obeyed orders his car would have been amongst a load of others in the car park of Rookwood Hospital. The police wouldn't have found it as the killer had plans for it to be collected later. There were still the likes of ex-car thieves whom he could make jump through hoops because he knew things about their past that they would prefer to remain buried.

He had seen the car as he had hurried away from the killing, but by then it was too late. His brain had gone quickly through the chain of events that he could see happening. It would start with the keys being found in Arthur's pocket, the car being discovered, and then the owner being identified via the DVLA database.

There was nothing the killer didn't know about his victims – after all, part of his game had been to study them for years. He knew the Taylors had moved house because some madman had been phoning them with threats to expose Arthur's dodgy car dealings. That had been good fun.

He also knew that their new address was not on any official documents because he had checked it out. They didn't want anyone to know where they now lived, but the killer had watched them move in during one of his many stakeouts.

He had enjoyed the times when, sitting in his BMW, he had watched each of his victims in turn, going about their day-to-day lives. They laughed, they shopped, they talked to neighbours, they went to the dentist, and did so many other things without once being aware of his presence.

He had sat in his car as some couple had helped Miss Rossiter move into her new house, and he had also watched the developing relationship between Martin Phelps and Shelley Edwards. He knew about Shelley's diabetic father and the Italian houseguest at Connie Jackson's. The antics of the staff at Watch Towers were well known to him and he had even sat at the next table to Victor Davies in his regular café. He loved the idea that he knew so much about his victims while they didn't even give a thought to his existence.

The killer couldn't dwell on his last murder as it represented something that was far from the perfect plan he had dreamed of. Usually, when it came to organising detail, manipulating people, and covering his tracks, he could give master classes, but this time he knew his efforts had been way off the ten out of ten he had come to expect.

All the more reason to concentrate on the rest of his plan and alongside the green envelope he placed a blue one and the remaining two colours. The blue one was the one that had always been his main focus as it represented the public humiliation and killing of DCI Phelps. He knew all about the way in which the detective worked – all about the questions he asked – all about his dogged determination to get things right.

He knew because he had been caught out as a result of those things. He had lost everything because of those things.

Martin Phelps had been one big thorn in his side, but now he revelled in the thought that after failing to solve the murder of Connie Jackson, Phelps would be ridiculed, not just by the public but by the whole of the police force that had until now held him in such high esteem. How he would enjoy watching the mighty fall from grace – and die ...

Chapter Fourteen

For three people Monday was three very different days. The killer was in a state of euphoric anticipation as, months ahead of his original schedule, he plotted the final details for the demises of his last four victims. He would not be caught alive, and without actually having the knife in his hand he practised the move on himself that he would execute if he had to. He anticipated giving himself the opportunity to practise for real at least four more times on others, before turning the knife on himself if he had to, so would be point-perfect by then.

The remaining four coloured envelopes were now all in a line on his kitchen table alongside the corresponding lengths of coloured cord. His eyes focused on the blue cord, and he imagined it tied around the dead wrists of DCI Phelps. The killer believed that in some way all his victims had in his lifetime tied his hands behind his back, metaphorically speaking, so in their deaths he was turning the tables.

He had used the same knife on all his victims, and it was now washed and sharpened to a razor-edge finish but not in its usual place. This time the killer had put the knife, safely within its leather sheath, not in his canvas bag but alongside the putter in his golf bag. He loosened the sheath and practised pulling the knife out quickly. He went over and over the movements he would have to make when saying 'goodbye' to Connie.

After much deliberation he had put aside the mistakes of the third murder, and spent the day congratulating himself on despatching three of his demons and savouring the thoughts of what he would do to the other four.

For Connie, the Monday was endless, although it should have been one of the happiest days of her life. Having yesterday received Mama's blessing Roberto had gone out early and bought a sapphire and diamond engagement ring which, if she was ever short of cash, would keep her suppliers happy for years.

He was suggesting that they take the first available flight to Milan, as the family wanted to celebrate their engagement and plan a real Italian wedding. The ceremony she had shared with her late husband had been in Cardiff: not traditional enough for the Giordano clan, who this time wanted the wedding to take place in Italy.

There was nothing Connie would have liked better than to jet away with Roberto, but a certain round of golf was hanging over her like a black cloud. She even contemplated suggesting they go to Italy and stay there permanently, but she knew such arrangements would take time – certainly enough time for her blackmailer to spread his spiteful knowledge.

She knew that she would have to meet him as arranged, and persuaded Roberto that she needed to do a bit more shopping before their trip to Italy. They agreed a Wednesday lunchtime flight from London Heathrow. Roberto had things to attend to and spent most of Monday in the Cardiff office, giving Connie too much time to worry. She took the opportunity to get her golf clubs into the boot of her car ready for Tuesday morning. She wouldn't tell Roberto that she was playing golf, it was not a game he had ever had any time for and he would persuade her to cancel. She would say she had yet more shopping to do – he would understand that.

For Martin the day was a very mixed bag and he found himself the centre of some unwanted attention from the press and from the hierarchy of his own organisation. True to his threat, Superintendent Bryant had taken advice regarding their altercation in the car park. Martin had been obliged to spend the best part of an hour giving his version of events to the senior personnel officer, who was looking into the possibility of a formal hearing on the grounds of misconduct.

He could hardly believe the super had been petty enough to

go ahead with his threat, but Martin wasn't unduly worried as he knew PC Lyons had overheard their exchanges and would ensure that only the truth was told. He became somewhat more worried when the personnel officer told him that they would not be involving PC Lyons as although he had been in the car park at the time he had not heard what had been said.

The situation reminded Martin of the time when he had just returned from Swansea as a newly appointed detective sergeant, and he had been told that some evidence he had regarding an officer under investigation was not needed. Perhaps PC Lyons had been told the same thing. Strangely enough, that had also been at the time of an investigation into the crimes of a serial killer. Maybe these horrendous occurrences just brought out the worst in people.

When he returned to the team Matt asked if everything was all right and Martin shrugged his shoulders. 'I thought it would be the media that would be jumping on my case, but when the boot comes from within its harder to cope with. Still that's not for today – I'll explain when we haven't got a murderer to catch. It would be helpful if we caught up on what everyone has been doing.'

'Everyone's been waiting for you before doing just that,' replied Matt. 'I'll kick off with what we were hoping was some positive information we got from the Prof, but it's not taken us as far as we would have hoped. He got it confirmed that Mr Taylor was being treated at Velindre Hospital and they were able to give him a change of address. It's a fair distance away, just the other side of Chepstow, but according to the local officers, who went to check it out for us, there was no one at home.

'They spoke to one neighbour who said that Mr and Mrs Taylor were just renting the house and she didn't know if they were coming back as she hadn't seen their car for a while. She hadn't got to know the couple very well but she did know that Mr Taylor had cancer and there was nothing the doctors could do for him.'

Matt continued. 'The woman told the officer that the couple

had moved there because some man in Cardiff was making their life unbearable but that it wasn't long after their move to Chepstow before he caught up with them and they were once again getting malicious phone calls. The neighbour had asked why they didn't notify the police and she had been surprised by Mrs Taylor's hostile reply. Apparently she said that she had done that once before and that her husband had been attacked as a result – but the neighbour didn't know what she meant by that.

'Another neighbour told the officer that Mrs Taylor had mentioned a holiday home that her sister had near the coast. She wasn't sure if Mrs Taylor had said Barry or Porthcawl or possibly Penarth, but she had said that Arthur might benefit from some sea air and this neighbour seemed to think the couple might have gone there – wherever there is!'

Helen Cook-Watts got to her feet. 'We have been cross-referencing every name that has come up in any part of this enquiry. There are pages and pages of names that relate to the children taught by Miss Rossiter. There are the official ones we have obtained through the Education Authority records and there are the names on the work we found in her home, probably left by some of children she taught outside school hours.

'We now believe that the children whose work was found at her home weren't pupils at her school, as we can find no trace of most of their names on the official records. The names that did match were ones like David Jones and John Davies, but there were lots of them on all the lists. It's possible that she was giving private lessons to some children, probably at her home, and that's why she still had those books.

'I don't know whether to concentrate on the school list or the smaller number of names from the home tutorials. I was hoping for some matches but nothing so far. As you can imagine there are a number of common names and so we still have hundreds of possibilities.'

Martin interrupted. 'Yes, but I am certain that the killer was taught by Miss Rossiter and so his name will be there somewhere.'

Helen continued. 'We have the names of the boys who were scouts during the time that Mr Davies was the scoutmaster, although we are pretty certain that this is an incomplete list. Apparently lots of boys join the scouts and only stay for a short while. It's not until they are officially enrolled that their names are recorded, and only then if the scoutmaster is competent. Mr Davies doesn't seem to have had that sort of reputation. Work is still going on with the cross-referencing of the pupils against the scouts but once again it's just the common place names that are found on both lists.'

Matt jumped in. 'We've given Helen's group the names of anyone owning a BMW of the type the killer was seen getting out of in Rookwood, but again there is the possibility that we won't have a completely accurate list. We have so far come up with a David Jones and a John Davies and both have been ruled out.'

'That's right,' said Helen. 'The David Jones on Miss Rossiter's list is not the same person as the man who owns a BMW. I have spoken to both of them and neither was ever a scout. The John Davies that is on both lists, and who was also a boy scout, made us hopeful – but I visited him and he is only just a bit taller than me, and skinny as a rake.

'We are nowhere near to finishing the exercise as we're spending time going down what turn out to be blind alleys – but we can't risk ignoring them, that's why it's taking so long.'

Martin nodded. 'This part of the process can be tedious and unrewarding, but it has also been known to come up with the goods, so keep at it.'

'I'm beginning to hate this killer's poems even more than some I was forced to learn in order to regurgitate for examination purposes in school. Still, we did use the third poem to help us consider the possible location of that murder and it was amongst the ones we came up with. How did we do that?'

'Well, we had the colour,' suggested Helen. 'As the first two locations had been colour linked we presumed that the third one would follow the same pattern.'

Martin agreed and then said. 'So we have had red, orange, yellow ...'

'Green, blue, indigo, and violet.' Helen completed the well-known sequence of colours. 'He's not just killing by colours, he is using the colours of the rainbow. A rainbow isn't a physical object – it isn't something we can touch – and maybe the killer thinks that by using its colours he too will become untouchable.'

Helen had become really excited and her suggestions seemed plausible but Martin reined her ideas in a bit. 'You may well have hit the nail on the head, Helen, and it's certainly something I could see the killer doing. It somehow fits in with the poetry and the colour thing in general, but there are other possibilities. For example, the first three colours are the colours of heat or sunshine, or possibly anger or fire, so will he keep to those types of colours?'

'Maybe,' agreed Helen. 'However, according to him he has four more murders to commit, and there are four more colours of the rainbow left – it all seems to fit.'

'OK,' said Martin, 'let's run with it.'

'In that case,' Helen said, 'we will be looking at a green location for the fourth murder. Do you want to take suggestions for possible murder sites?'

'It worked last time, so why not?'

Martin had barely finished his words when the ideas started flowing in.

'The Cathedral Green in Llandaff.'

'Cardiff Greenpeace – they meet in Roath.'

'Green bin recycling.'

'Golf courses – they all have greens.'

'The Cardiff Green Party.'

'The Green Lady – that's a pub in Caerphilly.'

'The Green Down – that's a pub in St Georges-super-Ely.'

'Green Bay – a media production company – think it's on or near Talbot Street.'

'Parks and green spaces.'

'Green Shoots Catering – they're based not far from Freshly

Squeezed.'

'Green Devil Tattoo – business premises on Clifton Street.'

'Green Willow Funerals – I think they have premises near the Heath Hospital, and they're certainly down in Dinas Powys.'

'There's a new dress agency called Mint Green where you can take your no-longer-wanted designer clothes and they sell them for you. Anyway, they're based in Llandaff.'

Martin held up his hands, as like before the suggestions were drying up and he had no more space on the whiteboard to write them.

'There are probably lots more we haven't considered but if we had just ten minutes to guess which of the suggested locations our killer would use next, which one would it be?'

The team talked amongst themselves, and after five minutes the only suggestions that Martin had left on the whiteboard were the Cathedral Green, both the pubs, golf courses, and the Green Devil Tattoo shop. The others had for one reason or another been removed but the actual location was still wide open.

Martin summed up what was left. 'Apart from the golf courses we have identified places that are relatively self-contained, and if we received a poem directing us to one of them we would soon get it covered. Golf courses on the other hand are a different kettle of fish. How many are there in and around Cardiff?'

'Well, I can think of ten or twelve just off the top of my head,' said Matt. 'I'm not a golfer, so maybe we should enlist the help of Superintendent Bryant – he's the man for the little white ball.'

Martin didn't even give that suggestion time to register and instead asked if there were any golf clubs that maybe had a reference to the colour green in their name.

Matt Googled the combination, but only got information about the green fees charged by the various clubs.

'Doesn't look like it,' he said. 'I'll get some work done on the location and layout of every club within a ten-mile radius of

Cardiff and have it at the ready.'

Martin tapped the board as the meeting was breaking up and he needed to keep everyone focused.

'This is a good suggestion that Helen has come up with regarding a possible sequence of colours but I want to take it one step further. We have just spent time considering locations associated with green and I now want groups of you to think about just about every other colour there is, including black and white. Go through the same exercise we have done here and for every colour get a short list of possible sites that could attract the killer. We will continue to concentrate on green but we were so close on the yellow clue and I want us to be ready for whatever colour the killer throws at us next. The other thing is the timing. The first two murders were two weeks apart and then we get a third just one week later. The only common denominator is that all three were on a Saturday morning. The last one didn't go according to plan, and the study of serial killers shows that once things start to go wrong they tend to escalate any programme they may have planned. I want to be as many steps ahead as is humanly possible. Let's be ready and let's get there before he stabs the next person to death.'

Martin left his team to get on with the task he had set them and made his way back to his office. What he wanted to do was take a brisk walk around Mermaid Quay and get some quality thinking time for himself, but one look through his office window soon pushed those thoughts away. The press were camped out on the doorstep and he knew that he would be the subject of their attention if he gave them half a chance.

He had heard the television news last night and had listened to his car radio on the way to work that morning. He was not the blue-eyed boy of a few months ago when he had solved the Coopers Field murder and uncovered some untimely deaths in a local nursing home. He had potentially saved dozens of lives by stopping a rogue doctor who was killing for the financial benefit of himself and the home owner.

The press had short memories and the news since Saturday had only spoken of tardy responses, incompetence, lacklustre performance, and issues of public confidence. Several of the newspapers had suggested that perhaps Phelps was past his sell-by-date and needed to be replaced. Martin was still one of the youngest DCIs in the country so the statement seemed to be aimed at his ability rather than his age.

It was an unpleasant and unfamiliar experience to be on the blunt end of these accusations and Martin knew that every member of his team was feeling the same hurt that he was. The killer would have been in his element if he could read Martin's mind at this moment. He had of course revelled in what the press was saying about the DCI – that part of his programme was going exactly according to plan.

Martin went through his tried and tested method of writing down the known facts of the case in one column and then writing second column where he ticked off one by one the facts that needed to be considered. They were all in the capable hands of his team. He concentrated his efforts on what was always his third and favourite column, headed 'What If'.

Today he hesitated over the page and then pondered, what if Helen's rainbow theory was correct? That would make the next colour green but from a personal point of view it was the colour that followed after green that scared him. Blue was the colour most people would give if you asked them for one they associated with the police force. Martin was sure that the killer would use that colour to target the boys in blue – and one in particular. What didn't fit for Martin was the fact that if the killer intended to kill him at that point what would be the significance of the indigo and violet deaths?

He sat and thought of the numerous criminals he had been party to bringing to justice during his career and wrote down the names of those that had particularly blamed him for their capture. Surely it had to be one of those people. It had to be someone who, if it were not for Martin's intervention, would still be doing whatever it was he had put a stop to – but who?

He crossed off two names because he knew that Sgt Evans hadn't been involved with either of the cases and was left with five seriously hard criminals. After making a few phone calls he crossed off four more names as the prison service had been able to confirm that the men he was asking about were still inside.

That left him with just one name, but Martin remembered that this man had hanged himself about six months ago. He had seen the grieving widow protesting her husband's innocence and blaming the prison for his death. What she hadn't mentioned was the fact that he had been caught red-handed bludgeoning to death a pensioner for the sake of £11, and that he would have got away with it if Martin hadn't persuaded two witnesses to testify.

So there were no names left on his list, and even though others were popping into his memory he put the paper back in his desk and went to see how the team was getting on. It had been a long day and although there had been some progress it was not good enough and he knew that unless he could come up with something in the next couple of days he would be seriously hung out to dry.

He praised his team for the work they had done and encouraged them not to feel despondent.

'It's almost seven o'clock,' he said. 'We have done as much as we can with the information at our disposal. Get home all of you, chill out, try to get a good night's sleep, and we'll all meet back here at 8.30 in the morning.'

No one needed second bidding and the room emptied quickly. Martin noticed a text message from Shelley asking him to text her when he was planning to leave the office. He did that.

She was leaning against the bonnet of his car and he caught sight of her before she noticed him. She wore a pair of cropped linen trousers and a long, pale blue cotton top, and with her hair tied back loosely she looked so young and carefree. He would not burden her with the worries of his day and he made her laugh with an appreciative wolf-whistle.

'Behave yourself,' she said, 'and come with me. If we walk away from the Quay and then turn back in a wide circle we'll miss running into the mob that's hanging around the side and front entrances. As long as they can see that your car is still in

194

the car park they'll assume you are still inside.'

She caught Martin's hand and pulled him in the direction she had suggested. Ten minutes later they were lost in the midst of the large numbers of people enjoying the temporary resurgence of summer. They found a bench and were sitting in companionable silence watching the boats, the birds, and the people when Shelley suddenly spoke. 'Those reporters don't know you. They don't know how hard you work. How dare they suggest you don't know what you are doing – how dare they?'

In spite of having similar feelings Martin laughed and kissed her on the tip of her nose.

'It's OK,' he said. 'It comes with the job. One minute you're the hero of the hour and the next minute you attract more pins than a voodoo doll. It will all go away once this killer is caught.' He hugged her and got tied up with the rucksack she had on her back.

Changing the subject he joked. 'What's with the backpack? Is it going to be a permanent feature? I know – you've discovered a way of avoiding having to pay the five-pence charge whenever you're out shopping and need a carrier bag. You are always going to wear one on your back.'

They both laughed. From where they were sitting they could see the Welsh Assembly government building, where the law relating to the payment for plastic bags in Wales had been passed. The exercise was part of an initiative to stop millions of bags ending up on landfill sites, and as the money for the sale of the bags had to be donated to charity it had been quite well accepted.

'No,' Shelley smiled. 'I enlisted the help of Iris to make us both a picnic and she insisted on putting it all into her granddaughter's backpack. Didn't you notice the Hello Kitty logo?'

'I thought it was a bit pink and girly for your taste, but never mind the outside – let's get a taste of what delights are inside.'

Martin took the bag from her and took out a container on which Iris had written *'Eat these first'*. They tucked into strips of toast topped with sardines that had been soaked in balsamic vinegar, and licked their fingers to show joint appreciation.

'They were good,' said Shelley. 'Simple but tasty, and they were certainly an appetite stimulator! What's next?'

Martin had already delved in, coming up with a couple of homemade meat and potato pasties and some thick slices of ham and cheese. 'What a lovely change – a picnic without a sandwich in sight. Iris has style!'

Although it had been a beautiful autumn day, it was nearing the end of September and approaching eight o'clock, and as so often happens at that time of the year the light suddenly faded. The sun had gone to bed and the lights from the bars and restaurants were starting to shine but they were unable to supply the same warm output and so the ambient temperature had dropped quite quickly.

'You warm enough?' asked Martin.

'I'm fine,' said Shelley, as she took the lid off the last container of the picnic and offered Martin a slice of lemon tart.

Ten minutes later, and with hardly a crumb left, they packed up and made their way back to Goleudy. 'Remind me to thank Iris in the morning,' said Martin. 'She's a lovely woman and a really good cook, and we are very lucky to have her.'

The interlude with Shelley, complemented by the culinary delights from Iris, had been just what Martin had needed but as they turned the corner that would take them back to the car park they received a sudden and unwelcome dose of reality. Without warning they were surrounded by reporters and microphones were being thrust into their faces from every direction.

'Taking time off from a triple murder enquiry, are we?' A man that Martin had never seen before shouted out the question. 'Must be pretty confident of a result – want to share the identity of the killer with us?'

Martin said nothing and with his arm around Shelley's waist he walked defiantly into the mob and guided her to the back entrance of the car park. Questions and open abuse followed them but he refused to rise to the bait and once inside the barrier of Goleudy car park he relaxed. The press would not pass that barrier without an invitation and Martin was not about to offer one.

'I'm so sorry about that,' he said. 'I should have realised that they would still be there. Presumably they were waiting for me to come out of the office as they didn't see me leave earlier. They'll put their own spin on how long I've been off enjoying myself while innocent members of the public go about in fear of their lives – but I'm way past caring what they say or print.'

Shelley responded. 'It's me who should be sorry, as I've probably made things worse for you.'

Martin lifted her chin so that she was looking directly up at him. 'You could never do that, you are the best thing that has ever happened to me.' He kissed her tenderly but the moment was ended abruptly as with the familiar sound of a camera and the sight of a flash they both realised that their kiss had been captured and would give the public even more reason to believe that DCI Phelps did not have his mind on the job.

They drove off in the direction of Shelley's home, but Shelley made him change direction. 'I want to be with you tonight,' she said. 'I need to make sure you are safe – I can't explain it, but don't argue with me, Martin, just drive to the cottage.'

Martin didn't argue. He had never felt less like wanting his own company, and falling asleep much later and with Shelley wrapped around him was just the comfort blanket he needed. He fell into a deep, dreamless sleep until he was aware of Shelley shaking him. Had he really slept the whole night without waking? It didn't feel like that.

'Come on, Martin, wake up. It's the second time your mobile has gone off. It was only at the end of the first call that I managed to gain consciousness but then the second one came almost immediately. I've answered it and Matt's on the line.'

Lifting his head from the pillow Martin took the phone.

'I won't beat about the bush,' said Matt. 'We've had a call from the Royal Mail and they have intercepted a green envelope addressed to you as the DCI, and intended to reach the cottage tomorrow morning.'

Chapter Fifteen

Martin had gone from the deepest of sleeps to being completely wide awake within nanoseconds, and even as he dressed he was recollecting the team's discussions of yesterday regarding possible locations for the next murder. If the killer had gone down his usual route of giving clues in verse they would hopefully be able to eliminate some of the suggestions and concentrate on the most likely places for the next planned murder. The killer wouldn't know that they had received his letter hours before he had anticipated. It was the best advantage they had achieved so far.

It was only 3.25 a.m., and the roads were quiet as he headed away from the coast, cutting ten minutes off the journey time to Goleudy despite dropping Shelley off en route. Helen Cook-Watts' car was already in the car park, but there was no sign yet of Matt, who had opted to personally pick up the letter from the sorting office.

Martin greeted Helen, who knew that something had been discovered but not what it was. 'It looks as if your rainbow theory is holding up,' he told her. 'The brilliant staff at the Royal Mail sorting office have discovered a letter addressed to me, and it's in a green envelope. So while we're waiting for Matt, let's have a look at some of the locations we considered yesterday that relate to the colour green. Let's get a supply of coffee sorted, because I suspect this is going to be a prolonged session.'

It was not that long since Helen had been a uniformed officer, and she knew all about working in Goleudy by night. Within a couple of minutes she had rustled up a kettle and some mugs, together with the ingredients for making some good strong coffee. Martin voiced his appreciation and had just taken the first mouthful when Matt joined them.

'Thought I could smell the coffee,' he said, handing the green envelope to Martin. 'I haven't opened it, but it looks exactly the same as the previous ones, and it's green, as Helen so cleverly anticipated.'

'So we can forget about the other colours we worked on yesterday – unless the evil bastard adds this murder to his tally and we have to move on to them.'

'That won't be on the cards,' said Martin. 'If we let him get away with this homicide it won't be "us" moving on.'

Matt raised an eyebrow and Martin continued. 'There are already issues between Superintendent Bryant and myself, and he will undoubtedly be getting flak from the top brass over the adverse publicity I'm attracting. Unless we can bring the killer in before his next murder I suspect we will all be replaced and a new team brought in.'

As he spoke, Martin remembered the photograph that had been taken in the car park last evening and shuddered at the thought of the kiss being published with a suitably vindictive caption. He would speak to the PR people as soon as they got in to see if, for Shelley's sake, he could prevent it being printed.

Martin checked the outside of the envelope. It was the same typeface, with a single stamp torn off a sheet. No doubt about the source, and the green sheet of paper inside was exactly what they had anticipated. Martin read out the poem.

That last one was a bloody mess
but still the job was done.
This time I'll use a different stroke
and get a hole in one.

The Greens are peaceful usually
but will not be today.
For somewhere on her final round
I'm going to make her pay.

No woman makes a fool of me
her story then to tell.
I'll show you how I deal with those
who make my life a hell.

You're just too honest Martin Phelps
to look the other way.
Without your questions I would be
a different man today.

'He *is* talking about a golf course as the location for his next planned murder,' said Helen. 'We got that right, and so we can forget about the Cathedral Green, the two pubs, and the Green Devil Tattoo shop.'

'Yes,' said Matt. 'But unfortunately, with it being a golf club, the location is still wide open. How can we possibly narrow it down to the one the killer plans to use?'

Helen came up with a suggestion. 'None of us are golfers, but when I went scrounging around for the coffee things I was helped out by PC Davies. He's a semi-pro, whatever that is, and a walking encyclopaedia when it comes to the rules of the game. Do you want me to give him a shout?'

'Yes, please,' replied Martin.

As Helen went in search of PC Davies, Matt drew Martin's attention to some additional work that had been done on the possibility of a green link to the actual club name. 'You remember my initial trawl came up with no results, but a closer look gave us four possibilities.'

'There's Greenmeadow somewhere in Cwmbran, and Greenway Valley near St Nicholas. Both these clubs actually have "green" in their name, and then we have two more tenuous links. The Llantrisant and Pontyclun club is in Talbot Green, and finally there's Bryn Meadows the other side of Caerphilly. Most people think of meadows as green areas, but I think that link is weak at best.'

Martin nodded, asking, 'What have we found out about the two main contenders?'

'Well, we know where they are, and I've visited their websites, but when we were looking at them last evening it was without the urgency of this latest poem.

'Some of the clubs have early bird tee off times, but even if they start at 7 a.m. there won't be anyone around for at least the next three hours. In any case, the killer talks about a round of golf today, so he's not going to be there until they open either.'

Helen returned with PC Brian Davies, who had been only too pleased to hand over his phone-manning duties and do something a bit more interesting.

'I understand you're a bit of a golfing aficionado,' said Martin. 'As none of the rest of us can identify our irons from our woods we could do with your help.'

PC Davies grinned. '"Aficionado" is not one of the words my wife uses, but if I can help I'll be happy to do so. What do you want to know?'

Martin thought for a moment and then posed his first question prefaced by an explanation. 'We think that this serial killer, the one the press keep calling the 'Bard', may be planning his next murder today, for one of the local golf courses. Would he have to be a member in order to book a game?'

PC Davies responded, shocked. 'Oh my good God, I've got a round booked myself this afternoon! Do you know what club? Sorry ... to answer your question, no, he wouldn't have to be a member. Even in the clubs where it is strictly "members only", there's the facility for paid-up members to invite a visitor to play with them. Different clubs have different rules but that's fairly general.

'Do you know who he's playing with? If he isn't a member then his partner would have to be. There are clubs that are open to non-members, but they tend to be used by less experienced players. Is he experienced? What's his handicap?'

PC Davies was asking as many questions as he was answering, but his knowledgeable questions were making his CID colleagues think outside the box.

'We know nothing about him as a golfer,' said Matt. 'Our

only image of him is as a killer.' He pointed out the image that was being used for identification purposes and PC Davies laughed.

'Well, he wouldn't be seen on any self-respecting golf course looking like that. Golfers do sometimes wear peaked hats, but that's very definitely a baseball cap, and would be frowned upon – as would his trainers. Another thing he would have to leave behind would be that canvas bag. Most clubs treasure their greens and don't appreciate people dumping any sort of random baggage around the place. Everything a golfer needs will have a place within the specifically designed golf bag. Dress and equipment codes are strictly enforced on the better golf courses.'

Martin remembered the Saturday of the first murder, when Superintendent Bryant had pitched up at the office in full golfing regalia, and could appreciate what PC Davies was saying.

'How would we find out who's arranged to play in any one of the clubs today?' Martin asked.

'Well, if you had the name of the killer or the person he plans to partner, you could simply ring around all the clubs and persuade them to tell you. If they were told it was part of a murder investigation I doubt there would be a problem.

'However if you just ask the clubs to give you a list of everyone who has a tee-off time booked today, I doubt they would be happy to oblige. Members don't always want other members and outside parties to know who they play golf with – it's not always played just for the sake of the game. There's a lot of business planned during a round of golf, and not all of it above board.'

'It's the lists we would need,' interrupted Matt. 'To compare them with a few other lists and hopefully come up with at least one common name.

'It will be a massive exercise anyway. We don't really know which golf course is in the killer's mind. We have two that we think might be possibilities but we can't take the chance of ruling out all the others. It could even be somewhere out of the area but the balance of probabilities is with it being around Cardiff.'

Martin changed tack and asked about timing. 'I guess there will be the possibility that other golfers will be in front and behind our killer. How does that work? How would it be possible for him to commit murder on the golf course without being seen?'

'Again, there are local variations,' said PC Davies, 'but in general we are allowed five minutes per person. So if a couple tee off at ten o'clock, it will be ten past ten before the next party follows. If there were four people in the next group they would be given a twenty-minute gap, and so half past before anyone followed them. That normally works but if a group is slow it can hold things up. Conversely, if golfers are cracking on they can get ahead and will have to wait for those in front.'

'OK,' said Martin. 'But what I'm really asking is, how much time would the killer have to stab his victim before being in the sights of the people coming behind?'

'Well, he couldn't really rely on any time at all, because he could never be sure that the following golfers weren't playing quickly – but maybe five minutes.' PC Davies looked at his watch and said there were things he should be doing before finishing his shift at 6 a.m.

Martin mentioned that five minutes was more than enough time for the killer to complete his handiwork and then thanked the constable for his input.

As PC Davies made his way toward the door he noticed the names of the two clubs that were the front runners. 'Now there you have two very different clubs,' he said. 'I have played in both, and was actually a member of the Greenway Valley club for about a year. The Greenmeadow is a smashing club that adheres to the spirit of golfing regulations but isn't bound up by them. Greenway Valley is a very different proposition, and in my view it's not for the serious golfer, more for the person who likes to be able to tell others that they play golf.

He winked. 'A lot of the great and the good are members there, including some of the top brass from within our own

204

organisation.'

With that comment he walked off and left Martin using a few expletives that he would not normally have used in front of Helen. 'Sorry,' he said. 'It would be just my luck to have this next murder on the superintendent's favourite golf course. Is it the one he uses?'

Matt and Helen shook their heads and confessed to not having a clue about the super and his little white balls.

'What do we do next?' asked Helen. 'It's still too early to be ringing around golf clubs, all calls would probably just go through to answerphones.'

'I agree,' said Martin. 'We need a strategy, so let's look at the list of all the clubs and find out their opening hours. Thank God the internet is a 24-hour system. We need an army of people to man the phones, and as each of them opens we need to get the names on their lists. I won't have any nonsense about members' rights to confidentiality – this is a murder enquiry and I will have anyone who doesn't cooperate arrested for obstruction.'

Extra pairs of hands and additional telephone lines were soon sorted and Incident Room One began to resemble a telephone exchange. As dawn broke, the numbers of all the golf clubs within a twenty-mile radius were being dialled and redialled way ahead of the clubs' advertised opening times. There was always a chance that one of the cleaners would answer the phone and be able to get a message to someone who could help. Gradually snippets of information were received and names provided for the all-important comparison.

Matt headed up that part of the operation, using the IT programme that Charlie had set up. The names of the boys that had been taught by the 'dragon' Miss Rossiter were on the system. There was the capability of cross-referencing them with the boys that had been scouts during Mr Davies' period as the perverted scoutmaster, and with owners of the relevant model of BMW. There was the list Martin had provided at an earlier point of the investigation, which included anyone he could think of who could know both his rank and his home address.

There could be names missing off any of the lists, and so even the names that appeared just twice were shortlisted.

What was missing, and would have been a great help, was the list of people known to Mr Taylor, and more particularly the name of the person Mrs Taylor had dumped in favour of her husband. That line of enquiry had so far drawn a complete blank, and it looked as if Mrs Taylor had disappeared off the face of the earth.

It crossed Martin's mind that she too had been killed and the body not yet found, but that simply didn't fit into the profile of the killer. It just wasn't his style to commit a crime and not brag about it.

No one knew how much time they had, but the sense of urgency was overwhelming. A few more lists dribbled through, and then just after 8 a.m. there was a flurry of activity as seven of the golf clubs responded in a group and hopes of a result were raised. But nothing matched and it was beginning to look as if all the golfers out this morning were women.

The clubs had been told that if one of their members was taking out a guest but there was no known name then that would need to be checked out by the police. They were given a description of the man the police were looking for. Over and over again the officers making and receiving calls were reminding club staff that on no account were they to confront any of the golfers. If they had doubts about anyone they were given a dedicated number to ring.

That number had already been called twice by 8.30, but the concerns of two clubs had been unfounded.

Martin was aware that they were putting a great number of people through a lot of anxiety, and that it wouldn't be long before someone told the media what was going on.

How much time did they have? Was the killer already on one of the fairways? Had the fourth victim already been stabbed? By 9.30 Martin himself was in a state of high anxiety, and realised that this was partly due to the thought of not being able to prevent this murder and also due to high levels of caffeine and lack of food. As if by magic the door opened and a

206

stainless steel trolley was pushed to the centre of the room. Iris guided the trolley with its offering of tea, orange juice, toast, preserves, croissants, cheese, and hard-boiled eggs.

She saw Martin's bemused look. 'It was Sgt Evans' idea,' she said. 'He suggested that as everyone up here was unlikely to have time to get to the canteen then maybe the service should come up here. It's paid for through the slush fund so I suggest you all help yourselves.'

Iris was concerned that her actions would be deemed inappropriate, as she was interrupting what even she could see was an intense operation. She needn't have worried, as her food was met by a spontaneous round of applause and eager hands were soon helping themselves to the offerings.

Martin thanked her and she made a quick exit, almost bumping into Sgt Evans as she left. Evans helped himself to toast and then took a small plate of food over to Martin.

'Here,' he said. 'Take this. Everyone in Goleudy knows the pressure you and the team are working under, but you'll be good for nothing if you don't eat. My brain only works if it gets regular fuel from my stomach.'

Martin took the food and in spite of himself enjoyed two large pieces of toast and some slices of cheese. He looked at the experienced sergeant and thought how much every organisation needed an Iris and a Sgt Evans. They were as vital to the smooth running of the service as the officers, the SOC people, the professors of pathology, and much more than the top brass.

Sgt Evans had already heard about the fourth poem and knew about the direction the colour green was taking Martin's team, but he was now reading all four verses for the first time. Although other readers had made a chilling mental note of the final verse, they had set it aside in favour of working on possible clues from the first three.

The final verse was the focus of Sgt Evans' attention and he read it over and over.

'You're just too honest, Martin Phelps,/ to look the other way./ Without your questions I would be/ a different man today.'

Evans was back with the feeling he had known since the first time he had seen the CCTV from the Red Dragon Centre and Martin noticed the intense look of concentration on the sergeant's face.

'It's got to be someone you've put away. Someone whose little empire you have tumbled. Or someone who's fallen foul of your determination to tell the truth and to shame the devil. The trouble is that over the years there have been so many people who tick those boxes. I instinctively want to go back a few years. I don't think this is someone that your current team will have had any dealings with – I think it will be one of your early collars. Possibly going back to the time when you cracked some spectacularly high-profile cases as a young detective sergeant – what do you think?'

Martin replied. 'I've not just racked my brains, I've been through all my old case notes, and there isn't one convicted criminal that matches this bastard's profile.'

Sgt Evans picked up the lists of names that Martin had just put on the table. At the same moment a PC came across with the latest set of names she had received from the golf clubs and announced with a sense of achievement that she had actually just managed to wake up the Greenway Valley club and get their bookings for the day.

Martin and the sergeant read the list and their eyes simultaneously rested on a name that was known to both of them. The name had never reached the shortlist because it hadn't appeared on at least two of the other lists. Martin asked Matt for the full list of pupils and scouts, and the name reappeared amongst the names of Miss Rossiter's pupils.

Sgt Evans stared at Martin. 'I would like to say it can't possibly be him – but it bloody well is – it bloody well is!'

Chapter Sixteen

The killer woke from a restless sleep and calmed his nerves by arranging and rearranging the envelopes and lengths of coloured cord on his kitchen table. He had spent all of Monday fine-tuning the timescale for his final three murders, and the blue, indigo, and violet envelopes were already addressed and stamped. With his usual degree of arrogance he was assuming that today's murder was already in the bag – it was certainly well prepared in his mind.

As always, it was the blue envelope that held the most sinister fascination for him, and he was tempted to open it and read yet again the words of that particular poem. He didn't really need to as he knew that one off by heart. How he wished he could be watching Martin Phelps when he read about the fate the killer had in store for him. He had relished rhyming 'booted out' with 'Shelley's doubt'. The suggestion that the DCI's precious organisation and his lover could both dump him would take Martin Phelps to the depths of despair – just where Phelps had put the killer.

During his original planning phase the killer had considered it would be futile to send the last two envelopes to Martin's home address, because dead men don't get mail delivered. However it would be another twist of the knife, both for the Phelps' team and Shelley Edwards to be told, even after his death, that their hero was worthless and that the killer had won.

He showered and shaved with more care and attention than he had taken for a very long time, and as he dressed there was no sign of his killing uniform. Today he would be immaculately turned out and just the sort of visitor any well-established golf course would want to receive. He still wore a wide-brimmed black hat, but this one was different. From the tips of his two-tone coloured shoes to the Galvin Green logo on his hat, he looked every inch the gentleman golfer.

He checked his image in the mirror and compared it with the pictures of him, as the killer, that were being circulated. Not even his own mother would have considered the two to be the same person – but then his own mother wouldn't know him anyway, not even if she was still alive to see him.

The bitch had left him in the dubious care of his father when he was just six and later in life he had used his contacts to track her down. Unfortunately he hadn't discovered her alive, because she had been killed in a house fire. The killer wasn't sorry she had died – just sorry that she hadn't lived long enough to be his first victim.

Picking up his golf bag he checked the contents. Yes, he was keen to ensure he had the required number and variety of clubs, but of particular interest to him was the contents of the deep front pocket. He practised, once again, removing the knife from this section of the bag. He couldn't remember how many times he had practised it but the movement was now as fluid as he had anticipated.

He had threatened to use a gun on Mr Taylor and he opened a drawer in the table and stared at his second choice of weapon. No, Connie was a woman, and although she kept herself in shape she would be no match for his physical strength. He would stick with plan A and stare her in the face as he thrust the knife towards her heart. The very thought of it made his own heart beat faster, and he looked at his watch to check on the time that was moving far too slowly for his liking.

He had asked Connie to book them in for the first available tee-off time and he had checked with the club to ensure she had done so. The receptionist had told him that they would be the second pair to tee off, as Tuesday was busier than usual and the second slot was only available because some others had pulled out. 'Typical of the despicable woman,' the killer said to himself, and was about to slag her off for not letting him know, when he remembered that he had blocked his number when he had phoned her.

Just so long as she turned up. He could of course carry out his threats to expose her drug habit to her friends and her new man but that was not what he wanted to do. He looked forward to the thrill of seeing the abject fear in her eyes, and then watching as her lifeblood drained from her and that wretched voice was silenced for ever.

It was with a strange, almost detached, interest that the killer realised the extent to which, with every killing, his enjoyment of the act was increasing and he was particularly revelling in the planning. The anticipation of the stabbing was almost better than its realisation – but not quite.

He heard a car pull up and was pleased that the taxi driver was on time. The BMW was going nowhere and he had rated the risk of hiring a car as being too great. A taxi would be fine: after all, the driver was not transporting a killer, just taking a perfectly respectable member of the public for a game of golf. Nothing sinister about that.

The Greenway Valley Golf Club was not one of those catered for serious early morning golfers. The membership was more of the social golfing and 'nineteenth hole' varieties, and in keeping with the needs of the members the first tee-off was never before 10 a.m. unless there was some sort of competition booked. Consequently the killer now knew that he and Connie were booked for ten past ten, but it was only nine thirty when the taxi set him down.

This had been his own club and he knew his way around. There were things he had to do. He made his way to the reception and watched one of the cleaners polishing the desk and tidying the magazines. She had been with the club for years and she recognised the man who walked towards her.

He smiled warmly as he approached and remarked on the beauty of the weather and complimented her on the job she was doing.

She smiled back. 'You're a bit early, sir, the receptionist doesn't usually get here until about 9.45.'

211

He nodded. 'Yes, I know that, I just want to check my booking – I think my partner has got the time wrong.'

He prayed that the woman wouldn't be one of the jobsworths who guarded the receptionist's books with her life. He needn't have worried, as she had already forgotten he was even there and was frantically polishing the front door handle.

So far, so good, and he took the opportunity of discovering who was booked to tee off after him. He had planned to draw a line through their names and facilitate a delaying tactic for when they tried to book in but he was given a better opportunity to not only delay but stop the next group of four being a worry to him.

He recognised two of the names and especially the lead for that party, Gerald Ashton. A phone call to a directory enquiries service gave him the information he needed, and he rang the number.

Sounding remarkably like the nice man from the garden centre who had given the news of the competition win he spoke this time of some bad news regarding Mr Ashton's planned golf round.

'It's quite unbelievable, sir,' he said. 'We've never been troubled by moles before, but at least two of the greens have developed what looks like a bad case of hives. There are bumps all over the place, and we've got experts here at the moment trying to sort things out.'

The killer was nearly blown off the phone by the force of the reply. 'What in the name of hell are you rambling on about? I don't pay your extortionate annual membership charges, and green fees on top, to be told a session with three business associates is cancelled at such short notice. Get someone to flatten the bumps – bloody hell, it can't be that difficult!'

Taking a deep breath the killer responded. 'If it was that simple, sir, we certainly would not have bothered you this morning, but our experts tell us that we need to kill the little blighters that are causing the problem. We're doing that now. We will ring you as soon as we are able to offer you something, but as for this morning I am afraid it is impossible for you to play.'

'Who the hell are you anyway?' asked Gerald. 'I don't recognise your voice.'

'I've been called in to help with the extermination of these undesirable creatures, and now if you'll excuse me, sir, I'll get on with the job.'

The phone call had amused the killer, and as he strode off to decide on the best of the eighteen holes for his mission his marching step was more pronounced than usual.

Connie arrived at eight minutes past ten, just as the killer was beginning to think that she had bottled out. She drove her black and white sports car much too fast and her tyres screeched on the surface of the car park as she came to a halt.

She was still a head-turner, but today she looked drawn and anxious. The killer was highly amused to see that she was wearing green cotton trousers and a pale green linen jacket. The green cord he had in his own jacket pocket would match the ensemble perfectly – life was playing jokes on people this morning and this time he was not the butt of the jokes.

He stepped from the doorway of the reception area as she got out of the car and he went forward to meet her. It looked as if he was going to greet her with a kiss, and so she sidestepped him and went straight to the reception desk.

Her avoidance tactics had not gone unnoticed, but the killer would get her for that, along with everything else, later.

Connie signed them in, and when doing so was pleased to notice that the group following behind them was being led by Gerald Ashton. 'Good,' she told herself. 'If this creep gives me any trouble it will be good to know that Gerald and his cronies are just ten minutes behind us.'

To any intelligent observer the couple would have presented a strange sight. They walked some distance apart, and no words were spoken between them until, as they arrived at the first tee, the killer said mockingly, 'Ladies first,' and Connie took her first swing.

The first hole saw them both take five shots to complete a par four and they moved to the second tee without speaking.

They stayed neck and neck for the next two holes, and it was not until Connie sliced her tee shot at the fourth that she broke the silence. 'OK, what is all this about? You didn't bring me here just to play golf – what exactly do you want?'

The killer didn't answer but took his tee shot, which was straight and took him very close to the green. He smiled. His day was getting better and better.

Connie was a good golfer and decided that if he was not going to talk then she would give this game her best effort and beat him. Accordingly she rescued her first rogue shot, and her second one for the par three hole took her to the edge of the green. It was unlikely that she would reach the hole with her next shot but she would have a damned good try.

He lifted his second shot onto the green within easy putting distance of the hole and then tapped the ball in before standing to one side to watch Connie try to match his par score. She concentrated with every fibre of her being and stroked the ball with her favourite putter. She knew the lie of the greens well and, although it initially looked as if she would miss, the slight slope turned her ball towards the hole and it dropped in.

As the ball disappeared so did the killer's upbeat mood. They had been playing for half an hour and there was no sign of the players that had started ten minutes ahead of them. Connie wasn't surprised by that, because she had recognised their names in the book and knew them to be two women whose idea of a game was to get it finished as quickly as possible and get back to the club house for a proper gossip.

What did surprise her was that she had not seen any sign of Gerald and his party, nor had she heard them coming up behind. On at least three occasions she had been one of his group and the rounds had always been raucous affairs. They were certainly quiet today.

The next two holes saw Connie move into a definite lead, and the more she improved her swing the more the killer's mood swung into a hole blacker than any of those being found by Connie's golf ball. He looked around. As far as the eye could see were rolling hills and beautiful countryside, but they didn't even register in his mind. All he wanted to see was the continued absence of other people.

Connie was becoming aware that her success over the past three holes was making her partner very angry and she decided to change her tactics. So far she had not indulged in conversation with the man, so she was no further forward in finding out what he really wanted. She had to do this. She had to find out if her future with Roberto was in jeopardy.

'Look, there's no point in us pussyfooting around, I just don't know what you want from me. We had a couple of dates but that was a few years ago and it didn't work out, did it? I'm with someone now, in fact we got engaged yesterday, so there's no possibility of us getting involved. You can see that – can't you?'

If Connie had expected a measured response from her partner she couldn't have been more wrong.

'What do you mean it didn't fucking *work out*? You made it your business to ensure it didn't fucking work out. You told everyone I was rubbish. You told them I was as hopeless on the golf course as I was in bed – words to that fucking effect.'

Connie felt scared. It had not escaped her notice that there was no sign of life anywhere on the golf course and that was really strange. They had slowed down quite a bit and she could have expected at least one following party to be on their tail by now. Where was everybody?

She tried to pacify her partner. 'I didn't say that, how could I have said that? We didn't have that sort of relationship. We had never been lovers.'

The killer responded angrily. 'No, I was never good enough, was I? Not that you've ever been choosy. There are very few male members you haven't slept with, and possibly some of the women too; you'd be happy with that provided your brain was stuffed with cocaine. What's more, most of them know what a crackhead you are. I don't know why you're so worried about me telling them – they already know.'

The killer was spitting out his words and Connie thought he was going to have a fit but even though she was truly terrified

215

his words had given her some courage. 'Well, if everyone knows, then I agree – there is no point in me jumping through hoops to prevent you telling Roberto. Either he already knows and isn't too bothered, or he's going to find out anyway.'

Connie summoned up all her nerve and, turning her back on her partner, started to walk back towards the club reception building, hoping it wouldn't be too long before Gerald and his party appeared.

She knew instinctively that the killer was behind her and she hadn't walked more than two steps before his arm circled her neck and pulled her backwards. The first thing she saw was a length of green cord, though she didn't realise the significance of it at first. The full details of the killer's use of colours hadn't been released to the press, but Connie had been following the recent activities of a serial killer and a few things seemed to fit.

She could imagine the man who had just attacked her in the clothes the television had shown – he was exactly the right build – and then there was the walk. One television presenter had suggested that the man could have been in one of the forces. Her partner walked exactly like that and now she was truly petrified and began to cry.

'Don't waste your fucking tears on me,' he spat. 'I'm the victim here, not you.'

He had seen the look of abject fear in her eyes, just as he had planned, and so now was the moment to watch her bleed to death. For some reason, though, the killer wasn't satisfied with letting her die without some more punishment. He thought that maybe she didn't realise yet that she was going to die. Maybe she just thought he was going to knock her about a bit. Well, that wasn't good enough, so he decided on the best way he knew to make her physically sick with fear.

'Got an inkling of who I might be, have we?' he teased. 'Well, let me put your mind at rest before I help your body to follow it – permanently!'

Connie felt in serious danger of losing control over her bodily functions, and in some bizarre way it was concentrating on not letting that happen that held her together. The killer seemed to be rambling on and Connie wasn't really sure if he was talking to her or offering up his words for some sort of judgement.

'Let me tell you a story of a boy who was abandoned by his mother, ridiculed by his teacher, and raped by his scoutmaster. Can you imagine how all that made him feel? There was never a single moment when he had any feeling of self-worth.

'He taught himself to hate back and it worked well. He learned to use and manipulate people in the way he had been used, and as he got older he became more adept at lying and bullying became a way of life. Most people are wimps, you know, and their biggest problem is that they like to be liked. Threaten them with anything that will tarnish their reputation and they will do anything for you.'

Connie didn't move a muscle. She knew that her partner was talking about himself but while he was talking he wasn't killing so she let him continue.

During the next couple of sentences he changed the subject from some anonymous person and began speaking in the first person. He wasn't making much sense to Connie as he moved through the various phases of his life and laid blame at the door of a number of people.

'I couldn't let them all get away with it,' he said. 'I am better than all of them. Everyone I worked with said I was the best – I even won awards.'

Connie strained her ears to see if she could hear someone – anyone – she had never known the place be so deserted. Someone called Martin Phelps was getting the sharp end of the killer's tongue and at first Connie didn't know who he was talking about. Then she remembered seeing a Detective Chief Inspector Phelps on the television saying he would find the killer and bring him to justice. Now would be a good time, DCI Phelps, she thought.

Connie shifted her position and in doing so caused the killer to regain his focus on her. He was pleased to witness her distress. He still had his arm around her neck and he forced her to her knees. The green cord that she had noticed earlier was wrapped around one of his fingers and he dangled it in Connie's face.

'Know the significance of this?' he taunted. 'This is you, reduced to a colour in a murder investigation. I was always fascinated by rainbows – always looking for my pot of gold – but like everything else in life they turned out to be just illusions of something perfect. I've changed their beautiful colours into pieces of death. There are plenty of people now who will never again look at a rainbow as a thing of beauty – just as the colours of killing.

'She said my poems were stupid and he said I was useless and couldn't even tie a reef knot. Let me show you how well I tie a reef knot – especially when securing the wrists of the person I'm about to stab to death.'

He pushed Connie forward and roughly pulled both her hands behind her back – and secured her wrists with his best reef knot yet.

No longer able to control herself, Connie screamed, but her mouth was clamped as the killer's hand covered it and she smelled the leather of his golf gloves before passing out.

This wasn't part of the plan and he was not going to be robbed of the thrill of seeing her fight for oxygen as her blood supply diminished. He pulled her back to her feet and shook her as he watched her eyes partly open and then roll helplessly around her eye sockets before settling down. She didn't want to open her eyes and she was half-hoping that she was already dead.

'Look at me,' he instructed. 'Look at me!'

Connie did as she was directed and stared into his eyes. If eyes are the window to the soul then she could only think that his soul had already been sold to the devil. She had never before seen anything that uncompromisingly evil. She shuddered and he laughed.

'Getting the message, are we? Good. I didn't want you to go without understanding why I have to do this. Let me tell you what will happen.'

Connie didn't want to know and closed her eyes again but he

218

demanded she keep them open. 'In my golf bag is a long sharp knife. I am going to thrust it into your pretty little belly and aim for the heart I know you haven't got.

'I will then sit with you quietly as you die of shock and internal bleeding, and this time I'll be able to stab you in the back in the way I always intended to with the others.

'They all stabbed me in the back, but for one reason or another I only managed to get at their necks – I messed that bit up, but with you it will be different.'

Connie was completely helpless and the killer seemed to be strengthening his grip around her neck, making her think he had changed his mind about the method of killing and was about to strangle her.

He pushed her forward in the direction of his golf bag and he opened the front pocket and she saw something that glinted in the sunlight. Already tortured beyond belief she had now closed her eyes tightly and was waiting to be killed – so why was nothing happening?

Chapter Seventeen

Having given orders to everyone regarding the way in which the operation was to be handled Martin drove with Sgt Evans in one of the squad cars to the Greenway Valley Golf Club. Armed officers were on their way, but Martin had made it clear that he wanted no action without his say-so. This operation would end with the capture of the killer either dead or alive, and hopefully before he had killed his latest victim – a woman whom they now knew to be Connie Jackson.

The club told them that Connie had booked in a guest that met the description they had been given, and that the pair had teed off at 10.10. Martin asked how many other golfers were actually on the course at the moment. They said that they had been expecting a party for the 10.20 slot, but no one had turned up and they were unable to offer any rational explanation for that. The receptionist told Martin that when she had rung Mr Gerald Ashton to find out why he and his party had not turned up, he had given her some incredible story about being contacted by the club regarding the course being out of action because of an infestation of moles. She went on to say that members were always coming up with excuses not to pay the late cancellation fees but this one was the best yet. Two other pairs had signed in within the past ten minutes so they were probably no further than the second hole.

Martin had no doubt that the Ashton group had received that phone call, but not from the club – it was the killer's way of gaining an extra twenty minutes' time alone with Connie Jackson. This was not his usual way of going about his business. He was not hiding his identity, and both the receptionist and the cleaner could describe him. More than that – they actually knew the man who had accompanied Connie Jackson to the first tee.

Sgt Evans took less than twenty minutes to reach the short lane leading to the entrance of the golf course but it had given him and Martin time to discuss the killer – time to discuss someone they both knew – time to discuss ex-Detective Chief Inspector Norman Austin.

Martin had opened the conversation. 'I personally detested working with the man, but I valued his skills as a detective – he always seemed to be able to find clues where others had failed.'

Sgt Evans stopped him and spoke much more sharply than usual. 'You were young and inexperienced when you joined us from Swansea, and yes, you were already a sergeant but CID was a new area for you. From the beginning I knew you were going to be good and from the beginning Austin resented your logical questioning approach. You said he was able to find clues – well I would say he was able to plant clues. He would do anything to get results, and although I couldn't prove it I took the risk of reporting something I thought he had done.

'You'll remember the prostitutes that were being murdered in the city centre – four in all and over a long period. The first one would have been killed about six months after you came to Cardiff and the other three during the next year. There was no real pattern, but they were all working on the streets around the Central bus station and all had their throats cut.'

Martin nodded. It was one of the things he would never forget and even now if he thought about it he could see the pathetic bodies of those women. During the course of that investigation he had spoken to many of the city's prostitutes, and had received a stark lesson in how not to prejudge the various groups of society. Some of those women had been amongst the most generous and caring people he had ever met.

John Evans continued. 'Austin was under a lot of pressure to bring in the killer and make the streets safe, and after the fourth woman was butchered he had us all running around like headless chickens.'

'I remember it well, John,' said Martin. 'I particularly remember being very surprised when my two weeks' leave wasn't cancelled.'

John responded. 'It wasn't cancelled because Austin wanted you out of the way. He could manipulate the other officers in his team but you always asked the difficult questions and had to see things for yourself. I don't think you realise, Martin, how much of a threat you were to that bastard's empire. He had all sorts of people in his pocket. He had the makings of a really great detective but he was and obviously still is rotten to the core.'

Martin agreed and added. 'But he did solve that case, and the killer was convicted of the four murders – it was all done and dusted before I came back from leave. Vincent Bowen, who had mental health problems, was seen in the vicinity of the crime scene at the time of the third murder, and a bloodstained knife with his fingerprints on it was recovered from his room. He lived in one of those "care in the community" accommodation units.'

'I'm very well aware of that,' said John. 'I was younger then, but I still had lots of experience as a sergeant and I was one of the officers involved with the initial search of Vincent's room. There was no knife found.'

'What do you mean?' asked Martin.

'Exactly that – not only was there no knife but one of the other residents told me that Vincent had been with him on the night of the fourth murder. He said they had bought a couple of cans from the shop and watched telly.'

Sgt Evans took a deep breath. 'When Vincent was arrested I asked where the knife had been found and was told it was hidden under the sink. I challenged that because I had looked in that area but was made to look an idiot for missing such an important piece of evidence.' He momentarily took his eyes off the road and glanced sideways at Martin. 'That knife was never there!'

'Why didn't you take your concerns to a higher level?' asked Martin quietly.

'Oh, I did,' was the reply. 'You will remember that Superintendent Bryant was appointed the very week the arrest was made, and for him it was a heaven-sent opportunity to gain himself some early positive publicity. He listened to me, but Austin persuaded him that the knife had been well hidden and that I, not being a detective, had overlooked it – but I can assure you, it was never there.'

'What about Vincent's alibi?' asked Martin. 'I went to the trial and I don't remember hearing anything about someone being able to vouch for his whereabouts at the time of one of the murders.'

Sgt Evans replied. 'He was considered to be an unreliable witness because he was on high doses of medication, but he was perfectly lucid when I spoke to him.'

'What are you saying?' prompted Martin. 'Is it that Austin planted a knife stained with the victim's blood and with Vincent Bowen's fingerprints on it – *and* silenced a potential alibi? What about the SOC team, where were they?'

John grimaced. 'You're getting today's excellent team headed by Alex Griffiths confused with a very different setup back there. They were all drinking buddies – you must remember – there was a group of them including a number of CID officers. There wasn't one of us uniformed officers that had any respect for CID at that time, and there were a few of my own colleagues who were more than a little intimidated by Austin. We lost several potentially good officers, and I remember you asking questions at the time that didn't go down well with your boss.'

Martin also remembered. It had not been the start to his CID career that he had envisaged, but he still couldn't deny the investigative brain of the then-DCI Austin.

'Do you know what happened to him?' asked Sgt Evans.

'Yes,' said Martin. 'He went up north to establish a criminal investigation unit but he was never on my Christmas card list so I didn't keep in touch.'

'Wrong,' replied the sergeant. 'He was arrested for the harassment and assault of his ex-girlfriend's husband.

Apparently, when the arrest was made he went ballistic and three officers were injured. By some means or other the powers that be kept the incident out of the public eye and dealt with the whole thing via the force's internal disciplinary processes. Anyway, his career was finished and I guess he's now taken his revenge on Mr Taylor. The yellow poem tells that story.'

'I can't get my head around it,' said Martin. 'True, I hated the man as a person – his attitude towards women wouldn't be tolerated now, and even then he was lucky to get away with it. There were times when I should have challenged the way he treated suspects, and even colleagues, but you tend to get carried along with simply getting the job done.'

Sgt Evans interrupted. 'The man wasn't stupid and he knew who was corruptible. He wouldn't have tried to get you on side, you were far from his idea of a perfect junior. He hid most of his activities from you, and if you think back you'll start to remember little things, things that have been worrying me for years.

'You asked far more questions than was good for you and from day one you were a real pain in his arse. He probably blames you for the fact that he isn't the commissioner now. He always had someone to blame. Nothing he ever did was wrong and if anyone ever crossed him he would make their life a living hell. Talk about harbouring grudges – he positively nurtured them.'

Martin had never heard the good-natured sergeant talk so bitterly about anyone and he thought back on what he had said. 'Whatever the outcome of this current situation, I can assure you that I will make it my business to get the case of Vincent Bowen re-opened. If Superintendent Bryant doesn't like it he can lump it. I hate to think that Vincent has spent years being punished for something he didn't do.'

'On the other hand, the killings did stop after his arrest so possibly they did get the right man even if the method was flawed.' Sgt Evans pointed out.

'The method wasn't "flawed",' said Martin. 'From your description of things it was in itself criminal. The other thing is that the following year several similar crimes were committed in Bristol, so perhaps the real killer crossed the Severn Bridge.'

They were seeing a number of other police vehicles heading in the same direction as them, but as instructed all were keeping a low key – no sirens or flashing blue lights, just a general sense of urgency.

'It's no wonder we both had a feeling of knowing this killer from the outset, but of course we were looking at criminal links, not at one of our own. Although he is no longer a police officer it will be that element of his life that will interest the press.' Martin frowned. 'They will jump off the back of one incompetent officer, namely me, and onto the all-too-familiar issue of bad apples within the force.'

'What sort of upbringing do you think he had?' asked Sgt Evans. 'If he murdered his teacher and then his scoutmaster one has to assume that they did something really bad.'

Martin replied. 'We may never know exactly what they did, but at least as far as Mr Davies is concerned there are very powerful rumours regarding his abuse of some of the boys in his care. If Austin was abused by him then I have a certain sympathy – I think I would want to murder someone if I was put in that position.'

'Yes, but wanting to murder someone and actually doing it are two different things. He could have used the legal system when he was a DCI, and knowing his methods of working I am sure he would have persuaded others to testify.' Sgt Evans thought for a moment, then shook his head and added. 'But that wouldn't have suited him. If he had admitted to being abused he would have presented himself as a victim, and although it looks as if he felt that way inside it would not fit the image of a macho man that he proclaimed himself to be.'

When they were less than five minutes away from the club Martin asked Sgt Evans how he thought Austin would react to being trapped.

Evans responded immediately. 'It's something I have been thinking about while we've been talking, and my guess is he won't want to be caught because that would be the biggest failure of all. I think he would rather die than go to jail – we both know how he'd be received there.'

Martin nodded. 'Do you think he would kill himself?'

An emphatic answer came from the sergeant. 'No. I think he may have plans to kill himself if it looks as if he's going to be caught, but from what I know of the man I would say he wouldn't be able to harm himself if it came to the crunch. He would probably like us to do that for him.'

Martin voiced something he had been turning over in his mind. 'In one of his poems he makes reference to a gun. Do you think he would use one, John?'

'If he has a gun with him and he's cornered, he will use it, and he was one of CID's top marksmen so he'll use it effectively.'

Sgt Evans turned the squad car into the car park and parked alongside three others and a number of unmarked police vehicles. Although there were now in excess of thirty officers on the scene there was an uncanny air of silence.

Martin spoke to the head of the Armed Response Unit. He knew Keith Patterson quite well and was pleased to see him. Keith was not one of the gung-ho brigade; he was known for his calm and patient approach to hostage situations and this was how Martin wanted this one treated.

He briefed Keith and his team. 'Somewhere on the course, probably around the halfway mark, we have a known killer and a woman who may already have been murdered. If he has not yet killed her and the killer sees that we are on to him, he is likely to use her as a human shield to get away himself. There's one thing I must tell you, Keith, and that is that you will know the killer when you see him.'

Keith raised an eyebrow and Martin continued. 'He was a DCI some years ago and may well have practised his gun skills with you – it's Norman Austin.'

The colour drained from Keith's cheeks and he swore under his breath before asking the obvious question. 'Has he got a gun?'

'We have no idea,' said Martin. 'A knife has been his

weapon of choice so far, but he did threaten to use a gun on one occasion.'

'If he has a gun, I don't relish our chances – he scored better than me lots of times in practice sessions, he's really good. Still, there are all of us with our guns, and at least he'll only have one. How do you want to play this?'

'We know there are three more pairs of golfers on the course, and the first thing we want to do is bring them in safely, so I'll get some officers to do that if you can ensure they are covered. The officers are being kitted out in golfing dress so they will be less conspicuous; in fact they're just coming out now, so we can move on the first part of the plan. The first pair of golfers is likely to be some way ahead, so they should be approached by walking from the eighteenth hole backwards over the course. I don't think they are in any danger but if things kick off I don't want any members of the public around.'

Keith nodded and directed one of the officers plus one of his team to the eighteenth hole.

'The other two pairs are my biggest concern,' said Martin. 'We don't know exactly where Austin and the woman are but there is the potential that the others could catch up with them and with dire consequences.'

Keith tasked two more of his team with the job of finding the other four golfers before they reached the killer. He then turned to Martin for his permission to go further with his plan.

'We've got maps of the course, so we know the spots that will give us cover, and I suggest we try to find exactly where Austin as soon as possible.'

He handed Martin a small piece of electronic equipment. 'These things are less noisy than mobile phones,' he said. 'I will keep you informed of progress at every step of the way.'

Martin took the gadget but protested. 'I would prefer to be alongside you, not just waiting here when we could be preventing a murder.'

'Look, Martin,' Keith said rather impatiently. 'This is our part of the job – when did you last crawl around on your belly and read the terrain like a terrorist?'

Martin gave a wry smile and resigned himself to watching the armed response team in a scene that was more like a film than reality. They wore camouflage clothing and merged with the trees and bushes so that even he found it hard to spot them and he was looking and listening.

He overheard a bit of a commotion as the two women who had reached the sixteenth hole were protesting loudly that their round had been disrupted. 'Shut those women up,' said Martin. 'Get them inside and shut them up – arrest them if you have to – just shut them up.'

The thought of being arrested must have been what did it as not another word was spoken and once again there was silence.

Martin's gadget vibrated and he listened as Keith spoke quietly but distinctly. 'Any moment now you should see some people walking towards you. They are the two pairs of golfers and our officers so we have no more members of the public on the golf course. Austin has been sighted at the ninth hole and two of the people who are walking towards you were caught up with as they went towards the tee for the eighth. A near thing!'

'Is there any sign of the woman – of Connie Jackson?' asked Martin.

'Yes,' was the reply. 'Austin's pacing around and I'd say he looks extremely unstable. He has his arm around her neck and appears to be talking to her. Some of my lot are approaching from a different angle so we'll get a better picture soon. I'll let you know as soon as we do.'

Martin moved to where Matt and Helen were standing, having dealt with the golfers coming off the course, and Matt took the chance to speak to him.

'We got a call on our way here from Barry Police Station. Apparently Mrs Taylor called in there this morning to report her husband missing. We got the officer to ask her a series of questions and she confirmed that when she had first met her husband she had been in a relationship with Norman Austin. She also told them that some years ago her husband had been brutally attacked by Austin, but the police had hushed it up.

'That's why she apparently has no faith in the police and

hadn't summoned up the courage to report her husband missing until this morning. The poor woman is obviously distraught so she may be rambling but they are sending a family liaison officer home with her and awaiting our instructions.'

Martin responded. 'The poor woman may well be distraught, but what she said about the attack on her husband did, according to Sgt Evans, happen in the way she describes.'

Once again Martin's handset vibrated and he heard Keith's voice. 'We've had a better sighting of the woman and I can tell you that he has tied her hands behind her back –'

'With green cord,' continued Martin. Keith was about to speak but Martin got in first. 'Is she injured?'

'We have telescopic lenses, so we're able to see her very clearly. She looks terrified but as far as we can see she is not injured. Austin looks like he's completely lost the plot.'

'Direct me on the best way to approach without being seen,' said Martin. 'We're going to have to take some action, and we must retain the element of surprise.'

'Stay where you are,' said Keith. 'I'll come and escort you in and I suggest no more than two officers come with you, we really can't risk involving any more.'

Matt and Helen had overheard the message and both volunteered immediately. Martin hesitated, remembering that the last time he and Matt had faced a knife-wielding criminal Matt had almost lost his life. But Matt was the most senior officer and would be expecting to accompany Martin.

This was the first time since Helen had joined CID that she was volunteering for a potentially dangerous mission, and Martin knew he couldn't exclude her just because she was a young woman. He was saved from having to make the decision to take her by Sgt Evans. 'As I know this man better than anyone else here I think it'd be a good idea if I was the third officer. You don't mind, do you, Helen? It makes sense.'

Sgt Evans had supported Helen when she was a PC and she valued his opinion and experience. She was disappointed not to be going into the thick of the action but nodded her approval.

'Take care, all of you,' she said as she watched the three

men walking towards where Keith was just coming into view. 'You've all got your stab vests, haven't you?'

'Yes, Mum,' called back Sgt Evans.

Keith gave them a bit more news as they followed him to a point where they could see where members of the armed response team had taken up positions, some crouched low, some lying in the rough, and some standing behind trees. It looked surreal.

'The woman's very much alive and she looks amazingly calm for someone in her position. I can't figure out at all what he intends doing. He's pulled his golf bag towards the woman a few times as if he has something in mind but then nothing happens.'

'We have to do something now,' said Martin. 'For his last three murders he's used a long sharp knife and we have CCTV images of him killing a woman in far less time than it would take us to get to him now.'

Keith tried to give some reassurance. 'He's under the closest of scrutiny, and if he went for her with a knife one of our snipers would take him out. We probably wouldn't kill him but he would be minus a few fingers.'

'But would that be before or after Connie Jackson was minus her life? No, waiting is not an option; we have to make the first move and be prepared for the consequences. Pass me the speaker, please.'

Keith signalled to all his men that primary action was the preferred way forward, and they all trained their weapons on the killer. Martin moved the switch to 'on' before holding the speaker to his mouth and shouting.

'Norman Austin, this is Detective Chief Inspector Martin Phelps, and I have to tell you that you are surrounded by members of the armed response team who will shoot if you make any attempt to harm Ms Jackson. Please raise your left arm slowly if you understand what I am saying.'

Austin looked for a moment as if he was responding as he started to raise his arm but then he executed a well-practised movement and the knife was no longer in his golf bag but at the throat of Connie Jackson. One bullet had already been fired, but Keith instantly gave an order for no further rounds to be used – there was too much of a chance that Connie would be shot by friendly fire.

'We wounded him,' said Keith. 'Look, you can see blood dripping down his arm – it looks like a shoulder injury, but unfortunately I don't think it will be fatal.'

He handed Martin the binoculars he was using, and as Martin focused them he found himself staring straight into the eyes of Norman Austin. For a moment he jumped because it really did seem as if Austin was just an inch away, but then he used the enhanced vision to check on Connie Jackson and the specific position of her body in relation to Austin.

Austin was gripping his shoulder and pressing the tip of his knife to her skin. He was content that she was between him and the line of fire, and the officers would know that one false move from them and he would finish her off. Not that he wanted to do that, because she was his only way out of there.

'I think he's been hurt more than we first thought,' said Martin, but then changed his mind as Austin's voice boomed out over the fairways. 'Long time, no see, Phelps, but I have enjoyed watching the press destroy you lately. No longer the blue-eyed boy, are you? You won't get me unless you kill her first and that won't be very clever, will it?

'I've got nothing left to lose but you'll lose everything when you mess this one up. Did you bring DS Pryor and DC Cook-Watts to help you? Don't tell me you came alone.'

Martin wondered why Austin was interested in whom he had brought with him and decided to humour him. 'DS Pryor is with me, Austin, but I also have an old friend of yours, namely Sergeant John Evans.'

Austin was seen to grip his shoulder tighter and a fresh stream of blood covered his right hand. This didn't stop him shouting defiantly. 'It was a toss-up between Evans and you, Phelps, both of you got in my way. Evans, don't think I don't know it was you who shopped me on more than one occasion. Did you really expect them to believe a fucking *sergeant* over me?'

Martin didn't know what happened next. All he saw was a contorted movement of Connie Jackson's legs, causing Austin to lose his balance, and all he heard was a single shot.

Chapter Eighteen

Helen Cook-Watts was pacing up and down on the patio outside the entrance to the reception area. Since the four men had left she had watched two vehicles pull up and they had added to her feeling of apprehension.

Alex Griffiths was usually at a crime scene before CID officers arrived, and it felt a bit like the cart before the horse to see him and his team turning up in their white van and waiting to be needed. She briefed him regarding what was happening and he gave a low whistle. He had heard about the reputation of the former DCI but hadn't met him.

When Alex had been appointed head of SOC, it had been with a particular remit to weed out some unsavoury personnel and to stamp on any unprofessional working practices. It had not been easy. DCI Austin was no longer in his post at that time, but he had left behind a legacy of collusion between CID and the SOC whereby the line of least resistance was taken, regardless of whether or not it had any scientific significance. It had been an 'anything for a quiet life' culture.

The first year had been hell for Alex, as he realised that some of the staff who had been SOCOs for years seemed to have been trained to ignore evidence that didn't suit and to find evidence that made closure of a case more probable. When challenged it was always a case of 'that's how DCI Austin wanted it, so that's what he got'.

Alex made rapid inroads into changing the methods of working but it was not until a few key officers had been given their marching orders that things improved. The promotion of Martin Phelps to DCI brought a fresh approach to the working relationship between SOC and CID. Now, Alex was proud to be part of a team that was getting a national, even an international, reputation for coordinated criminal investigations that produced first-class results. If Austin had been festering in retirement and witnessing the team's success via the media, then he would have had every reason to hate the little upstart that had once been his dogsbody.

The second vehicle that Helen saw was a fully equipped ambulance serviced by four senior personnel. Matt had spoken to the ambulance service earlier. The situation was outside the parameters needed for instigating a major incident response but was considered to need something more than the normal course of action. Consequently one doctor and three experienced paramedics had been sent, together with additional medical supplies.

Helen explained to them that injuries commensurate with stabbing could be expected and also that there was an armed response team on site so gunshot wounds could also be possible. The ambulance team took on board her words and began organising equipment for such eventualities.

Helen walked back towards Alex, and as she did she heard Martin's voice in the distance speaking into a loudhailer. She recognised the voice but it was too far away for her to be able to pick up exactly what he was saying.

Alex helped out a bit. 'It sounds as if DCI Phelps is issuing some sort of ultima –'

He stopped in mid-sentence as the sound of a shot was heard.

It was followed by an even more frightening silence.

'We can't just wait here,' said one of the paramedics. 'Someone may already be injured.'

'Possibly,' replied Helen, 'but there's an experienced armed response team out there and they know what they're doing. We'll get a call as soon as we're needed.'

Not long after she had finished her sentence, the second shot was heard and the ambulance staff could contain themselves no longer. 'The shots seemed to come from over there,' said the doctor. 'At the very least we should get the vehicle a bit nearer – it could save us time later.'

Helen sensed their frustration and didn't want them heading off in the wrong direction. She had seen the path her DCI had taken and it wasn't where the doctor had pointed. She looked at Alex and suggested he drive towards the ninth hole and the ambulance could follow.

The two vehicles churned up more earth on the golf course than an army of moles, and as Alex drove down a second slope the scene of the action was visible. Helen's phone sprang to life – it was Matt, asking for medical assistance.

'Help's right here,' said Helen as the ambulance drew to a halt and the team headed for the injured.

Matt assured the team as they approached that the area was safe for them to work in and directed them to the man sprawled out in a pool of blood. 'He was hit in the shoulder first and I think that's where most of the blood is coming from, but a second bullet may have hit him somewhere else. He seems to be unconscious but he is breathing.'

The doctor and one of the paramedics began working on Austin and within minutes he had an airway in situ, was attached to various pieces of equipment, and was receiving intravenous fluids. Matt watched, impressed at their teamwork and at the speed of their actions.

'We'll need to get him to hospital as quickly as possible,' said the doctor, and she shouted to one of the other paramedics to get the stretcher.

'I'll have to come with you,' said Matt. 'As soon as he regains consciousness this man will be charged on several counts of murder.'

'If he regains consciousness,' came the reply. 'His vital signs are deteriorating. He must be still bleeding, but it's not from any obvious source so we need to get him where we can have a better look. Feel free to join us.'

As she spoke her two colleagues were transferring Austin from the ground to the trolley and she asked them about the woman who the fourth paramedic was sitting with. One of them replied. 'Nothing we can't cope with, but if you and Dave can manage this one I'll stay and help Paul and bring her in at a more leisurely pace. We've sent for a second ambulance and it's on the way.'

Sirens and flashing lights paved the way of the ambulance from the golf course to the Accident and Emergency Unit of the University Hospital of Wales. Matt had been involved with some high-speed chases in police cars, but this experience was more nerve-racking than any one of those. It was not just the speed and the drama it was the feeling of not being in control. He sat in the back being thrown around and watched the doctor in what was looking like a losing battle to save the life of a killer.

Connie, on the other hand, had insisted on sitting up and was demanding a drink.

Paul shook his head. 'No can do,' he said. 'Your feet are swelling, and it looks like some broken bones, so nothing to eat or drink until we know what's what.'

He took out a flask of water, soaked some tissues, and wet her lips, receiving a nod of approval. Martin came over to them and introduced himself.

'I'm Detective Chief Inspector Phelps,' he said. 'I'm trying to make up my mind if you are the bravest or the most stupid woman I have ever met.'

Connie grinned because she knew what he was talking about. 'Nobody has ever called me brave – but stupid – that's one I've heard more than once. I go to the gym regularly, Inspector, and I've probably got stronger muscles in my legs and back than you have. More to the point, I wanted it to be me that knocked that monster over – you won't believe what he said he was going to do to me.'

Suddenly every vestige of a smile left Connie's lips and tears started to roll down her face. Seconds later her sobbing was out of control, and the paramedic rocked her gently in his arms.

Martin could only guess at the trauma that she had endured, but she was alive and a woman with the bottle to do what she had just done should recover from any mental scars the killer had inflicted on her.

Keith came over to confirm that the armed response unit had been stood down and to arrange a time for the statutory debriefing. Martin thanked him and walked over to where Alex was standing.

'It's unusual for us to meet at a crime scene without a body, and no Professor Moore either, but well done – great result. Even without a corpse this is still a site that needs investigation, so we'll just get on with the job.'

'I'll need you later too,' said Martin. 'As soon as we establish where Austin has been living I suspect we will find that BMW and maybe some of Mr Taylor's blood. Hopefully a few other things as well, as I've got to make sure he gets done for all three murders and one attempted murder – and we may also be able to prove he was planning three more.'

'He looked pretty out of it when they stretchered him to the ambulance. Is he going to make it?' asked Alex.

'I sincerely hope so; dying will be too good for him,' Martin replied. 'I want the opportunity of making him face up to what he has done. Alex, can you believe that I worked with the guy for the best part of two years – was I deaf and blind back there? I certainly didn't anticipate he would turn into a serial killer.'

'Hey, mate, don't beat yourself up on his account. I dismissed a lot of what I heard about him as being some sort of urban myth, but on reflection it was probably all true.' Alex left Martin and went to give his team some instructions.

Helen was sitting with Connie Jackson and rose to her feet as Martin approached.

'Stay where you are,' he said. 'Wait until the paramedics are ready to move Connie and then I want you to go with her.'

He turned to Connie, who was now much more composed, and asked if there was anyone he could contact on her behalf. She managed a smile as she gave him Roberto's telephone number. 'Just tell him I've had an accident playing golf, but don't be surprised if he tells you that I'm not playing golf because he thinks I'm shopping. It's a long story, Inspector, and one that I may have to lie my way out of later.'

'I'll need to talk to you, but there's no urgency now. Let the doctors sort you out first and we'll take it from there,' said Martin.

He watched the second ambulance drive off – no flashing lights this time. He thought for a moment that it could have been Alex's team transporting Connie's body if there had been a different outcome.

Martin walked back to the reception area with Sgt Evans, and for the first time he took in the beauty of the surroundings. The course had been developed making the most of the natural rises and falls of the ground. At one moment there was a clear view for miles around and the next one could see only trees as the course sloped downwards. There was no sign of twenty-first century life, no traffic noise, and Martin could suddenly see the attraction of spending hours in such a setting.

Sgt Evans had picked up the same vibes. 'Peaceful, isn't it? It could have been so different.'

When the two men reached the reception area it was to see a very relieved group of police officers being served coffee by the receptionist and the cleaner. They had all heard the news that the situation was now under control, and offered drinks to Martin and Sgt Evans.

After five minutes of general debriefing Sgt Evans dispatched some of the officers back to base and posted two at the entrance to the golf club. There would be no golf played today, but the place would be inundated with ghoulish sightseers and hordes of media people as soon as the news broke.

Martin knew he had a duty to inform Superintendent Bryant of the outcome, as he had been the one who authorised the use of the armed response team and would be waiting for a report. However, his first phone call was to Roberto who, as Connie had anticipated, was more than a bit confused, as he had been expecting his fiancée to return soon and with designer bags full of shopping. Martin did as Connie had suggested and spoke of an accident on the golf course.

Roberto didn't question why a DCI would be involved in such an event, and a phone call didn't seem to be the appropriate way to tell him that Connie could have been murdered – he would find out about that when he saw she was alive and relatively well.

Martin phoned Superintendent Bryant who told him that he had already heard that the armed response team had been stood down, as some people seemed to understand their chain of command and act accordingly. Not a word of 'well done' or 'good result' or even 'it's a relief to get that over with no fatalities'.

Sadly Martin realised that he had not expected those words anyway, and listened resignedly as the superintendent announced that there would be a press conference at 2 p.m., and that he would attend.

Martin had promised Sgt Evans that when this was all over he would ensure that the case of the murdered prostitutes would be reopened. From what Evans had told him, the superintendent had been in a position to at least ask questions at the time and Martin was determined to hear him answer some now.

Putting that to one side for the moment, Martin spoke to the receptionist and the cleaner.

The cleaner recalled. 'I recognised Mr Austin as soon as I saw him this morning. He used to be a member here, but he was always such a miserable sod that I was prepared to ignore him. I was really surprised when he started talking to me, first about it being a lovely day and then saying how hard I must work to get everything so spick and span. It was nice to be appreciated, but I had work to do so I just got on with it. He did keep talking – something about checking a tee-off time, and I know he looked at the book on the reception desk but I didn't speak to him again. Is he really the killer that's been on the news? I was here on my own with him, I could have been killed!'

Martin gave his usual reassurance about the killer's selective nature, and then listened as the receptionist told the story of the molehills. She was able to give the name and a contact number for the man who had been contacted by the killer, and Martin thanked the two women for their help.

'We will need formal statements from both of you later,' said Martin. 'There will be a police presence here for the foreseeable future, but here's my card and you can ring me directly if you need to.'

Martin walked back out onto the patio and asked Sgt Evans if he was in a position to drive him to the hospital and then back to Goleudy. John nodded.

Back in the car, and driving away from the Greenway Valley Golf Club, both men were silent. Both were locked into their own thoughts and when Sgt Evans finally spoke it was nothing to do with the current murders.

'Don't let my old grumbles ruin things for you. I may have got things wrong back then when Vincent Bowen was arrested. I don't want you opening up a can of worms and annoying the hierarchy.' He grinned. 'We've all got you named as the next superintendent and I don't want to be the one that stops that happening.'

'Thanks for the vote of confidence,' said Martin. 'But that job's not for me – at least not yet, John. What you told me about the Vincent Bowen investigation only served to make me remember that there were always issues that bothered me. On reflection, I think I was deliberately sidelined, but I shouldn't have allowed that to happen and I owe it to that boy to take a fresh look. It will open a can of worms, but so be it. If we find discrepancies with the evidence in that case it will lead to other cases that Austin headed up being scrutinised. You're right, John, it certainly won't make me popular with the powers that be – but so what?'

They reached the University Hospital of Wales and parked outside A&E. From there they were offered the choice of two locations for both their enquiries. Norman Austin was either in the Surgical ICU or actually in the operating theatre. According to the receptionist surgery was certainly planned. Connie Jackson was either on the orthopaedic ward or still in the X-ray department.

By mutual consent they headed for the Surgical ICU, and

242

found Matt talking to a short, thin woman dressed in blue scrubs.

Matt made the introductions. Mrs Harrison, a Senior Registrar in vascular surgery, had just started to tell Matt what was happening.'

'Good timing, Chief Inspector,' she said. 'Now you can all hear things at the same time and save me repeating myself. We were told there could have been two bullets, but you will know more about that than I do.

'Certainly a bullet shot clean through the brachial artery, and you would have seen a lot of bright red blood spurting out. Bright red because the blood in that artery is oxygen-rich. The speed at which it was forced out would depend on the person's heart rate.'

'I suspect that this man was really pumped up when he was hit, and so he would have lost a great deal of blood very quickly. As the blood flows from the artery in synchronisation with the heartbeat, it would have looked as if less was flowing out as he got weaker and his heart rate slowed down. But it won't stop completely until either he dies or until the artery is repaired – and that's what's happening now: he's undergoing arterial surgery.

'We have supplied him with replacement blood and prevented further blood loss from the artery but he is in a very weak condition and we have been expecting him to arrest. He's a big man, but not particularly fit, and there may be other factors preventing the response we would have hoped for by now. One factor could be that possible second bullet that so far has eluded our detection.'

'Anyway, Chief Inspector, it will be a long time before he is able to talk to you, so why don't you leave him to us and we'll give you a call when we have any news. Oh by the way, do you know if there any relatives that we should notify?'

Martin shook his head and looked for help from Sgt Evans. 'We could have a look in his old file – there might be something there.'

The surgeon acknowledged his words and at the same time

her pager bleeped and she raised her eyebrows. 'My consultant is obviously useless without me, so I need to go.' Turning on her heels she quickly disappeared into the operating theatre.

'She's right,' said Matt. 'The nurses tell me that this type of surgery can take hours and hours and that's when things go according to plan. After surgery he'll be on a ventilator in the Intensive Care Unit so there's no fear he will get away, other than escaping justice by not recovering.'

The three men left the surgical unit and headed for the orthopaedic wards. 'This looks a bit mob-handed,' Martin said to the other two. 'Why don't you both go to the concourse and get some coffee and I'll follow you shortly.'

Connie Jackson was lying on a bed with her legs elevated. She looked somewhat frail, and was being comforted by Roberto, who stood up as her visitor approached.

'I think it's all starting to sink in,' she said. 'I only got away with what I did because he wasn't expecting me to do anything. I don't think if I had realised the possible consequences back there I would have been able to kick both my legs backwards with enough force to make contact with his knees and cause the bastard to fall directly onto his injured shoulder.'

Roberto tutted at his fiancée's language, and it caused both Martin and Connie to laugh.

'That's mild compared to what we've been calling him since the start of this investigation, and it's all completely justified,' said Martin.

Roberto nodded. 'If he had killed Connie I would have killed him.'

Martin ignored the suggestion and asked Connie what was happening with her.

'I have my legs up in the air in an attempt to reduce the swelling,' she said. 'At first they were sure I had broken bones in my ankle but now there's a chance that it's just bruising caused by the impact, they are taking a close look at the X-rays – pray for the latter, Chief Inspector, because then I'll be able to get home. There are things there that will help me get over this.'

Assuming she was talking about her home comforts and not a line of white powder, Martin agreed to pray and updated Connie on what was happening with Austin. This seemed to unnerve Roberto. 'You mean to say that man is here, in this hospital? What if he finds out where Connie is?'

Connie gripped Roberto's hand and Martin explained that Austin was in theatre and surgeons were fighting for his life. 'I hope this is one fight they lose,' snapped Roberto.

After explaining that he would visit her at home if she was discharged or else come back to the hospital later, Martin went in search of his colleagues and half an hour later all three were back in Goleudy.

As always when a case was solved the incident room looked a little like a bomb had been dropped. The poems now made complete sense and lots of little pieces of evidence added up. There were still things that would need to be followed up but they could be dealt with at a reasonable pace.

The team was normally on a high at this point, but today that euphoria was severely tempered by the fact that the captured killer had at some time in the past actually been a DCI. Although there had been a healthy degree of staff turnover since he was in office there were still some people who remembered DCI Norman Austin. Everyone had a pretty good idea of what the press would make of the killer being an ex-police officer – it would certainly be their focus.

Martin knew he had to speak to Superintendent Bryant and decided it would be best to do so before the press conference, but there was one particular thing he had to deal with first. He couldn't believe that it was only a few minutes past twelve o'clock. Since that unwelcome very early morning call from Matt it felt as if he had lived through two whole days at least.

Mrs Taylor had reported her husband missing several hours ago and had not yet been told of his murder. Martin knew that he should be the one to tell her, and used his Alfa Romeo to drive Helen to the address given to them by Barry police station. Matt was left in charge of clearing up a number of loose ends and keeping in contact with the hospital.

The journey was only eleven miles and so took just twenty-five minutes. The Taylors had certainly wanted to be left alone, as their temporary home was a static caravan parked in the grounds of a small farm near the coast. As they approached they could see one of the small police cars parked outside and a young female officer came out to meet them.

They all introduced themselves, and PC Ana Mason told them that Mrs Taylor was expecting the worst possible news and was as prepared as anyone could be.

'I've been here for the past three and a half hours,' said PC Mason. 'She's talked non-stop and I know more about her family history than I know about my own. Her husband was terminally ill and I think Carol is expecting to hear that he simply went somewhere to die and that it's all over. Apparently they talked a lot about it, and he never wanted her to actually see him die but rather to remember him living. They seem devoted to one another, but no matter how prepared she thinks she is it will still be a shock when she hears of his death.'

'Even more so when she hears exactly how he died,' said Martin. 'Come on, let's get this over with.'

The inside of the caravan was much larger than Martin had expected it to be, and extremely light and airy. The early afternoon sun streamed in through a window that formed almost the whole of one of the end walls and bounced off the silver streaks in Mrs Taylor's hair. She would normally be considered a good-looking woman, but today her mouth was downcast and her eyes were without light.

As Martin approached to introduce himself she said, quite simply, 'He's dead, isn't he? Arthur's dead.'

Martin nodded and moved to one side to allow PC Mason to pass him and take hold of Mrs Taylor's hands.

'It's what we thought, isn't it?' Mrs Taylor was gripping on tight and looking towards Ana Mason, who had become her confidant and could give her some of the strength she needed. 'Did he die alone? He wanted to be alone you know, it's one of the few things we totally disagreed about.'

For the next ten minutes Martin talked the grieving widow through the details of what had happened to her husband and watched as each piece of his account brought new and unexpected horror to the woman's face.

There was no point in him holding back some of the facts about Arthur's actual murder, as there had already been a lot of media coverage from the Primrose Garden Centre.

'So that was my Arthur,' Carol said quietly. 'I would have preferred to hear that the cancer had got him than for him to be murdered. It doesn't seem fair …'

She started to lose control, and PC Mason put one arm around her shoulder and wiped away her tears.

If the conversation had been difficult up to that point Martin knew that what was to come would be horrendous. He had sat down and moved his chair closer to Mrs Taylor. 'Carol,' he said gently, 'I have to tell you that we have caught your husband's killer.'

She raised her head for a moment and looked directly at Martin. 'Oh, well, that's good isn't it? It's good you've caught him. It wasn't only my Arthur he killed, was it?'

'No,' said Martin. 'We know of at least two other people he killed, and today he attempted a fourth murder which was when we caught him. He knew all the people he killed and believed he had good reason to kill them.'

Carol sat upright and challenged Martin. 'No, you're wrong there, Arthur never gave anyone cause to kill him, he was a good man. He was useless as a second-hand car dealer because he went to the nth degree to sort out vehicles with problems and that often left him out of pocket.'

She suddenly stopped short. Martin had seen the flash of a possibility cross her mind and jumped in quickly to prevent her having to second guess her own thoughts. 'I think you will know someone who has caused you both a lot of angst over the years, and who may well be the reason that you are currently living here.'

'We're here because we were getting some very spiteful phone calls from a man who was threatening to expose what he said were Arthur's "illegal trading practices". Most of what the caller said was untrue, but as we already knew that Arthur had very little time left to live we didn't want to spend that time fighting anyone. We didn't know who the caller was or why he hated Arthur so much. There's one person who hated my husband, and now I see why the police in Barry were this morning asking me about my relationship with Norman Austin ... was it him? Is he the man that killed Arthur? Is he the serial killer? He was a policeman, you know – a detective at the same rank as you. Is it him?'

Martin nodded and was then almost shaken out of his seat by the howl that came from Carol Taylor. It was followed by another, and several more before she broke down in sobs and shudders that caused her whole body to shake.

After a few minutes Martin started talking and filled her in with what had occurred at the golf course that morning. He explained what was happening to Norman Austin.

He hadn't expected any comments and didn't get any. His words had been intended more for PC Mason than Mrs Taylor.

The family liaison officer would stay with her and be able to reiterate what Martin had said at a time when she was more ready to accept the information. Martin got up and put his hand on Mrs Taylor's arm as he placed his business card on the table. 'You or PC Mason can contact me directly if you want to, and I know you will have her support for as long as you need it.'

Helen was quiet for most of the journey back to Goleudy and Martin asked her if she was all right.

'I keep thinking about the fact that this man who has terrorised Cardiff for the past three or four weeks was once a senior police officer. Was he mad or just bad? The rumours flying around the station at the moment are sickening. Some officers are even saying that he persuaded people to testify to things they could not possibly have witnessed and that evidence was planted in order to secure convictions.

There are a few people who seem to think that he was just of the old school, that he got the job done, and they still see

248

nothing wrong with that. Most people are worried that we'll get a load of very negative publicity and our relationship with the public will be damaged. What do you think?'

Chapter Nineteen

'We can't do that,' said Superintendent Bryant. 'What you are suggesting is preposterous, we all agreed at the time on the package that was given to the Crown Prosecution Services. It's water under the bridge and in nobody's best interest to go raking up things that you, and only you, seem to think resulted in a miscarriage of justice.'

Martin responded sharply. 'I can think of at least one person whose interest will be served if a new enquiry deems his conviction to be unsafe. Vincent Bowen was only twenty-three years of age when he was given a life sentence for the murder of those sex workers. His mother has campaigned for years for a new enquiry. Psychiatric reports said that although he had some mental health problems he was capable of knowing right from wrong and he was sent to an adult prison. God knows what that has done to him, particularly if the poor sod knows he was never guilty in the first place.'

'But he was,' said the Superintendent. 'All the evidence pointed to him. The knife, covered with the last victim's blood, was found under the sink in his room – it was an open and shut case. People were rejoicing in the city when that killer was arrested and the streets were safe again.'

Turning to Martin, he said accusingly. 'You weren't even around – apparently you were unwilling to give up some planned leave in order to help with such a high-profile case. Now, it looks as if there is no doubt that Norman Austin committed these latest murders, but I firmly believe our best course of action will be to say that he was suffering from some sort of severe mental breakdown and that while he was a police

251

officer he did some fantastic work that we can all still be proud of. Now is not the time to be suggesting things could have been wrong when he was still a DCI – the press and the public will crucify us.'

Martin listened in disbelief. 'There is no way we can say that! It would take the press no time at all to discover it wasn't true, and then we'd all be blown away by the storm that would follow.

'And regarding the Bowen case – I offered to defer my leave but was told it had to be taken. Do you really think that if the then DCI Austin had wanted me around he would have allowed me to swan off on annual leave? He once stopped one of his sergeants from going on honeymoon! He obviously wanted me out of the way.

'If your intention is to tell the press, this afternoon, that Austin committed these crimes while the balance of his mind was disturbed, then I have to tell you that I will not be a party to what I believe to be a total lie. In my view he knew exactly what he was doing and had been planning the whole sick programme for a long time.

'The really sad thing is that during the time I worked with him I saw him figure out some of the most difficult cases, and if he had chosen to take a different path he could have ended his career at the very top.

'I would like to make a suggestion.' Martin didn't wait for the superintendent's approval and continued. 'We use the press conference to state publically the horror we all feel that someone who was once a police officer has been the person behind these cruel murders. We make no excuses for him. You could then go on to say that since his capture there have been issues brought to your attention regarding one of the cases that Austin headed up while he was a DCI. Take the moral high ground and say that you will leave no stone unturned to discover the truth and that you will personally authorise a full internal investigation into that case.'

The superintendent suddenly looked as if he was ready for retirement, and not even the buttons on his immaculate uniform

252

shone as brightly as they usually did, but even so he defiantly stood up and pointed a finger at Martin. 'Don't you know the expression "let sleeping dogs lie"? Why can't you do just that? The press conference is in twenty minutes. You will be there and you will take your lead from me. I will not be washing our dirty linen in public and if you make any attempt to do so I will take appropriate action.'

Martin shook his head and turned towards the door.

'I'm not finished,' said Superintendent Bryant.

'No, but I am,' said Martin, slamming the door behind him.

As before, the heated exchange with his senior officer had caused Martin to feel hungry and he made his way to the staff café. He was not the only one who had suddenly needed to satisfy a basic need for food and the place was packed out. With only about fifteen minutes available to him he chose the ubiquitous sandwich, not even bothering to check what the filling was, and joined a table where Matt and others were finishing off their meals.

'I came looking for you,' said Matt. 'I figured you would be hungry as Iris's breakfast trolley is a dim and distant memory and we've done a lot of running around. Where have you been?'

Martin ignored the question and took a mouthful of what turned out to be a tuna mayo sandwich. His mind was on other things. 'What's the news from the hospital?' he asked.

'Connie Jackson has been discharged. No broken bones, but she may well have a few nightmares or flashbacks to deal with in the future. I've sent one of the Victim Support staff to speak to her and suggested that we leave the taking of her formal statement until tomorrow. Is that OK?'

'Yes, that's more than OK – thank you Matt. What about Norman Austin?'

'The last thing I heard was that he was still in theatre and that was just before I came here. I spoke to one of the charge nurses on the Surgical ICU and he told me that Austin had arrested twice but that things were now under control and the arterial grafts were going ahead. We have a dedicated number to ring for information because apparently the hospital has been

253

bombarded by the press and even the public who have just been randomly asking for news of the killer. Some people have sad lives.'

Martin pushed his plate away with only two thirds of his sandwich eaten and Matt looked quizzically at him. 'You OK?' he asked. 'Are you worried about the press conference? They'll have a field day regarding rotten coppers but hell, that's not your fault.'

'No, but there are some things about Norman Austin that I need to tell you, and I'm not sure how Superintendent Bryant is going to play this one – it could end up going badly wrong.'

As Martin spoke the puzzled look on Matt's face intensified, but then he jumped up. 'Well, if that's the case let's get it over with and let's not be late.'

Both men made their way down the back stairs to the large conference room on the ground floor. They were followed by several members of the investigation team, including Sgt Evans, who had no wish to miss this particular press conference.

The usual paraphernalia that accompanied these sessions was apparent as soon as Matt opened the door. A room full of noise and excitement and an atmosphere of anticipation and speculation hit the two men like a physical force. There was the usual mass of equipment and the usual jockeying for positions as microphones were held higher, with some being manoeuvred by the use of robotic arms.

Everything was exactly as Martin had expected and the table and the three front seats set out as usual for the two detectives and their senior officer. That person was already there, but it was not the one they were expecting. Superintendent Bryant was not sitting in the middle seat this time – it was Chief Superintendent Colin Atkinson.

Matt whispered. 'What's all this about?' Getting no reply from Martin he simply nodded in the direction of the chief super and took his seat.

As Martin also sat down the Chief Superintendent spoke quietly to him. 'I'll fill you in on why I'm here later, but for now leave this session to me – I think you'll be content with what I have to say.'

Martin didn't really know Colin Atkinson other than by reputation. He was new to South Wales, having recently been promoted and transferred from the Greater Manchester force, and was known for his fair but no- nonsense approach. Matt didn't have to do his usual banging on the speakers to get order because as soon as the Chief Superintendent got to his feet he was greeted by complete silence. He was an unknown factor as far as the media in Cardiff were concerned, and what they saw was a plump man with prematurely white hair and thick-lensed glasses, standing no more than five feet nine inches tall. His appearance was not one that called for immediate respect, and belied his ability to exude authority, but when he spoke his blunt northern accent quickly cut straight through any suggestion that he was a soft touch.

'For those of you who don't know me, I am Chief Superintendent Colin Atkinson. I have been waiting for a suitable moment to meet the press since my transfer from Manchester, and what better way than to be able to tell you all about the successful capture of a serial killer.

'I take no credit for the hard work and the brilliant leadership that has brought this killer to justice – and some of you that have given DCI Phelps such a hard time of late may want to rethink your positions.'

Martin noticed Matt grinning. This was something that would never have happened if Superintendent Bryant had been fronting this press conference, and they both waited expectantly for what would come next.

Colin Atkinson continued. 'I will come straight to the point regarding the killer. He is a man called Norman Austin, and some of you will remember that for many years he was a police officer in Cardiff, reaching the rank of detective chief inspector in this very criminal investigation department. He is currently being operated on at the University Hospital of Wales, because a bullet from one of our armed response officers severed his brachial artery. His condition is critical.

'I have been briefed on the circumstances surrounding the

255

time he left the force, and I want to take this opportunity to tell you that there are issues that give me cause for great concern. This will not be the first time in my career that I have looked back at cases when the conduct of a police officer has been questioned.'

A ripple of excitement broke out in the audience and a few questions were fired. The chief superintendent ignored them and continued. 'A respected member of the force has already brought to my attention that there may have been some unanswered questions relating to the arrest and subsequent conviction of a young man by the name of Vincent Bowen.'

The ripple of excitement turned into a storm of emotions as reporters shouted out questions and demanded answers.

Colin Atkinson was not fazed, and just stood completely still and in silence until the commotion had died down.

'There is no point in you asking questions about what I have just told you, because at present I have no answers but I am using this opportunity to tell you that the case will be re-opened, as will any others where Norman Austin was involved and there are question marks over procedure, evidence, or witnesses.

'The vast majority of our officers work extremely hard and are honest and dedicated individuals, but as in all organisations there are and have been some bad apples – and I will make you a promise, here and now, that if I ever get to hear of one, he or she will be booted out, and I will happily do the booting.

'Now the main reason we're here is to tell you about the events that led to the capture of Norman Austin this morning, and on that note I will hand over to Detective Chief Inspector Martin Phelps.'

Martin couldn't remember when he had last felt such a degree of respect for a senior officer and he looked forward to having this guy around. He hoped he would get to know what had happened prior to the press conference, but picking up on a few comments he guessed that Sgt Evans had stuck his head above the parapet.

DCI Phelps got on his feet and if anything upstaged even the chief superintendent's performance. He took his audience back to the first murder and for the first time they were given the full details of the colours and their connections, and the actual wording of the poems. He explained how the team had gone about identifying possible sites for the murders and as he spoke he noticed a visible shift in the opinion of the media.

A few days ago he was considered to be an incompetent plod, promoted beyond his capability and incapable of solving even a simple crossword puzzle. Today they were lapping up his words, and with the subsequent questions came comments about 'a job well done' and about how 'Cardiff was lucky to have such a good team' – and so on, ad nauseam. It was a good feeling to have them back onside but it would be a long time before there was any trust – from his side at least.

The questions petered out and people were starting to leave when Diane Cummings, the local television crime reporter, made a comment and then asked what was to be the final question.

'DCI Phelps, we all offer you our congratulations on a job well done, but you know how fickle our audiences are. Now that the killer has been stopped this story will soon be yesterday's news. However, the possibility of Vincent Bowen's conviction being unsafe will cause a furore – you will know that one of the local rags has been supporting his mother's campaign for a re-trial. When will we know what's happening with that?'

Chief Superintendent Colin Atkinson stood up alongside Martin and answered the question.

'You will know as soon as we do,' he said. 'Good afternoon, ladies and gentlemen.'

Matt walked back up the stairs ahead of the other two men, as he thought they would want to speak privately and was surprised when Martin caught him up even before he had reached his office.

'The chief superintendent has got some urgent business to attend to, but will be back in his office by five o'clock and I plan to see him then.'

'What's going on?' said Matt. 'What's all this about an

unsafe conviction? – I didn't have a clue what he was going on about but he was good, wasn't he? He's a bit of a contrast to Bryant – and where was he?'

'Matt,' said Martin. 'I do need to bring you up to date with what I've learned since driving with Sgt Evans to the Greenway Valley Golf Club, but you must remember that before the press conference I couldn't even finish a tuna sandwich. Now I'm absolutely starving and I am going to look for my guardian angel, Iris. One of her famous cheese omelettes is the only thing that will sort me out! Join me if you will.'

'I will,' said Matt. 'There are things I need to let you know, but I did eat earlier so a coffee will do me.'

To begin with it was Matt who did the talking, because Martin was savouring the delights of his king-size cheese omelette and the buttery mini new potatoes that accompanied it.

'We had no trouble finding the address of Norman Austin and Alex has taken a team there. The BMW is in the garage, and according to Alex there's still a cardboard coffee cup in the driver's cup holder stuffed with blood-stained latex gloves. I can't believe Austin would have forgotten to remove those, but he did seem to go to pieces after the garden centre murder. He made too many mistakes and it unnerved him.'

'That's brilliant,' said Martin. 'What else have they found?'

'Enough to prove that Helen was on the button with her rainbow colours theory because there are apparently blue, indigo, and violet lengths of cords and envelopes.'

Matt drained the last of the coffee from his mug and added. 'They haven't opened the envelopes, they're waiting for you to do that.'

Martin dipped his last new potato into the buttery sauce and popped it into his mouth as he rose to his feet.

'Come on then, what are we waiting for? I can just as easily update you on the way there. We'll take my car.'

On the way to the killer's home, which turned out to be just two streets away from where Matt lived, Martin updated his sergeant regarding the dark side of Norman Austin's character and career.

'I confronted Superintendent Bryant with my concerns just before the press conference and I suspect that at the same time John Evans jumped over a few ranks in his part of the organisation and decided to speak to the new man, Colin Atkinson.'

Austin's home was what an estate agent would describe as a 'townhouse with an integral garage', in which sat the grey BMW. The garage door was wide open and the area surrounding the house was sealed off with blue and white 'scene of crime' tape. A few onlookers had gathered at the corner of the road and as Martin pulled up a reporter stepped forward.

'Absolutely nothing more today,' said Martin curtly. 'You're wasting your time here.'

He acknowledged Alex who left the garage and joined his colleagues in the lounge/diner. Although Alex and his team were kitted out in their usual 'space suits', he indicated to Martin that there was no need for him and Matt to put suits on. However he did hand over a pair of latex gloves, and Martin set about opening the letters.

They were all addressed to him, as before, and he had already anticipated that the blue envelope could contain his death notice.

He was right, and this poem really did make him feel physically sick. The reference to his head being used as a football and the whole issue of the colour blue led him to believe that Austin could have been planning to murder him at the Cardiff City Stadium, home of Cardiff City Football Club.

The mention of Shelley in the blue poem angered Martin more than anything else had done, and he couldn't bear the thought of the killer even writing down her name. There was nothing to suggest that she was going to be one of his targets, just that the killer plotted to rubbish Martin in her eyes. None of this was of any real significance now and Martin handed over the blue sheet of paper for Matt and Alex to read. The air was as blue as the paper as they both described in detail what they would like to do to Norman Austin.

The indigo poem described the way someone he believed had swindled him of some money would be dealt with. He referred to the greed of the man who was the head of Indigo Investments. As before Martin's team would have considered locations linked to the colour and the first one he thought of was The Indigo Indian Restaurant on Albany Road.

He and Shelley had bought a fabulous takeaway from there recently. Their king prawn karahi was a lovely blend of Indian spices cooked with sliced onions, peppers, and tomatoes. Thank God he now didn't need to think of that place as a possible venue for murder.

Opening the violet envelope he could only think that the killer had completely taken leave of his senses. This poem didn't even rhyme but was clearly aimed at a woman called Violet. It was all in the past tense and in it the killer expressed regret at not being able to kill the bitch because the flames had already got her. What was that all about?

Alex had now bagged all the envelopes and the coloured cords. He turned his attention to the laptop computer that was attached to a laser printer and remembered a promise that had been made by Charlie.

'I know someone who would like to take a good look at this,' he said. 'I think her boast was along the lines of making the machine tell her every key that was ever pressed as she believes that there's no such thing as a deleted file. If he planned anything on this laptop Charlie will provide us with the evidence.'

Martin imagined Austin sitting at the computer and the thought sickened him. How did anyone's mind get to the point of being so warped planning murders in such a systematic way?

There were things that Martin was desperate to ask Norman Austin and he prayed the man would live not just long enough to answer some of his questions but to endure the punishment he deserved.

'There's nothing else here, is there?' he asked Alex, and the head of SOC shook his head but then added.

'Nothing here, but just to let you know that we found both

260

bullets at the scene. One certainly had traces of Austin's blood but the other looks to have ricocheted off the handle of his golf bag.'

'OK,' said Martin. 'I was wondering about that and now I'll be getting back. It's amazing how much the fact that Austin was once one of us has taken the shine off the solving of this case. I need to get that feeling of success across to the team and I usually fork out for the drinks and nibbles on such occasions. Matt and I will collect some on the way back and we could have a round-up session at four thirty. I need to be somewhere at five so that should be fine. Does it suit you?'

'Absolutely,' replied Alex. 'We'll be finished here in about ten minutes so I'll see you back at base.'

Fifteen minutes later, after a quick session in the supermarket, Matt was complaining. 'I can't get used to having to pay for carrier bags. I must have dozens of "bags for life" in my car and now I've got four more.' The four bags in question were stuffed full of savoury and sweet nibbles and a variety of drinks.

News soon spread around the station that a debriefing session with DCI Phelps was on offer and by four thirty Incident Room One was crowded. The atmosphere was becoming more and more positive and the team was starting to recognise Norman Austin as a deranged killer and not as an ex-police officer. The two were very different and the officers had needed to separate them before moving on.

Alex opened the door for Charlie to weave her way through and help herself to some cheese and onion crisps. 'Can you believe it?' she asked. 'Of all the expensive and exotic things I could have had a craving for, I've plumped for cheese and onion crisps.'

One of the PCs overheard what Charlie had said and raised her eyebrow.

Charlie smiled and looked at Alex. 'Oh, go on, let's tell them,' he said. Banging his fist on one of the tables he called for silence. 'Ladies and gentlemen,' he announced in an over-the-top flamboyant style. 'It gives me great pleasure to announce that Charlie and I are about to give birth.'

He laughed as Charlie drove her wheelchair straight at him. 'Don't listen to him,' she pleaded. 'Yes, it's true that I am pregnant, but it's early days so I am *not* about to give birth – and he never will be!'

Cheers, applause, and lots of words of congratulation followed her words. The couple was extremely popular and the announcement really raised the spirits so that at last the atmosphere was as would normally be expected at a successful debriefing.

Matt walked over to Martin and pulled him to one side. 'I've just had news from the hospital,' he said. 'It would appear that the arterial surgery has been successful, and although nothing is guaranteed yet it looks as if Norman Austin will pull through. The senior registrar told me that the next twenty-four hours will be critical but she sounded optimistic.'

'It's strange to think we're rooting for a killer to survive,' said Martin. 'In my mind it's the only way that justice will really be served – he has to be made to answer for not just these murders, but for some of his past mistakes.

'Matt, do you think you could ensure that everyone finishes off these nibbles and drinks? I don't imagine I will be long, but my meeting is with the chief superintendent and I don't know how he operates.'

Martin left the room and made his way past Superintendent Bryant's empty office and on to the top floor of Goleudy, where there were just two main offices and some secretarial pods.

It was only on high days and holidays that Martin visited the top floor, and although the offices were spacious they were too modern for Martin's liking. They had been stripped of the Victorian detail that he had on his office ceiling, and even the view from the windows was not as good as his.

He had obviously been heard walking along the corridor, as even before he had knocked the chief superintendent called out for him to enter.

'You did well at that press conference,' he told Martin. 'We need a few more people who aren't reduced to quivering wrecks when they are faced with the media. I didn't get a chance to speak to you before that meeting but I'm sure you will have guessed that I had a visit earlier from Sergeant John Evans – what a great chap.'

'I'm not going to go over everything he said because I know he has already spoken to you. Immediately after his visit I paid a call on Superintendent Bryant, and in my blunt northern way I will tell you that I was hacked off with his petty excuses and blame-dodging.'

'He is currently on "gardening leave" and will remain so while the investigation into the conviction of that young man for the murder of the four prostitutes is re-examined. That leaves me with a problem, and you with a number of opportunities.'

'You can stay as you are and no one will blame you for that. Your results are first-class and you are heading up a smashing team.

'Or, you can stand in for Superintendent Bryant as acting super and give that energetic sergeant of yours a shot at being an inspector.

'Or, you can lead the team I will be setting up to reinvestigate the conviction of Vincent Bowen. What's it to be Detective Chief Inspector, Phelps – what do you want to do next?'

Author Inspiration

When attempting to identify the possible locations of the murders, DCI Phelps and the team take readers to a variety of well-known landmarks, so choosing one was difficult. Seeing the colours of the Welsh flag framing the entrance to Cardiff Castle seemed to fit the bill.

Cardiff Castle is situated at the heart of the capital, and a visit to the castle will take you back through two thousand years of Welsh history. When the Romans invaded Wales they built forts and sited these strongholds strategically, including near to where the River Taff flows into the Bristol Channel giving them easy access to their ships.

Until the fifth century Cardiff Castle was the base for the Roman army, but after they left it was at the mercy of foreign invaders. The next people to occupy the castle were the Normans, who recognised the value of its strategic position and built a keep on the site. Throughout the ages different features were added, and the castle was occupied by various families of the nobility. In 1766 it passed by marriage into the Bute family.

It was the second Marquess of Bute who transformed the fortunes of Cardiff when he built the docks and enabled the port to become world-famous for exporting coal. The family became very wealthy, and when Cardiff Castle and the Bute fortune passed to the third Marquess he was amongst the richest men in the world.

Money was lavished on the castle, and architect William Burges added Gothic towers, stained glass windows, and amazing carvings. The rooms within the castle are a testament to the wealth of the family with elaborate wall hangings and gold and crystal ornamental features. Each room is different and quite spectacular and it is generally believed that the third

Marquess achieved his ambition to build a Welsh, Victorian Camelot.

The grounds are magnificent and of great interest to visitors is the famous animal wall. After the death of the fourth Marquess, the family gifted the castle and the adjacent grounds known as Bute Park to the city of Cardiff.

Today the castle welcomes visitors from all over the world and is one of the biggest tourist attractions in Wales.

Wonny Lea

The Fourth DCI Martin Phelps Book

Money Can Kill

A school trip to the National History Museum of Wales at St Fagans ends early with the disappearance of a child. Is he just playing hide and seek – or is it the work of a criminal? Perhaps a kidnapper with designs on the boy's mother and her recently-acquired millions?

DCI Martin Phelps and his team are back together just in time to take on the case – one that starts off as a possible kidnapping but soon descends into something even more sinister ...

As the investigation exposes the complexities of family relationships, another long-standing mystery is solved – all while Martin and his colleagues anxiously await the results of a major police review that may result in them losing their jobs ...